the BRIGHTEST SPARK

the BRIGHTEST SPARK

VICTORIA LUM

Cover Design Copyright © 2023 Y'All That Graphic
Editing by Becca Mysoor, Grace Bradley, and Amy Briggs
Proofreading by Virginia Tesi Carey
Formatting by Elaine York of Allusion Publishing
www.allusionpublishing.com)

Author's Note: Please note this story may contain
areas that may be sensitive to some readers.
For a list of potential areas of sensitive content, please visit:
https://www.victorialum.com/sensitive-content-information

To my readers, this one is for you.
Thank you for reading my books and for all
your support. You make the journey worthwhile.

She's here again. The angel.

Her hair shimmers in a unique shade between rose gold and copper under the golden rays of the waning afternoon sun, with some sort of emerald-colored barrette in her hair, as if she's wearing a crown of rare metals and gems, befitting a princess like her. The soft curls dance around her silky face before cascading over her shoulders, an errant lock resting on top of the upper swells of her ample curves.

I never thought I'd be jealous of hair. But here I am.

I also never thought I'd be a poet, but I guess I can surprise myself sometimes.

My breath freezes in my chest and I stand as still as a statue in a corner on the outside patio of Grocery for Less during my mandatory fifteen-minute break from the tedium of restocking shelves and mopping the scratched linoleum floors. A sharp winter breeze attempts to pierce through my flimsy shirt—an oldie I wear with pride—but I pay no attention, my senses only attuned to the brightest spark of my days here at this dingy grocery store.

Someday, I'll be able to blow this joint and get out of here. My fingers twitch, aching for a smoke. Usually, that means I'm craving a jolt of something to get through another mindless shift. But now that she's here, I'm all juiced up for the evening.

In the last year or so, I've seen her at the store during my breaks, sometimes laughing with her friends, an infectious smile on display, other times wandering the aisles as if lost in thought. Based on the sexy cheerleading outfits she's usually wearing and the hulking jocks sometimes by her side, my guess is they're stopping by to pick up some snacks or drinks before or after some game. Normally, a beautiful girl at the supermarket is nothing I'd pay attention to. Hot chicks are everywhere these days. But there's a stillness, an essence radiating from her which beckons another glance. And another. And another.

Before I knew it, I was addicted. Perhaps I just traded vices.

It's not only her appearance I'm drawn to. It's also the way she carries herself, the way she behaves. And it's consistent. In the times I've seen her here, I've witnessed her buying sandwiches for a few homeless people who sometimes dig through the trash bins by the exit. Or the other day, another customer knocked over several tall stacks of boxed Japanese curry powder and fled in apparent panic, and instead of walking away because it's not her business, she stopped and help a flustered Fred, another staffer, stack them up piece by piece. It must have taken her at least fifteen minutes.

Kindness seeps out from her pores. Effortless. And she never seems to care about others' physical appearances or apparent station in life.

She looks like someone who wouldn't care about my junk car and subpar GPA.

She looks like someone who may see the real me. Or at least the me behind the tats, piercing, and the so-called pretty face.

Like I'm someone who is perhaps capable of more than being a delinquent.

I choke back a laugh. That's something even my parents don't believe in.

The angel is now talking with Bernice, the Salvation Army representative, at her table, which is bare except for some supplies and the classic red tin donation bucket and a small, ridiculous, white plastic Christmas tree, which should be called a Christmas twig instead, since most of its "branches" are as bare as a monk's head.

Even the tree looks pathetic and half-dead, just like the rest of this corner of the city, but it's part of a campaign, "A Random Act of Kindness," the store is trying out. A stack of flimsy, numbered paper tags is next to the tree, and a stranger can fill out the tag with a Christmas wish or sentiment and hang it on the tree, and if they want a response from another stranger—or in this case, probably one of us from the store—they can fill out their email or mailing address in the binder under their number. This is supposed to be festive and get people in the spirit of the holidays and whatnot. It's Christmas season and everyone and their grandmothers are trying to appeal to the do-gooders inside us. Make a donation and earn a chance at salvation or a spot in Heaven's line.

I snort. If it were only that easy.

The angel's eyes, a color I can't make out at this distance—my mind whirring with the possibilities—alight with laughter as her lips split into a wide smile. My heart gallops, and I wish the smile were directed at me. Bernice, with her usual stern set of brows and thin lips, even lets out a few chuckles, completely transforming her usually dour face into something more...approachable.

The irony of the grumpy, ham-fisted Bernice working behind a table designated to entice closet philanthropists to empty their pockets is not lost on me. But Bernice is now grinning broadly and one may even mistake her as the doting Nana who'll bake your favorite chocolate chip cookies when you visit. Of course, the angel can melt even the coldest of hearts. Maybe even spread some Christmas cheer around this dump.

It has to be magic. Nothing can explain this transformation.

The angel is now staring at the ugly Christmas tree of kindness with curiosity. Her fingers graze the two lonely wishes on the tree, one of which is mine—not by choice, but more by order from management. My heart skips a beat and I find myself holding my breath, wondering what she'll do next. She lets go of the thin paper tags, reaches out for a brand new one and starts writing on it. Her eyes take on a faraway look as if mulling over life's big mysteries before she scribbles something on the paper, her lips quirking up in a grin. The angel hangs up her wish on the tree and suddenly, the tree appears transformed, an ugly duckling changing into a beautiful swan.

She then fills out her information in the binder, and she reaches up toward the tree once more, her fingers pausing by my wish. My heart is now in my throat as I watch her flip over my message and read the contents. The angel smiles—glorious and blinding—as she grabs a new tag and writes her response to my message, before attaching it to my tag with the tack provided by the store.

She pulls out her wallet from inside her small tan purse inscribed with a logo-pattern I recognize as a brand I'll probably never be able to afford and removes a few crisp bills before dropping them into the donation can.

"Two hundred dollars?" Bernice exclaims, her raspy voice pitchy.

The angel shrugs, her hands falling to her sides as she rocks on her feet, the movement causing the short navy-and-green skirt of her cheerleading outfit to sway side-to-side, highlighting her curvy hips and slender, long legs. Legs I can imagine being wrapped around my waist while I—

"Heeey, Jack, what are you doing standing over there?"

Teasing fingers drag themselves across my chest before I can even turn toward the disruption. A sweet, sickly scent of pungent perfume reaches my nose and I hold my breath, rearranging my lips into a half grin, one I know the ladies always love. I spit my chewing gum into the trash can next to me. This is my third attempt at quitting smoking, so instead of a pack of cigs a day, it's a pack of Spearmint Delight a day.

"Just chillin', Nancy. Starting your shift? You look hot today."

The compliment automatically slips through my lips before I smirk and attempt to shift away from handsy Nancy. She's been trying to get into my pants since she started two months ago, but I'm firmly on the fence. She's got curves for days, but something about her rubs me the wrong way.

Perhaps it's her desperation. Maybe I like the thrill of the chase. Perhaps I like the unattainable, like the angel with red hair wearing a cheerleading outfit.

"Ugh. I need to get out of this place." She glances at me, her cherry-red lips pursed in what I assume is supposed to be a sexy pout, and her fingers settle on the collar of my well-worn blue shirt. "You know, I get off at eight tonight. No morning classes tomorrow." She leans in, her breath ghosting my ear. "Want to come over to my place and hang out later on? We can do...*whatever* you want." She doodles on my chest with her index finger; the motion doing nothing for me.

My eyes dart over to the angel, finding her *finally* staring at me for the first time since I've seen her around. My breath catches in my throat. My heart pounds so loudly I'd swear others can hear it, and this is something which never happens to me with beautiful girls.

Swallowing the pins and needles in my throat, I hold my gaze to hers, my tongue darting out and slowly caressing my lip ring, a move that has earned me smiles and flushes from hot chicks in the past. Her eyes widen a fraction and I wink. Instead of the expected grin or pinkened cheeks, her elegant brows furrow, a steeliness reflecting from her gaze, her jaw tense. Her frown deepens when I throw in a flirtatious cock of my brow, then she whirls around, her hair whipping behind her as she steps inside the store. A few of her classmates, from the looks of their identical uniforms which whisper of their wealthy status, join her from the parking lot and follow her into the store.

My heart pinches, followed by a burgeoning spark in my gut.

Of course my angel doesn't behave like other hot girls.

I want to know why. Is it because she sees something when she looks at me?

An unfamiliar heat rises to my face and I roll my lips inward, an unusual heaviness settling into my chest. I grip the frayed edge of my beloved shirt, my palm suddenly clammy, and smooth the hopeless wrinkles before taking a deep inhale of the crisp winter air. I poke at the small hole forming on the thin fabric. I struggle to get my bearings before raking one hand over my thick locks, which have, as usual, fallen over my face.

But I'm not a man who gives up so easily. Maybe it's the beginnings of an obsession. Maybe it's an unquenchable thirst to know why she doesn't smile back at me.

Glancing up, the tip of my tongue snakes out to give my silver lip ring a swirl before I force out a grin, fighting the disappointment-laced curiosity currently circulating in my veins. I need a distraction to get me out of this funk.

I eye the buxom blonde before me, her teeth biting her plump bottom lip in invitation and suddenly, my mind is made and I curl my arm around her waist, reflexively kneading the soft flesh there.

"Sure, babe. I think it's time for me to have some fun with you."

"Finally, my turn. I can't wait. I expect orgasms all night long. And don't worry, I know better than to expect any commitments from you."

I give her a half grin as a familiar chill settles inside me, and I steel myself for the curl of self-loathing, which usually makes an appearance about now.

That's who I am.

Mr. Good Times.

A guy who knows his way around a female's body, always getting them off in each romp, which apparently is a rarity among nineteen-year-olds, from what I hear. Good enough for a tumble or two in the sheets, never enough for anything more. After all, who'll expect anything more from someone who barely graduated from high school and is at the edge of being flunked out from community college? I'm the shame of my parents, hardworking Chinese immigrants who expected their son to graduate with honors and become a lawyer or a doctor or something fancy like that. My chest pinches and I crack the tense joints in my neck.

Nancy giggles as I lead her back inside the store for a few more hours of brainless work, my hand swiping the angel's wish from the tree as we pass by the table. Bernice glares at me and I wag my brows at her, earning myself a *harrumph*.

My mind flutters to the angel with her alabaster skin and fiery hair.

The heavy block of lead sinks deeper in my chest and I curl a hand into a tight fist. Smothering the pangs of craving in my gut, I straighten my shoulders and walk to my station like I couldn't care less.

I'm Jack Szeto, and nothing can faze me.

. . .

"Who are you calling a loser?" Heat rushes up my spine and I growl as I take a step toward the big, blond jock in front of me and Adrian Callahan, my best friend, stops me with his arm.

"Ignore them, Jack," he murmurs, his voice deep and laced with venom.

The holidays have come and gone, and the store looks even more pathetic without the faded Christmas decorations and non-stop holiday music. But at least I have my best friend working here as well, suffering alongside me.

A pitfall of working at Grocery for Less as a side gig, earning minimum wage, is seeing these rich-ass prep school kids prance around every so often, high school sporting fans—an unfortunate side effect of being close to a school with a decent athletics program—like they own the place, like everyone is beneath their brand-name shoes and flashy cars.

Case in point, the blond jock in front of me has been calling my homeboy here all types of names, which pisses me off because Adrian is the best man I know. He's sharp, hardworking, and loyal, but is dealing with some difficult circumstances in his life. Unlike me, he has the brain and the grades. He's just missing the right opportunity.

He's going places. I might not be book smart, but my gut is never wrong.

He was held back a year because of his many absences to take care of his family while his mom is sick, and now he's in this lame-ass rich kids prep school on scholarship, which apparently this jock takes offense to. Adrian and the idiot are now standing close to each other in some sort of showdown and my hands curl into fists as adrenaline surges through my body, ready to back up my friend when the shit blows up.

"Ryan? Adrian? What's going on?"

I glance away from the imminent fight, past the rainbow assortment of jars and jugs of cooking oil and condiments to two svelte figures ambling our way in the cropped tops and short skirts of cheerleading uniforms. A voice echoes from the speakers with some announcement I don't pay attention to. A concerned brunette, who just asked the question, rushes toward Adrian and Ryan, the jock, while my gaze snags to her friend next to her in her ethereal glory. Suddenly, the burning heat in my veins runs differently, the spicy warmth spreading through my body as my heart threatens to crawl out of my chest.

Even though she appears to hate me, I'm drawn to her, a diamond in my rough. Even if this means only admiring her from afar, the way you would admire beautiful artwork in a museum.

The angel's eyes flicker to mine briefly, a coolness in her expression, before she turns to look at her classmates. Words are exchanged, but I don't pay attention because the thudding in my chest is now a roaring in my ears, eclipsing everything around me, my senses only attuned to the redhead in front of me.

Utterly captivating. Effortlessly breathtaking.

Her Christmas wish sits heavily in my pocket, and I'm afraid it may burn a hole in my pants and reveal the paper-stealing thief I am.

Adrian's voice pierces through the veil. "We're fine. I think Ryan and I have just come to an agreement on some things."

"Whatever." Ryan shrugs and turns to the girls, barely sparing Adrian and me a glance. "You guys got what you need?"

The brunette nods. "Why don't you guys go and pay for the stuff? I'll be right there."

My eyes are pinned on her friend.

Look at me, Siren. Let me see those pretty eyes.

After what could've been seconds or minutes, her eyes—warmest hazel rimmed with dark green with small flecks of brown—finally find mine again. My foolish heart can't help but try again. Can't help but hope my angel will dole out a grin or something beautiful my way. My lips curve into a smile, no doubt showcasing my left dimple, and I arch my brow, an expression that has worked on all the chicks in the past but hasn't been sincere until now. My pulse is thready, my breathing light as I anticipate her response.

Instead of smiling back, her muscles tense up and she rakes her eyes over my body before flattening her lips into a thin line as if displeased.

My grin falters and I can feel my forehead furrowing as Emily says something. An ache settles in my chest as I chuckle halfheartedly in response. My eyes reluctantly leave my goddess, who is currently shooting ice daggers into my chest, and turn toward the brunette. Maybe this is punishment for all the hearts I've broken in the past.

How fitting.

"Well, aren't you cute?" I brush my hair to the side and flash another bright smile, trying once more. "I'm Jack, and who might you be?"

The brunette blinks and stares at me. She quirks a sarcastic brow.

My angel laughs. She *fucking* laughs at me. But her voice is sweet with a tinge of smoke at the end. Sultry. Too bad it isn't friendliness I'm hearing from her right now. "Please don't try that on her. It doesn't work."

I take a deep breath, noticing a light scent of orange blossoms drifting to my senses from her direction. It's almost like the addictive nicotine hitting my system. An unsubstantiated high running through my veins as I face my goddess once more. "Oh *hello,* beautiful. I love your orange hair. Reminds me of the most beautiful of sunsets." I wiggle my brow and throw out an easy grin.

Adrian shakes his head, his pale-blue eyes dancing in laughter. "Ladies, meet my friend Jack, who's mostly harmless. Jack, this is Emily and her friend..."

"Sarah. We're obviously cheerleaders. The basketball team was playing a game around here and we just stopped by to pick up some snacks and stuff." Sarah directs her answer at Adrian, completing ignoring me. "It's strawberry-blonde, dumbass," she mutters under her breath, then winces as if she's regretting her words.

Her friend stares at her in surprise, as if she too is shocked at Sarah's outburst, because if I were a betting man, Sarah isn't a cruel person and the furrowing of her brows and the look of guilt on her face seems to confirm that.

But why is she this way toward me?

I swallow and roll my shoulders back, adopting a devil-may-care attitude, my lips curved up in what Adrian nicknamed the Casanova smile, the very one making all the ladies swoon. The pinch in my chest mixes in with a heady burn in my gut, the predator inside me wanting to chase after her and unravel the mystery.

Sarah.

It means princess, something I learned in the Bible class I was forced to attend when I was a kid. What a perfect name for her.

She glances up once more, noting my brilliant smile, and her brow is now arched high as if she's daring me to call her out on it. My pulse picks up and I bite my cheek, amused by her response. I don't know whether I should be offended or appalled. Or should I be pleased? It's as if she's immune to all my charms.

I don't know what I've ever done to piss her off, but I can't find myself caring too much right now.

Sarah just spoke to me. She directed her barbs at me.

No girls have ever reacted to me this way before. A sick, perverse twist of pleasure snakes through me, and I find myself wanting to learn more about Sarah, wondering why she doesn't seem to like my flirting, wondering what I can do to win her over.

After Emily exchanges a few words with Adrian, she links arms with Sarah and drags them both toward the doors. I glance at my best friend, finding him staring at Emily like a lovesick puppy.

"Holy shit," I murmur to Adrian.

"What?"

"You're so fucked, dude."

He doesn't answer me. I keep my eyes on the retreating backsides of the two girls, my words sounding loud to my ears. Sliding my hands in my pockets, I roll out my shoulders, my body suddenly wanting to chase after Sarah, to find out why she seems to hate me. To hear her smoky voice once again.

I pull out my wallet, carefully taking out the paper tag and read the words I've long memorized, her response to my message on the tree.

> Merry Christmas, mysterious stranger. I know the pain of not feeling enough, of thinking others only want something from us and not caring about who we really are inside. I believe in you. You have something worthy to offer to the world and one day, others will see it too. You are enough.

A lump appears in my throat as my fingers trace the delicate cursive writing.

Perhaps I'm fucked too.

But angels are here for us to pray to, for us to admire from afar.

They're definitely not here for a sinner like me who's probably destined for hell.

Present Day—New York City

Jack

"Is it always so quiet here?" the teasing voice next to me asks.

"Don't jinx it, newbie. Enjoy these moments because they don't happen very often."

I arch my brow at Roxy, a cute, bubbly brunette we just hired as part of our trainee program. She's making moon eyes at me, her lashes fluttering. If she survives the next year of rigorous training, learning the ins and outs of the main levels of The Orchid, which is only the tip of the iceberg at this establishment, then she'll earn herself a coveted junior staff position. Just the starting salary and the benefits alone have people lining up around the block to apply.

"Jack, New York City Philharmonic just pulled out of the Christmas ball. Something about their conductor getting into an accident over the weekend and their backups are unavailable," Julia, my trusty assistant, materializes next to me and whispers urgently in my ear.

I swallow a groan. The Christmas ball is one of the biggest and most high-profile events at The Orchid, and is also the only event allowing paparazzi in our doors. Everything has to—no, *needs* to—be perfect.

"Can you get me Enrique Sandros on the phone?" I smile at a few patrons walking by. *Nothing to see here, move on guys.* A few bejeweled ladies I vaguely recognize as top-billing actresses in Asia wink at me and I nod in response. Roxy stands listlessly next to me, her eyes widening as if she knows something is amiss.

Julia checks her phone, no doubt verifying the time difference between here and Spain, and taps on a few buttons on the screen before handing it over.

"Sí," Sandros's baritone voice filters through the line.

"Enrique! This is Jack Szeto from The Orchid. How is my infamous piano prodigy doing? I saw your performance in Vienna online last month. It was marvelous." My hand clenches but I slide it into my pocket.

"Jack! So good to hear from you. Vienna was wonderful, but I miss your city and The Orchid."

I chuckle, remembering the handsome world-renowned pianist sampling all the flavors of entertainment we had to offer, and then some. He was fun to hang out with, if not a bit young and unsure of what to do with his fame.

Enrique rambles on, "I still remember when you saved my ass in New York last time I was there. Those paparazzi are ruthless. I thought for sure you were joking when you said you can get them to stop the photos of me with that *bella* girl from coming out, but you did, you magician."

"Small favors, nothing to thank me about, Enrique." I motion to Julia and Roxy to follow me as I stroll around the lobby, checking to see if anything is amiss.

I rap my knuckles in an erratic rhythm on the mahogany receptionist desk in the dimly lit lobby as my eyes rove over the large, luxurious room, an automatic habit to confirm all is in order. The tear-drop crystals from the chandeliers sparkle as if they're brand new, reflecting slices of rainbows off the dove-gray patterned wallpaper. I squint, making note of a crooked strand that must have dislodged during the daily cleaning. Strolling past the dark-blue jacquard and silk seating, my nose picks up the delicate scents of amber and sandalwood wafting in the air, and I skim my fingers on the settee, frowning at the wrinkles in the luxurious fabric. The music playing from the speakers is some melancholy aria from a famous opera.

This shit won't fly.

"I owe you one, Jack. Anything you need, let me know." Sandro's grateful sigh comes across the line. "My uncle won't be pleased if those photos came out."

Bingo.

"Actually, Enrique. I'm in a bit of a bind and want to get your thoughts on something."

"Sí? What's going on?"

"We need a conductor to direct the NYC Phil for our Christmas ball...you know, *the ball*. Everyone who's anyone will be there, and we only want the best of the best. We have a few candidates in mind, but as you're my friend, I was thinking—"

"Dios mío! Why did you wait so long? My uncle would love to be there for Christmas! He's been clamoring for an invitation to The Orchid after I sang praises of it."

My shoulders relax as I take in a deep breath. Quirking my lips to the side, I reply, "That's why I thought of you first. Everyone wants to be here, but I prefer working with people I trust. I know it's only a few weeks away and your uncle will need to fly out very soon to rehearse with the orchestra here, but he'll have everything The Orchid has to offer—"

"Say no more. This is a brilliant opportunity! Fantástico! I'll be his favorite nephew. And he's one of the best conductors who's performed with the Vienna Phil, so everything will be excellent!"

Roxy coughs and I turn to stare at her and Julia, who's wearing a bemused expression on her face and shaking her head. "My assistant will be in touch. Send me your uncle's contact information."

"Gracias, my friend. I can't wait to see you again in a few months when I'm back. I owe you one again! Thank you for thinking of me."

Laughing softly under my breath, I hang up and hand the phone back to Julia. Another crisis averted. This is what I'm good at. A rush of satisfaction flows through me.

"I can't believe you just did that," she mutters, her eyes dancing in mirth.

"What did I miss?" Roxy grasps my arm, eager to understand what just transpired.

"Jack here just secured one of the top conductors of the best orchestra in the world and made it sound like he's doing them a favor."

"Semantics, Julia. To cater to the rich, you need to speak their language."

Julia makes a tiny bow with her hands. "I will never reach your level, master."

Shaking my head, I gesture toward the hidden employee door camouflaged against the wallpaper in the room. "Coordinate this for me with Sandros?"

Julia nods before she spins around, her bouncing curls flying behind her as she sets off toward the offices.

I may not be a billionaire or an Ivy League graduate like most people here, but I'm damn good at reading people and killing it at my job as one of the entertainment managers, which is really a fancy name for jack-of-all-trades, but I tend to focus my time on resolving conflicts involving our pickiest patrons, overseeing our larger events, and occasionally training some of our new hires. Adrian got me this job when he secured a membership because as I predicted all along, my best friend dug himself out of his lowly circumstances and became a rags-to-riches success story, and is now one of the richest billionaires in the world. He gave me the opportunity to turn my miserable life around. And I won't repay him by half-assing this job.

Plus, the money is good. A quarter of a million plus a generous bonus per year is nothing to sneeze at.

"Roxy, come over here and bring your notepad."

She scurries over, her eyes wide as she awaits further instructions.

"Tell housekeeping to fix the chandeliers and be careful when they clean them. The strands are delicate, and if broken, we'll need to send for parts from Austria. Have them re-steam the seats as well. The wrinkles are an eyesore and look like wilted lettuce. Also, adjust the music to something that doesn't sound like I'm at my funeral. People are supposed to feel relaxed when they come here, not depressed. Amanda over at the desk," I motion to one of the three receptionists working behind the tall counter, "can help you."

Roxy nods and scribbles on her notepad. She scrunches her delicate nose. "Isn't all of this a little over the top? The place already looks great."

I flatten my lips, my fingers twiddling at the stainless-steel cufflinks on the sleeves of my bespoke shirt underneath my suit jacket. "You're working at the crowning jewel of Fleur Entertainment Holdings. This is not one of their entry-level nightclubs you've probably partied at before. This 'place' is not only a club or a resort, it's an experience. Anyone you encounter here is influential, rich, and expects the best of the best. We have senators, billionaires, world leaders, judges, and other powerful people as members here. We know everyone by face and name. We know their inseams and dress sizes. We know how they take their coffee and which side of the bed they sleep on. Being a member here means the rules don't apply to you. They can get anything they want here."

Nodding at a few staff members walking quickly but silently toward the back rooms—they're to be seen and not heard—I stroll to one of the few antique tables dotting the space and pick up a few scraps of paper littering the surface. Roxy follows as I finish my sweep of the lobby.

"They're here to escape the pressures of their daily lives, to relax without the prying eyes of the public and paparazzi. The Orchid not only provides a place for them to do that, we fulfill all of their needs, whether it's a scrumptious meal from the Michelin restaurants or a drink from the gentlemen's club or ladies' lounge on-site, the best medical treatment from the top surgeons in the world, front-row tickets to any sporting event, to even providing dates or companionship for our members if desired. Our patrons only need to walk through our doors, and everything they could possibly want is taken care of."

"Isn't that illegal?" she whispers, snagging on the last part of my explanation, as all newbies do. Something about potential illicit behavior or sex always seems to interest them. I fight the urge to roll my eyes, my mind already hedging Roxy won't survive this training period with her inane questions and lack of research. I don't even know how she got through the vetting process. Something I'll need to talk to the hiring team about.

"Roxy, the politicians and selected high-ranking judges are members here. They are clamoring to be part of this establishment. You're still young, but you'll soon learn the world isn't black and white. Furthermore, we don't explicitly offer sexual services. What the girls and gents do on their own time is their business, provided they follow our usual health and safety rules."

I don't add the escorts who provide services here have different classifications based on the level of "services" they are willing to provide. I also don't let her know that the private Rose floors of this building are reserved for adult entertainment, including sex clubs, strip clubs, kink rooms, and suites for members with amorous pursuits in mind. That's classified information she doesn't need as an entry-level employee in her training period, and most likely will never know about.

I lean closer to Roxy and murmur, "But remember this, the one golden rule. Since you and I aren't working as companions or dates, there's absolutely no fraternization between employees and patrons. It's a zero-tolerance policy and any violation will result in immediate termination and blacklisting of most hospitality establishments in the city and beyond. No one will hire anyone who has been fired from The Orchid in disgrace."

Roxy nods, her face paling a smidge. Unfortunately, this is a reminder I have to dole out to many trainees because the temptation to flirt or "something more" with our rich clientele can be too enticing for some folks.

The *clicking* and *clacking* of high heels strutting on the marble floors alert me to a newcomer. I straighten up and smooth out the lapels of my crisp, black suit, and smile, making sure my dimple is showing. A petite, forty-something brunette is striding toward us with the determination of a tiger on the prowl for his next meal. "Ms. Marceau, welcome back to The Orchid."

"Jack! I've been looking for you. This just won't do."

Flashing a reassuring grin, I take in her flushed appearance. She's bundled up in some sort of black-and-white fur coat, reminding me of a certain cartoon villainess. Her hair is coated with a light dusting of snow and is sticking out of her usually coiffed updo. Apparently, she's worked herself into a fit and is probably *this close* to blowing up and causing a scene. I motion to one of our waitstaff to come over to retrieve the coat from her.

"We can't have a frown like that marring such a beautiful face." I wink, enjoying her pinkened cheeks. After all, my charm is one reason I was hired here. "I'm sure no problem is too big for us to resolve for you."

"I've talked to my cover designer, my agent, my publisher, and everyone is saying they can't pull this off because Christmas and New Years are in a few weeks. Like they can't make adjustments to accommodate. That's utter bullshit. I'm Juliet Marceau, the *only* author whose *entire* backlist has graced the *New York Times* bestseller's list for three years consecutively. I'm also the *only* romance author who has been *Time Magazine's* 'Person of the Year' five times in the last decade. I am fronting the entire cost for production and all I need are their resources for the project. I probably generate most of their revenue and they're saying no to me. It's appalling. Unacceptable."

Placing my hand lightly on the small of her back, I usher her toward one of the few decorative offices next to the lobby. "I'll take care of you. When have I ever disappointed you?" I murmur, keeping my voice gentle.

Juliet melts under my touch and sighs. "I know you can fix this for me. You always do."

I glance back at Roxy. "Go shadow Amanda at reception and remember the tasks I mentioned earlier." Roxy scampers away, closing the clear glass door behind her, and I return my attention to the high-strung and demanding author, who is sitting in one of the dark leather chairs in front of the oak desk. I amble to the wet bar and pour two glasses of Chianti, her favorite, and set one glass before her before taking a seat across from her.

"So, what can The Orchid do for you?"

She takes a large gulp of wine, her flushed pallor from earlier paling a smidge. "I had a vision last week for my next bestseller and I spent the last three days holed up in one of your suites, writing what I know will be a list topper. My editors and publishers are all on board with it, and I want to release the book shortly after the holidays before my vacation to Turks and Caicos. Everything is lined up except for the cover and the promo video trailer and materials! It's a MFMMM to MF romance and I have the male models secured, but I still need a female model."

I blink. "MFMMM?" *What in the motherfucking world is this?*

"It's why choose," she says, as if that means anything to me. Upon seeing my lack of reaction, she lets out a deep exhale. "It's a romance between four men and one woman. The story starts out with four men and a woman with some group activities and ends up with a main pairing of a male/female couple."

"That sounds...thrilling. Lucky girl."

She waves her hands in the air, her voice increasing in pitch again. "Yes, yes. But I don't *have* the girl. The cover and promo materials need the *right* girl. I have scenes planned out in my head already."

"Surely your team can find you a suitable model?"

"Apparently not right now because of the holiday season. Everyone is booked up."

I pull out my phone, scrolling through my contacts. I know quite a few models who enjoyed spending a few nights of good fun and pleasure with me during New York Fashion Week in the past.

"Charlene Stevens? Annalise Hopkins? Belinda Kang?" I cite a few of the supermodels in my Rolodex I can probably woo to do me a last-minute favor.

"No. No, no, no. That won't work! My vision is an ingenue and these girls are too famous for my girl-next-door role. Also, they don't have the exact shade of strawberry-blonde I'm looking for."

Which can come from a bottle. But I refrain from speaking.

"None of the dyed crap. She needs to be an *au naturale* beauty. It's all part of my vision." Juliet taps her fingers on the desk. *Clack clack clack.* The sound of her nails scratching on the wood is like the nuisance of the woodpecker hacking at the electricity pole at six a.m. each day outside my bedroom window in my Brooklyn apartment.

Taking a deep breath, I nod and reach out, closing my hand over her jittery one and she stills before glancing at me.

"I'll talk to our companionship department. We employ beautiful women of all attributes and ethnicities here. I can—"

Suddenly, Juliet gasps, her eyes widening. She wrenches her hand from underneath mine and points toward the door, her other hand fluttering to her mouth. If she wasn't an author, she'd make a superb actress with her theatrics.

"Her. I want her. She's the perfect girl for the cover."

Arching my brow, I turn toward the glass door and my heart revs up and skips several beats.

On the other side of the door is *her*.

My angel. My Siren.

Sarah Winstead.

She's a vision in white, the orange flames of her hair curled in waves, cascading down her back. Hair I want to wrap my hand around while I kiss those soft, pink lips, teasing out a moan or whimper.

Or at least, I've imagined it many times over the years. After Adrian left for college all those years ago, I lost touch with Emily and, by association, Sarah. For those earlier years while my best friend was on the East Coast writing his own rags-to-riches story, I was bouncing from odd jobs and aimlessly trolling bars and clubs on the weekend, but the angel with strawberry-blonde hair never strayed far from my mind, and I find myself always looking for her in the hordes of people on the dance floors or hunkering behind the bar top trying to signal for a bartender's attention.

But of course, she would never be there, and why would she? I went to seedy clubs while she frequents establishments such as The Orchid.

But I still remember as clear as yesterday when I first bumped into her at The Orchid. It was a sweltering summer day, and I was letting out a sigh of relief as I stepped through the main entrance with Julia, reveling in the crisp air-conditioning while my skin was slick with a thin layer of sweat after my brief excursion to a restaurant nearby for lunch. As I took out a tissue to blot off the stickiness of a humid New York day, I pulled Julia in for a brief hug, once again congratulating her for her incoming bundle of joy. She wasn't showing yet, but Julia was absolutely glowing with happiness.

As I pulled away, my eyes caught a flash of copper, my nose picked up a faint scent of orange blossoms, and my heart stopped as Sarah's eyes locked with mine. We stared at each other for what could've been minutes but was probably just seconds, and it was as if my heart was restarted, finally kicking into a ferocious rhythm as the woman in my dreams walked back into my life. Her wide eyes softened, her lips tipping into the beginnings of a smile before Julia murmured something into my ear—something inane I don't remember—and when I finally pulled away, the hazel eyes were cold before she whirled away, disappearing into an open elevator.

Our paths have since crossed multiple times because of our mutual friends and here at The Orchid, second home to the rich and famous. Yet another sign of how different our stations are. Sarah sitting in her gilded throne while I'm the lowly employee, a shadow to be seen and not heard.

Our interactions are mostly passing glances, jokes and cutting remarks thrown at each other in half-jest or half-seriousness, me trying anything I could to get her to respond to me, to talk to me. But somehow, while I can decode the inner workings of supermodels and actresses, I can't seem to break the codex that is Sarah Winstead.

My angel today is glorious as always. Her pale skin is pink from the elements, and she slowly tugs off her black leather gloves as a footman waltzes up and retrieves her thick, white coat, revealing a deep-turquoise dress that wraps around her abundant curves. Those tits, that ass. The curves that have grown more enticing, more luscious over the years.

Attributes I can only admire from afar.

My breathing quickens as a muscle tics in my jaw and heat slowly travels from my chest to my extremities.

Sarah turns her head, and our gazes meet, and I swear I can feel the animosity radiating from those hazel gems in torrents. But I can also feel the sharp zing of electric current as our stares hold each other, neither of us moving. I never figured out what I ever did to offend her, but despite the barbs and comebacks she usually doles out to me, I've always sensed a hidden current of something... something headier. As if insults are an extended foreplay between us. My nostrils flare as the blood finally reaches my stiffening hard-on.

It's like the room has vanished, and the world only contains Sarah and me.

Sarah flinches, as if jolting out of a trance, before her shrewd eyes narrow at me. She tosses her hair and walks away, her hips swaying like the Siren she is.

"...She's perfect. That's who I want. No one else will do."

The room refocuses and I realize Juliet is still babbling, her voice now animated in apparent excitement. I blink a few times and swallow the lump in my throat, my heart still racing as if I just finished a marathon.

Turning back to the woman before me, I let out a quivering smile. "You were saying you wanted who?"

"The woman who just walked by the door. Wearing the turquoise wrap dress. I only want her."

My eyes bounce between Juliet and the door before I let out a halfhearted chuckle. "She's a member here, not a professional model or actress."

"I don't care!" She thumps her hands on the table, her manicured nails clacking on the wood. "Isn't this establishment famous for meeting all our needs and demands? God knows I had to endure a five-year waitlist, three interviews, and an ungodly six-figure annual fee to be here. Don't disappoint me, Jack."

The air suddenly feels thin, and I fight the urge to loosen my perfectly knotted tie. I cough into my fist, needing to do something with my hands that doesn't include reaching out and strangling the woman in front of me.

Fuck my life.

I need to convince the one woman who seems to hate my guts and doesn't fall for my looks or charm to star in what'll probably be a racy photoshoot. Juliet might as well put a bullet through my brain and throw me into the Hudson.

"Jack? You'll make this happen, right?"

Cracking my knuckles, I force out a wide smile and lean back in my chair, faking confidence I suddenly don't have. "Of course. I'll make the magic happen."

Juliet releases her breath and tilts her lips up in a grin. She reaches out and grazes her fingers on my hand on the desk. "I know I can count on you, Jack." She stands and strides to the door, her hand pausing on the doorknob. "I feel so much better now. I'm in suite 302, if you want to come by later. We can celebrate my upcoming success..."

"You know the rules, no fraternizing between employees and patrons. But I appreciate the thought. I'll have someone send over a bottle of champagne to your suite tonight."

She pouts before curling her fingers in a wave and exits the office.

"Shit," I mutter under my breath, raking my hand through my hair. "Shit, shit, shit."

My mind swirls through various strategies of eking out a yes from Sarah. There's one thing I know for sure, she definitely won't say yes if the ask comes from me.

Buzz. Buzz. Buzz.

The vibrations from my cell phone disrupt me from my impending headache and I stare at the caller ID, my lips tilting up into a smile, before answering.

"Adrian, your timing is impeccable. Can I ask you and Emily for a favor? It's about Sarah..."

Emily: Pretty, pretty please? Do it for me? Your best friend? Your one true love? I'll buy you drinks?

I roll my eyes, my lips tipping up in a grin. My fingers fly across my phone as I compose my reply. Mom blathers on in the background as I put her on speakerphone, momentarily tuning her out.

Sarah: I thought Adrian was your one true love. I'll think about it. I'm not sure if I want to flaunt my body in front of a camera...seems to add fuel to the fire, you know? And when are you going to buy me drinks anyway, with me moving to New York?

Emily: I'm an equal opportunity lover...and you're hot. If you're trying to hide your curves-for-days bod, because of what those stupid idiots from the past said, ignore them. Don't live your life because of what other people think. Sorry for the tirade. I just get pissed thinking about the assholes you've dated in the past.

My heart warms at Emily's text. It's hard to shake the feeling I'm more than tits and ass and a rich last name sometimes. Especially when my asshole exes or dates in the past have led me to believe otherwise.

"Don't be such a bitch. You have a body made for fucking and you don't want to put out?" Tim's voice, asshole number five, echoes in my mind, like a ghost haunting me.

"Please Sarah, if it wasn't for your last name and your rich dad, people wouldn't put up with your shit. You may be hot, but the sex isn't great enough to make me stick around." Courtesy of Evan, asshole number seven, when he broke up with me because the romance fizzled out.

I swallow, a familiar burn appearing behind my eyes. I shut those remarks down as soon as the assholes laid them on me because no one has time for such bullshit, but that doesn't mean what they said doesn't hurt. As much as I don't want to let these idiots run my life, their criticisms and insults always seem to weasel themselves in through the chinks of my tough armor. Especially during my lows. The pain inflicted by words and self-doubt can be much worse than the wounds from physical injury.

Mom is now talking about holiday plans. Something to do with traveling. I make the obligatory humming noises and she's none the wiser while my mind reflects on my unfortunate romantic history.

I love myself, love my curves and my heart. And perhaps, it's time for me to take charge of my own narrative. I'm proud of my body and what better way to give a middle finger to all the assholes out there than to celebrate it in a photoshoot by a world-renowned portrait photographer for a bestselling author whose work I love? Perhaps Emily does have a point. And I'll no doubt earn some money to tuck away for a rainy day when the funds from my family are cut off.

A few moments later, another text appears.

Emily: Aaaaand, if I can't buy you drinks, I'll force Steven... no, *ask* Steven to buy you drinks. And he'll be happy to do it.

I laugh at her text, imaging my petite best friend wrangling her tall, muscular, King of Wall Street of a younger brother into doing anything. Maybe back in high school that was possible, but definitely not now. I type in my reply on my phone.

"Sarah? What are you laughing about? It was embarrassing to be seen in the same outfit as her and—" Mom's shrill voice is dripping with censure.

I clear my throat. "Sorry, I just saw a funny text come through. Please continue."

Mom launches into another complaint about some society squabble, and my fingers fly over the keypad on my phone.

Sarah: I'll think about it and let you know, Ems. And if you can get Steven to stop being such a workaholic in order to even go out for drinks, that'll be nothing short of a miracle.

Despite being born into a world of privilege, I've tried my best to not let that get into my head, because frankly, I've seen what money can do to people and the desperate measures people will go to keep it or to gain more.

Perhaps it's naïve, but I'd like to think a measure of a person's quality isn't defined by the number of zeros in her bank account or how gorgeous or put together she appears to be. It's defined by her character and what she does with the resources she has.

Too bad most people in my family's circles, except for Emily and her siblings, don't feel this way. My parents, especially, don't subscribe to my thinking. I always wondered how we're even related. To the family, money and power reign supreme. There's never enough of either. And for the women, well, we are beautiful decorations and bobbleheads touting the family name, helping to preserve our high society image.

I scoff at the thought. It's part of the reason why Emily and I are such good friends. We're both rebels in our circles.

And perhaps that's why I've always felt like a bit of an outsider.

Emily: You'll do great, and it's an adventure! Weren't you saying you wanted to try different things, break away from your family? While you're interviewing for your dream job, why don't you start with this gig? Maybe modeling is your calling!

I snort. Who wants to hire a thirty-year-old model? But Emily does have a point. I have been talking about trying new things. To get away from my family's control. To live for myself and not for the broader Winstead name. It's been a long time coming and perhaps turning thirty finally closed the deal for me, but I've had enough of being another cog in the Winstead engine, doing what's expected of me instead of what I want to do.

And it's part of why this conversation with my mom is necessary even though it's going to be painful.

"Sarah? Sarah! Do you hear me? What do you mean you're moving back to New York? Linda from HR sent me your resignation letter. I thought you were joking before." Mom's polished voice flits across the speakerphone, finally piercing through the storm in my head and drawing my attention back to my call with her.

I'm curled up in the thousand-dollar cream basket-weave desk chair that just wraps around your body like a pillow in my suite at the Kensington Hotel.

Better enjoy these luxuries before they cut me out of my trust fund.

My pulse picks up in speed as I contemplate a future where I'm on my own without relying on my family.

The freedom. The guilt. The tiny pinch of fear.

Will I make it? Or will I come crawling back into the fold with my tail between my legs?

I let out a laborious breath, my eyes unfocused as I force myself to say the words I've been holding in for so long.

Five years, to be exact.

I've done my time with the family business. I've put my dreams on hold. Now, it's time to spread my wings and fly.

"Mom, it's time for me to step back from the company. It's something that has been on my mind for years. And I'm going to do it. It's the end of the year, the marketing campaigns I set up are doing well. My projects are all wrapped up. I'd like to start the new year in New York. I've always liked this city."

"Why would you do such a thing? Your dad and I give you everything you can possibly want. Money. A job you don't really need but want to have. Why would you give it all up?" Mom's voice turns shrill and I lower the volume on my phone. "I knew we shouldn't have let you go to college all the way out there."

Burying my face in my hands, I groan. "This has nothing to do with where I went to college years ago. I want to pursue my dreams, to do something that actually makes a difference in the world, rather than to add more zeroes to a bank account that clearly doesn't need more."

Not to mention, working for the snake that is my dad is exhausting. The man is reprehensible and having him continue to control me is unthinkable.

"Sarah, what is going on in that pretty head of yours? You should be more like your friends. Attend the right events, the best parties, represent our family in a good light. Or better yet, find a man to marry, have children. Make connections. What are you even going to do out there?"

"I've applied to quite a few nonprofits to run their marketing departments."

"Nonprofits? Your family is rich and you're going to leave the family to work for pennies? I swear, we didn't raise you like this..."

Like what? Like someone who actually cares about the good of society? Someone who actually wants to help people less fortunate?

I bite my lip and don't reply. She's a hopeless cause. It's useless to argue with her.

She sighs, as if I've disappointed her by wanting to be more than a pretty figurehead, sipping martinis, and smiling for the press. "Your dad won't like this. He'll cut you off, you know."

"I don't—"

Ding.

My inbox chimes with a notification of a new text. The sender is Aunt Christy, and the message is addressed to Mom and me.

Aunt Christy: What can George possibly be thinking? Flaunting that whore around the country club for all to see. Linda, didn't you have an agreement with him to keep his "friends" outside of our circles? And they're saying she might be pregnant? I got five texts from the girls in the book club, and I don't know what to tell them.

She then sends over a link of the front-page article on *Gossip Times*, the go-to website in America for all things entertainment and gossip-related, which has a photo of Dad grabbing the ass of a curvy blonde who is quite possibly younger than me. The unflattering angle of the photo does make it seem like she may have a baby bump.

Despicable. Disgusting. Revolting.

Heat spreads from my chest to my face as I swipe close the open browser, not wanting to look at the offending photos of Dad acting like a horny teenager with someone who isn't his wife. Unfortunately, this isn't the first time it has happened, and it definitely won't be the last. But this is the first time there's a baby rumor. The thought of him turns my stomach. Heated blood churns through my veins and I clench my hands into tight fists.

If this is what it means to be part of the Winstead family and lofty circles, I want none of it.

I'm done. So done.

The room is silent except for the quiet hum of the AC and I sneak a glance at my phone, seeing the call still connected.

"Mom? Did you see what Aunt Christy sent?"

The silence sounds eerily loud for a few seconds before I hear the faintest sigh.

"And what of it?" I hear some rustling and a creak of the door before a muffled, "Anna, get me a size 0 in this color, please."

"You're shopping!" I stand and pace around the windows overlooking Central Park in all of its winter glory, the snow blanketing the ground like a scene from a postcard. My French braid whips around in a blur of orange and fire. "How can you sound so indifferent about this? For all these years? And now there may be a baby!"

More rustling comes across the line. "This is our way of life, Sarah. The sooner you learn it, the better. Men like your dad will always want younger, prettier women to play with. But he only has *one* wife, and that's me. And your dad isn't stupid. I'm sure there's no baby and if there is one, he'll pay her a nice sum to get it taken care of."

Bile threatens to make its way up my throat and I curl my lips in disgust.

"So, you just look the other way? What way of life is this? Don't you have any *self-respect?* Thank you for confirming for me I want to leave the family business for good because this...I want *nothing* to do with this type of life."

I clasp my hand over my mouth as the last words flew out without thought. Hurting her intentionally isn't something I take pride in, despite everything I feel about her choices. But it's as if a higher power out there is giving me a sign, telling me to run away while I still can.

"Sarah Elizabeth Winstead! I won't have you speak to me this way. I put up with everything for *us.* Who else will provide us with money to spend, houses to live in? Vacations in Europe? Who can accommodate our lifestyle? Those women mean nothing and—"

Slapping my hand on the cold glass, I grit my teeth, the heat in my chest burning hot. "Mom, I don't need these things. Don't use me as an excuse. This is all for you. I'm so sick of this bullshit and seeing how other people look at me in pity because Dad is dipping his dick in every available pussy—"

"Young lady! This language is unbecoming. I won't have you disrespecting me like this. What do you think you'll achieve by alienating us? You won't survive out there by yourself."

Burning acid travels up my throat and I shake my head while I try but fail to focus on the tiny dots of New Yorkers braving the winter weather on the streets. "I...can't talk to you. My mind's made up. I'm quitting the business and staying in New York, and I don't care what you and Dad do to me. I. Am. Done."

My fingers tremble as I disconnect the call, and suddenly, the world comes into clear focus. I notice small birds flitting across the gray skies, undeterred by the freezing temperatures outside. A few brave folks bundled up in winter gear and beanies jog on the periphery of the park. I imagine they have souls of warriors, not letting inconsequential problems like weather prevent them from achieving their exercise goals. I can be one of those people down there, braving the elements, giving the middle finger to Mother

Nature as they persist and persevere. The aching pressure in my chest loosens up gradually, as if there were invisible cinder blocks weighing me down all this time.

I take a deep breath and finally notice a faint scent of mint and jasmine, Kensington Hotel's signature aroma.

For the first time in a long time, I can breathe.

My lungs drag in ragged inhales as I walk back to the desk and take out the message a stranger mailed to me all those years ago during the holidays, a token I've laminated into a bookmark and carry with me always.

> There's beauty in uncertainty, in fear, in anticipation; because the future has endless possibilities. The world hasn't met the real you yet and when you step into the sun, everyone will be dazzled by your sparkle, your energy, and most of all, you. I believe in you. You are perfect. You're an angel among mankind. Go get them, angel.

A warmth bleeds into my chest as I smile at the sentiment. Whoever this person was, it's as if he knew the depths of my soul without ever having met me. It's kismet. Magical. A token from my soulmate out there...somewhere in the vast world.

Unlocking my phone, I scroll to the text messages between Emily and me. Time for me to take the road less traveled, grab risks by their horns, do something different for myself without a care to the Winstead name.

> **Sarah:** Screw it. Let's do it. And you owe me drinks for a month.

• • •

I spot him before he sees me.

Jack Szeto. The man who can drive me up the wall by simply looking at me. He's precisely the type of man I'd avoid with a ten-foot pole. The insincere flirt and womanizer. When we met all those years ago, I knew he was trouble the first moment I laid eyes on him at the grocery store. The teasing, wicked grin, the sexy swipe of his tongue on his lip ring. The effortless and meaningless compliments he doles out like second nature. The girls draped all over him on the occasions I've come across him. And every time, it's a different girl.

And sometimes, I see those girls staring forlornly at him after they have "broken up"—if you can even call it that since he never settles down. It's as if women are disposable and replaceable. I've been around men all my life who think women should fawn over them because of their family or their money. Jack gives off the same attitude, but he uses his looks and body as bait.

I remember when he came to pick up Emily from senior prom to escort her to the beach for a clandestine date with Adrian like something out of a Shakespearean play, how he strutted up in his casual, ragged rock-band T-shirt, his confident swagger earning whispers from classmates nearby. He may be a bad boy from the opposite side of the tracks, but he worked that to his advantage. And somehow, even after all these years, none of his behavior seems to be sincere. The nicknames, the casual remarks, and even his entire unflappable personality. He gives off the "I'm sexy and I know it" vibe and it completely turns me off.

I see through his act.

In the last five years, after I bumped into him in the lobby when he walked in, his arm curled around another beautiful woman, I can count our interactions on two hands. And each and every one of those interactions, he would seek me out, flash me one of those dazzling smiles, his eyes showing the faintest lines which only made him sexier, and then would proceed to bestow me the Jack Szeto experience of fake charm, nicknames that'd be sweet coming from anyone except him, and him volleying my snide remarks back with more compliments or annoying barbs in a twisted game of tennis.

And yet he makes you come alive more than ever, Sarah.
Damn it.

He's leaning casually on the crystal bar top at The Menagerie, a small wine and cocktail lounge tucked into the back of the second floor of The Orchid. This is one of my favorite places within the fifty-plus stories establishment in the heart of Manhattan. The space is small, intimate, and perhaps only fits around ten tables and four to five private rooms. The walls are adorned with dark-green wallpaper threaded with hand-drawn vines and leaves in shimmering gold, a nod to the natural theme of the room. The glittering pendant lights are shaped like low-hanging tree branches, interspersed across the space, lighting up the tables in a dim, warm glow. Sunken seating dressed in delicate embroidery adds to the finishing touch. I always feel like I'm not in the middle of one of the busiest cities in the world when I step through these doors.

I'll miss The Menagerie when The Orchid revokes my membership. Why would they keep me on after Dad disowns me?

But it's a small price to pay for freedom and change. To be myself without the Winstead name being the first thing people see. To do what I want to do with my life. To meet people who'll want to be with me not because of my trust fund or my associations with one of the wealthiest families on the West Coast, but because they like me for me. Someone's whose coffee order may be two shots of integrity, a swirl of heart, a drizzle of impatience, topped with a sprinkle of bravery.

Without a penny to her name.

Everyone will be dazzled by your sparkle, your energy, and most of all, you.

My heart warms at the memories of the masculine scribble from the mysterious stranger. Someone who, despite not having met me before, seems to know me better than most people.

Slowly, I traipse over to the compelling, yet infuriating man, my fingers gripping the edge of my wool blazer as my heart pounds in anticipation. He's a beautiful man, tall, sleek lines, graceful as a panther in the rainforest. The years have been wonderful to him. Where he was attractive as a sexy bad boy back then, he's downright lethal now in a suit with a streak of devil inside him.

Muscles bunch under his well-fitted suit as he leans over the bar counter, his deep voice chuckling at something the bartender is saying. His hair, perfectly styled, the color of midnight, sparkles under the spotlight. I swallow as I approach him, a mere few feet away, bracing myself for the inevitable when Jack unleashes his smoldering charm when he spots me.

Suddenly, his casual frame freezes, his body so still, one may believe he's a statue. He cocks his head to the side and inhales, as if he's picking up on something...or someone.

"Sarah." His voice is a whisper, my name fleeting like the wind.

The drumming beats in my chest are loud in my ears as I stand in place behind him, finding myself unable to move. My breathing quickens.

He slowly turns around, pinning me with his intense, coal-colored eyes. His face is half shadows. A trick of the lamps. But the light lovingly caresses his strong nose, sharp jawline, and the silver lip ring glints as his full lips tip up in a half smile.

The dimple makes an appearance. My chest flutters.

"Thank you for coming. I've been waiting for you."

He stares at me, his eyes penetrating, and I fight the urge to turn around and run away. His intensity this time is different. Unsettling. Something I rarely see from him when he's usually all sex appeal and surface-level charm. Grins that don't reach his eyes.

"W-Waiting?" I've been rendered into an incoherent parrot. My breathing quickens.

"Always."

The words echo between us like a vow.

I bite my cheek at the insane thought.

Jack's lips tip up in an infinitesimal smile as he steps away from the counter and in a few quick steps is mere inches before me. He slides a palm to my back, the pressure light, and ushers me toward one of the private rooms. My heart thuds loudly in my chest and I can't help but feel shaken from the last few moments, even though nothing happened.

But the beating organ in my rib cage seems to tell me otherwise.

Juliet Marceau is chatting quietly with a man and a woman when we step inside. She stands, her eyes lighting up, when she sees us.

"Jack!" She hurries over, sliding her hand up his chest and leans in, pressing a soft kiss to his cheek. "I knew you could do it."

He grins, bestowing one of his dazzling smiles and a wink to her. He leans in, pressing a brief kiss on her cheek, his hand giving her arm a squeeze. "Of course. I aim to serve and please."

The earlier warmth in my insides is doused with ice and I flinch. The photos of Dad and the buxom blonde and, frankly, all his other women in the past, resurface in my mind. I vividly remember the pain of the kids sneering at me at school whenever Dad headlined another scandalous liaison with another bimbo. Some of those women were young enough to be my sister.

Flirt. Womanizer. Philanderer. Casanova. Conqueror of Females. Pussy King, as they called him back in the day.

The nicknames are endless. How could I forget?

My stomach roars in protest. I want to puke or slap myself for falling for his smolder.

The same Jack Szeto I met all those years ago is still alive and well. Whatever happened minutes ago must have been a fluke, faulty electrical wiring, hallucinations from lack of sleep.

I shift away as Juliet greets me, pulling me in for a light hug. "Sarah, so nice to meet you. You are my vision. The exact person I imagined for my Joanna when I wrote the story. When I saw you the other day, I knew it had to be you. I begged Jack to ask and am so glad he pulled through."

"I didn't do it for him," I mumble under my breath. Jack stills, the earlier smile wiped off his face, but Juliet doesn't appear to notice. I tear my gaze away from him and focus my attention back on Juliet. "I'm happy to help. I'm a huge fan of your novels. Your book boyfriends are probably why I'm still single. Who can measure up in real life?"

Juliet laughs, apparently pleased at my compliments. We take a seat at the small table as a waiter magically appears and takes our drink orders.

"I'm so excited about this photoshoot. This is Amelia Lansing, renowned cover photographer, and that is Drew Chang." She points to the handsome Asian man next to an elegant brunette with a pixie cut. "You may recognize him as the hunky model from the show *Glitter Empire*. He's the model for the main male character. You'll be partnering with four male models for this shoot. There'll be two more male models joining on-site later."

Drew gives me a charming grin, his eyes glinting with humor. "Can't wait to work with you." His voice is hoarse, like he spent too many nights partying.

I smile at him but something nags at me. Turning back to Juliet, I ask, "Two more male models? With Drew, that'll be three models. Didn't you say there were four men?"

Juliet claps her hand, a gleefulness emanating from her being. "You're correct! The fourth model will be dear Jack over here."

Her words rob me of my breath and I stare mutely at her. My ears hear her words but my brain doesn't seem to understand them.

She nods and grins, rubbing her hands together like a toddler on Christmas morning. "You're surprised. We are so lucky, aren't we? Jack is going above and beyond his job description to help me along. We're so, so lucky."

"The luck is all mine," Jack drawls, his voice pulling my eyes to him. He arches his eyebrow as if daring me to make a scene in public. "And trust me, I'm as surprised about this as you are."

No. There's no way I'm taking sexy photos with Casanova by my side. No friggin' way.

"Did you know this in advance, Jack?" I glare at him.

Amelia interjects, "Oh no. This was a last-minute change. One of the models ended up with a bad case of the flu and Jack offered to step in."

I let out an awkward laugh. Somehow, the idea of Jack being in the photoshoot with me is enough to have me second-guess everything. "This is so unexpected. Surely there's—"

"Trust me, we've looked high and low and couldn't find a last-minute model to fill in. Thank goodness Jack agreed and saved our asses." Amelia lets out an exaggerated sigh of relief and sneaks a glance at Juliet, whose jovial mood is still in place.

"Sarah, thank you for sending over the signed contract. The terms and fees are standard, so if you have any questions, don't hesitate to ask me." Amelia clasps her hands in front of her, a picture of professionalism. "You're in for a treat, since this type of production doesn't usually happen, but Ms. Marceau has a definitive vision, and we will be traveling far and wide for the photos and videos. The shoot will take place in both Los Angeles and New York. We'll fly out next week and stay for a week, so we'll have plenty of time to take the photos, video footage, and also accommodate Juliet's busy schedule. I have an entire wardrobe, hair, and makeup team, so you just need to show up, and don't worry, I'll give you prompts and guide you every step of the way. Ms. Marceau has footed the cost for everything. It'll be fun and you'll do great."

She pauses, staring pleadingly at me, then glancing at Juliet again. I suddenly get it. This project is a big deal for Amelia and she's hoping I don't complain or make a fuss about the last-minute change of models. My eyes trail over to Jack, only to find him standing there, his arms crossed over his chest, a hard glint in his eyes as he waits for my next move.

Seconds pass as our gazes lock on to each other. I narrow my eyes and he quirks a half smile followed by another one of his sardonic arch of brow.

Fuck this. I was going to do this before he decided to come join the party. Why should that matter?

"Sure thing. Can't wait to try something new." I take a sip of the dirty martini I ordered, hoping the alcohol will give me the confidence I'm currently not feeling. My mind is spitting out scenario after scenario where this is all going to end up in flames.

Maybe Jack and I will kill each other on camera.

"You'll be perfect."

Three simple words, spoken by a voice as rich as dark chocolate, pull me out of my mental spiral and I glance up, finding Jack staring at me, his playboy façade slipping away, staring at me with something indecipherable in his dark-brown eyes.

The strange fluttering returns in my gut. It has to be indigestion.

I nod and take a deep breath. I can do this. New risks. New beginnings.

His lips tip up in an enigmatic smile again, and he gives me a quick wink. This time, his wink doesn't feel flirtatious, more like a silent reassurance, a vote of confidence. I look away, my face suddenly feeling heated. He raises his glass up for a toast.

"Let the show begin."

"**D**rew, stare into Jack's eyes like he's the steak you'll reward yourself with after the shoot today. Unless you've turned vegetarian after all the 'meat sandwich' you've been in today."

The room erupts in laughter at Amelia's quip as she directs the four gorgeous men dressed in suits into various poses for the MMMM portion of the shoot today. The preparation and flight out from Newark to LAX went without a hitch. Even without the photoshoot, I was excited at the prospect of coming back to LA for a brief visit to say goodbye to friends and to get my things squared away for my move back to the Big Apple. My plan is to covertly move everything and get settled down before I see my parents in person again. No need to subject myself to more in-person lectures and arguments when my decision isn't going to change.

Drew's loud chuckles draw my attention back to the group of men.

The current pose? Drew cupping his hand on Jack's jaw as Kevin Townsend, the rich, handsome influencer, rebellious son of a senator I recognize from a business dinner a few years back, reaches out from behind Drew to place his hands on Drew's chest. Tyler, a ginger with biceps as thick as my thighs, hovers behind Brad, his lips a few inches away from Jack's neck.

My eyes can't help but focus on Jack, who, despite his lack of modeling experience, oozes charisma in front of the cameras. The suit fits his body perfectly, his hair messier than usual, bringing back a bit more of the bad-boy vibe from the bygone era. I glance down his body, noticing how his muscles seem to ripple under his dress shirt, how the pants cling to his strong thighs, how—

I freeze, mentally slapping myself for my train of thought.

I quickly look away, my eyes finding Kevin next. When I found out he was one of the models after I signed on for the photoshoot, my heart sank. Unfortunately, our paths have crossed in the past before and he is a guy I don't have any fond memories of. He didn't take it particularly well when I rejected his offer to go out with him, which he doled out by flashing his hotel room key and telling me his "calendar" was open for the night. The smarmy grin. Alcohol-laced breath. A holier-than-thou attitude because of his powerful father. And since I'd already signed the modeling contract and he hadn't done anything untoward to me, I decided I could be a mature adult about all of this.

But still, just my luck.

Despite my misgivings toward Kevin, I'm capable of separating my personal life from my professional life. And I'm also capable of recognizing the deliciousness of the gorgeous men in front of me.

A sexy man-wich.

I twist my lips in a grin, enjoying the man-candy before me just as Amelia excused Jack from the group photos for the next segment, which only requires three men per Juliet's instructions.

"I can practically see your drool from here." Jack's low murmur sends a frisson of awareness through me. He saunters over and takes a seat next to me.

Blowing out a sigh, I keep my face straight and don't look at the maddening man beside me. "The difference between you and me is, I only admire from afar, whereas you sleep with anything that moves."

"Variety is the spice of life, right? They enjoy it. Trust me, I make sure they *enjoy* it multiple times a night." His voice is a raspy, lazy drawl, a gentle breeze caressing my skin. "Never had any complaints. Always five-star, glowing reviews."

My empty core involuntarily clenches. Damn these pheromones.

"You pig."

"Jealous, Siren? Wishing you were one of them?"

I snort. "One night with Casanova? To be used and discarded? Psssh. Poor me. I'm keeling over in sadness and jealousy, Jack."

"One night will never be enough," he murmurs under his breath and my head swivels toward him, wondering if I've misheard.

Jack stares intently at me, black coals with banked heat, any semblance of teasing gone from his piercing eyes. He doesn't speak. Doesn't elaborate. A muscle twitches in his jaw as the air between us thickens, the invisible smoke filtering into my senses, heating my skin, lighting up my nerves.

Swallowing, I look away, emitting a half-convincing *harrumph*. "Men like you can never be trusted."

He flinches, the shadow of hurt flashing in his eyes, gone as quickly as it appears, and a pinch of guilt takes hold in my chest, my barb coming out sharper than I intended. My fingers tremble as I brush a curl of hair behind my ear and go back to ignoring him, focusing my attention on the scene before me once more.

I want to apologize, but somehow, I can't bring myself to utter those words.

I groan inwardly. He brings out the worst in me.

"Kevin, relax your face. You look constipated, and Tyler, let's go for sexy, like you want to suck on his neck. Don't purse your lips like a fish."

Amelia's snarky comment breaks the tension like a sledgehammer to glass. I bite my bottom lip to keep from laughing as Jack chuckles on the stool next to me. I'm sure the results of the photoshoot will end up sexy and gorgeous, but so far, the process is anything but arousing.

Click. Click. Click.

"Hold that pose, wonderful. The lighting is just right for me to capture the sunset with the Ferris wheel in the background."

Amelia captures more photos, with Juliet hovering in he background like a starstruck teen, her eyes glued to the models. She claps after each shot is taken as if she's a kid in a candy store.

My eyes sweep to the large windows in our suite at the Kensington Santa Monica Hotel. The skies are painted in a swath of pinks and oranges, a few clouds kissing the striations in a lover's caress. An impressionist painter's dream. The iconic Ferris wheel at the Santa Monica pier stands proudly on the shoreline, its twinkling lights sparkling like fireflies dancing in the skies. This is the million-dollar view appearing in postcards of the city around the world. If I were to step outside now, I could almost imagine the briny breeze grazing my face, the sweet and savory smells of buttery popcorn and snacks in the air, the happy shrieks of kids running around the pier, no doubt sampling all types of delicious food or enjoying the rides.

My breath catches in my throat as my eyes suddenly prickle with moisture. An unexpected wistfulness threads through me. I'll miss LA and my friends here. But it's as if this sunset is the city's farewell to me, wishing me well in my next chapter in life. Nature is giving me a sign that my decision and move is the right one, finally sawing off the shackles binding me to the family name, setting me free in another city I love to start anew.

A beautiful closure. The lasting endnote of an aria.

"You know, they probably could've photoshopped the pier into the background instead of shooting it on location."

Keeping an eye on the stunning scene before me, one that'll burn itself in my brain forever, I let out an exasperated sigh. "Jack, why are you even here? Isn't this above and beyond your job description?"

"Someone has to make sure our top clients are happy, and everyone is comfortable. Juliet asked and I couldn't say no," he murmurs as he leans back in his chair. "Plus, gorgeous people in a beautiful place. How could I miss it?"

"Because you're a consummate professional and not just here to 'please' Juliet. I saw her batting her eyes at you earlier."

He laughs, the sound drawing a curious stare from Juliet, who is frowning in our direction. "Do I hear jealousy from you, Siren? Yet again? Careful there, if I didn't know any better, I'd think you have a thing for me."

"You wish." My skin prickles, the heat from earlier surging back. "I'm not a Siren. How many times do I have to tell you that? And I'm definitely *not* jealous." *Nope. Definitely not. There's no way on earth I'm jealous. Ha.* What I'd give to have a cup of ice water right now.

"I don't know. It sounds awfully like jealousy to me, ice maiden. And it's okay, I understand the frustration of not having my attentions on you."

"Can you cut it with the nicknames? How is it possible to be a Siren and an ice maiden at the same time, anyway? And does this Casanova thing ever turn off? It's extremely annoying."

He stays silent for a few seconds before murmuring, "They both lure unsuspecting men to their deaths."

"What?" Frowning at his cryptic response, I turn to him, finding his face once again devoid of a smile, his penetrating eyes holding me captive. His whiplash moods are the heavy currents at sea, and I'm the poor sailor trying to find her sea legs, holding onto the railing for dear life, and quite possibly regretting my decision to step aboard the ship.

He keeps his gaze on mine, the blacks of his pupils slowly invading the dark chocolate browns of his irises. A lighthouse in the stormy ocean.

Shaking my head at my nonsense, I intake a sharp breath, my heart kicking up a quick rhythm, and yet I couldn't bring myself to look away. It's as if he sees through me somehow. The one person who annoys me to no end is staring at me like he can see into my soul and pick apart every thought whispering through my mind.

My chest feels heavy as the seconds stretch between us and we're ensnared in this strange tension. His eyes slowly sweep to my lips and I fidget, wanting to, but still unable to move. My tongue swipes out to wet my parched lips and I suddenly feel lightheaded.

His nostrils flare, his eyes darting up to mine. Jack shifts in his seat and clears his throat. "Nothing." He whispers softly, "It's working, right? I have your attention."

His deep voice is a gentle breeze, yet so tangible I could almost feel its caress across my skin. The hairs stand on the back of my neck and I tremble, wondering if he's the Siren, or the male version of the temptress, and I'm a hopeless sailor lured by his raspy voice. "I...You..."

"Sarah! We're ready for you now. Jack, come back to the party."

Flinching, my body jolts at Amelia's voice and I tear my gaze away from him. Amelia beckons me to the men on the set. The lighting assistant adjusts the angles of a few spotlights as the others wait expectantly for me. Taking a deep breath, I dry my perspiring palms on my thighs.

Slowly, I stand up and remove my thin cotton coverup, revealing a low-cut, slinky, black sequin minidress held on by the thinnest spaghetti straps. It's something I'd never choose for myself back when I was the living model for the Winstead family, with my cleavage practically dripping out of my dress and the material clinging to my round hips. But now, I'm embracing change, which includes wearing what I choose for myself to wear, whether it be loungewear in public or, in this case, a sexy dress. I think I hear Jack's sharp inhale, but I don't turn toward him to confirm.

Goosebumps pebble on my arms as the AC hits my skin, and I slowly walk toward the group gathered in front of the large windows. My hair was meticulously curled by the hairstylist this morning and is skimming my bare back with each step. My makeup is light, with only a pale-green shimmery eyeshadow to make my eyes pop. Everything feels so unlike me, someone who already gets a lot of unwanted attention based on my body alone and yet, it also feels freeing. I'm taking the power back and controlling my narrative.

I'm sexy and confident.

I blow out a deep breath and crack a smile. Let them all look.

Drew doles out a grin, dragging his eyes lazily down my frame and back. Kevin stares at me, focusing his attention on my swaying breasts, his tongue dipping out to swipe his lips. My steps falter, the familiar sensation of ants crawling up my back returning as a result of his leering. Something about his gaze unsettles me and gets my hackles up. Drew coughs, drawing my attention back to him. He winks and gives me a thumbs-up. My shoulders relax as I step in between the two of them. Jack shuffles to the outskirts of the group.

"You look gorgeous, Sarah." Amelia grins before swiping on her phone and putting on some fast hip-hop music. "We'll start with a few group shots and then move on to photos with you, Drew, and Kevin."

She snaps her camera as we strike random poses, and I pretend these men are my best friends from college and we're just gathering for some group shots. I can feel the tension in my body melting away as we fall into a natural rhythm, shifting our positions every few seconds.

"Excellent. Loving the camaraderie there. Sarah, turn your head toward Drew, and tilt it up to the left a little more. Yes, that's right."

Click. Click. Click.

My head is now at an odd angle as I'm trying to meet Drew's eyes, but my chin is tilted in an opposing direction. My arms hang limply at my sides. My mind flits back to the covers of the spicy romance novels on my shelves, and I bite back a grin. Nothing about this process is sexy. It's a miracle the end products look so hot. Amelia barks out instruction after instruction, and my body parts are arranged in strange positions.

I definitely don't think modeling is my calling in life.

"Kevin, put your hand on her stomach. Everyone, crowd in a little closer. Jack and Tyler, reach toward Sarah, but let your hands graze Drew and Kevin."

Click. Click.

Kevin's roaming fingers trail downward toward my crotch area and I freeze, unsure if it's accidental or on purpose. I throw him a stern glare and he shrugs, appearing nonchalant, as if he isn't doing anything out of the ordinary.

Turning back, we pose for a few more photos as Amelia climbs onto a stool for a different angle and suddenly, Kevin's hand resumes its crawling, downward slide and just as I was about to give him a piece of my mind, Amelia clears her throat and Kevin stills.

"Perfect! Jack and Tyler, you're good to go. Thank you for your services. Tyler, my admin will be in touch with payment in the next few days, and Jack, I guess you're sticking around to help with the rest of the shoot. Let's take a fifteen-minute break."

I heave out a sigh of relief as we disentangle from each other, my brows furrowing as I glance at Kevin, who is staring at me with an uncomfortable intensity which has me inching back toward Drew.

"Great job, Sarah." Drew throws his arm around my shoulders. "You're a natural."

"Thanks. This feels so weird. Not really what I had in mind." I chuckle halfheartedly, the earlier unease slowly dissipating as I glance around the room, emptying the stale air trapped in my lungs.

"Not as sexy as you think it'll be, right? Holding your body still in odd positions?"

"Exactly!" I laugh at Drew's accurate assessment until my gaze lands on Jack, who's sitting rigidly in his chair, the muscles tense under the thin button-down shirt he has on, his jacket discarded to the side. His eyes are bottomless pools of darkness, his lips flattened in a thin line. A vein pulses on his forehead.

My stomach flips at his smoldering attention and I turn back to Drew and chat with him about his time filming *Glitter Empire,* the celebrities he met, and whether he's planning on returning for a future season. Drew launches into a vivid description of his time on set, but my body is still very attuned to a searing intensity on my back, unable to shake off the feeling Jack is probably still staring at us with his air of mystery and a leashed heat which threatens to burn us all alive.

"Okay, I want to try a few poses by the settee over there. Drew, sit down, and Sarah, lay your head on his lap, and stare into each other's eyes. Kevin, hover over Sarah and gaze at her, like both of you want to have her for yourself, but it's up to her to choose."

Drew squeezes my arm before threading his fingers with mine, as if knowing I need the encouragement. He settles into position on the large sofa, which is covered with a thick black blanket. Getting onto the settee, I tug down the hem of my dress, which has ridden up, and lay my head on one of his outspread thighs before gazing into Drew's eyes, which are shining with mirth. Kevin slowly climbs above me, hovering a little too close for my taste. I can smell his stale breath and I fight an impulse to roll away as my stomach churns.

He hasn't done anything yet for me to outright complain, and with his father being one of the most powerful men in the state, I'd rather not ruffle any feathers unless I have to. One thing I learned in my years of swimming in the murky pools of high society—men have fragile egos, and powerful, rich men are especially dangerous, capable of inflicting lasting damage with their fragile egos. A fine balance and careful navigation are needed.

"You look so hot laying there like that." His words graze my skin as he dips his head to my ear, his whisper so soft only I can hear him. I shudder, my hand pushing at his chest to keep him from flattening himself on me.

"You're too close," I grit through my teeth, but he doesn't move, staring at me with a sleazy grin. I bend my leg, ready to knee him in the balls. "Stop it."

I don't care if his dad is a senator. If this asshole doesn't stop, I'm going to inflict bodily pain.

"Back up a little, Kevin, you're too close to her." Amelia's stern voice cuts through the tension. "You okay, Sarah?"

I swallow and nod. "Fine." Sweat beads on the back of my neck. Okay, he's backed away. Everything is kosher.

"All right. Everyone, look in my direction."

Turning my head toward Amelia, my gaze catches with Jack's in the background. He's standing now, the sleeves of his shirt rolled up, exposing his muscular forearms. His hands catch my attention first. They're curled into tight fists, trembling slightly by his legs. I drag my eyes up his frame and what I see on his face takes my breath away.

If I thought his earlier expression was intense, it's nothing compared to the scowl decorating his beautiful face now. A lock of thick black hair drapes down his forehead, partially covering his left eye. His brows are pinched, his eyes piercing and steely. Murderous. Spewing venom. The usual flirtatious charm nowhere to be seen. His jaw flexes as if he's gnashing his teeth.

"Yes, you're in the arms of two hot men you love. That expression is perfect..."

The clicking of the shutter, the heavy breaths of the two men near me, the shuffling of the lighting assistant working the equipment all fade into the background. I don't hear Amelia anymore. My pulse is a beating drum in my ears as I stare at Jack, the man who has infuriated me and confused me since I was a senior in high school, the bad boy my family would never approve of, the man, with his Casanova, bed-hopping history I detest. But he's also someone who has never truly been out of my mind, always seeming to creep in at random moments, in my dark and lonely nights alone in my bedroom, or whenever I see a handsome man with raven hair on the streets.

It's hatred. Dislike multiplied by passion. That's what this is.

Except he's staring at me like I'm the only woman in the room. Like I'm someone he wants to devour whole. Like he's my avenging soldier, willing to fight and die for me. Juliet hovers over him, murmuring something in his ear, her body practically plastered to his, but he doesn't seem to notice. He's rigid, his focus on me searing, and a heat blooms in my gut and travels to my core. My breath catches, and I fidget to avoid clenching my thighs together.

"Fuck, you're so sexy," Kevin whispers again, and I tense up once more.

"Knock it off, dude. You're making her uncomfortable," Drew grunts under his breath. He squeezes my hand in reassurance.

Jack's eyes turn darker if that's possible, the color of death and destruction, as if he hears what Kevin is saying all the way across the room, as if he senses my discomfort. He takes a step forward, his arm shaking off Juliet with a roughness I've never seen him exhibit before. A sharp slither of concern for the man snakes through me, surprising myself.

"Okay, we're done for the day. Thank you, everyone."

Amelia's voice cuts through the dense fog in the room and I quickly scamper off the sofa, my heart pounding rapidly, my mind a rioting mess, trying to make sense of my emotions, of Jack, of Kevin, of this entire situation.

"You okay, Sarah?" Amelia scrunches her brows, her eyes brimming with concern.

I let out a shaky exhale. "I t-think so."

She scrutinizes my face before nodding and turning away.

The pulse thrums a delirious beat in my ears and my flesh feels hot to the touch.

The truth is, I'm not sure I'm okay.

At all.

want to kill the bastard. Kevin.

Heck, I want to murder both of them for touching her. But Kevin, I'll enjoy strangling with my bare hands, watching his mouth parting for air he won't receive, slowly enjoying the life leaching out of his eyes.

Because he made her uncomfortable.

Because he *dared* to make her afraid.

I was standing too far away to hear what he said to her, but I saw the flash of unease and fear in her eyes, occurring each time he was near her. I saw the way her muscles stiffened, the desperation in her gaze when she looked in my direction, the way she shrunk from his advances.

When his hand was traveling too far south in the group shoot, when he was crowding her on the sofa, the fire burning inside me churned into a raging inferno. I was a millisecond away from snapping, from saying bullshit to "the client comes first" philosophy of The Orchid, from rushing over there and throwing a right hook at the asswipe, rearranging his face so he can no longer model in the future.

"Jack, do you want to go to dinner together? Jack, Jack!"

Panting harshly in the dimly lit hallway, I stroll toward the elevators, eager to escape the room and find respite in my suite. I lift my phone to my ear, pretending I'm on a call and don't hear Juliet screeching like a banshee behind me.

Calm the fuck down, Jack. Nothing happened. Calm down.

Except the fire burns through my veins, my fingers tingling. My vision is black at the edges.

Light footfalls pound behind me as I walk faster to the elevator bay, eager to get away from Juliet, from anyone in the room because I'm losing the grip on my control, something that never, *ever* happens to me.

The elevator doors slide open, and I slip inside, my finger jamming the close button as the pounding footsteps sound closer.

"Close, dammit." I jab the button harder. The doors finally begin to slide shut, but at the last possible second, a slender hand slides in and the doors bounce open immediately.

"Ms. Mar—"

My words are cut off as the faint scent of orange blossoms travels to my nose, rendering me speechless as the doors widen enough to reveal my angel in her full glory, her luscious locks voluminous and loose around her face, her cheeks pinkened, and her parted lips dragging in quick gulps of air, as if she ran a mile to catch up to me. Her hazel eyes, the color of New England foliage in the fall, snare on my face.

Even after all these years, the vision of her steals my breath and robs my voice.

Wordlessly, I back away, letting her into the elevator before the doors glide shut again.

"You haven't pressed a floor yet." Her sultry voice is like a fine Cuban cigar. Addictive.

At my inaction, she quirks her brow before my brain belatedly catches on to her words.

"What floor are you?" My voice sounds hoarse and thick.

"Fifth."

"Same here." My finger trembles as I press the button. The quiet chimes fill the space as the elevator begins its slow descent from the fortieth floor.

"Why did you chase after me?"

She blushes, her eyes looking at everything except for me. "Who said I was?"

"You're panting. Out of breath like you ran a marathon."

"You're overthinking." Her response comes with a quiver at the end.

Our heavy breaths fill the air as a tense silence settles upon us. The scorching heat in my veins transforms into a sultry blaze with each inhalation of orange-scented air. I sneak a glance at the beguiling woman standing next to me, her arm hanging limply, a mere centimeter next to mine. My hand clenches, fingers twitching. It's as if I could physically feel her against me despite the air between us.

I absorb every excruciating detail of her, the dusting of freckles on her cheeks, the perfect cupid's bow of her upper lip, the plushness of her bottom lip, the smooth expanse of silky skin revealed by her tiny scrap of a dress. Her creamy tits moving gently with each breath she takes. Blood travels south. Unbidden images of her on the settee moments ago with Kevin and Drew ogling her flicker to the forefront and the spicy heat is now mixed with the earlier burning inferno.

I can't think. I can't breathe. I want to haul her in my arms and shake her. I want to do many unspeakable, dirty things to her.

Swallowing the ball in my throat, I hit the emergency stop button on the elevator.

"What are you doing!" Her voice is a half-squeak.

Her eyes dart to mine as I glare at her, my hands curling into fists once more, my internal barometer going haywire from the emotions churning inside me. The arrow spins faster, finally landing on the most identifiable emotion—anger.

"Why didn't you tell him to back off? Tell Amelia you were uncomfortable?"

"What?" The earlier hesitancy disappears in her voice, replaced with a sharpness.

"Kevin. You didn't like him too close. It was all over your face."

"It's none of your business. And who said I was uncomfortable? Why would I be unhappy with two hot men paying attention to me? You think only you're allowed to have the opposite sex draped all over you?" A flush spreads from her chest to her face as she flays me with the weapons of her words, a pain only reserved for me as I've never seen her lose her temper with anyone else before.

Turning, I lean toward her and watch her eyes widen in surprise.

"So, is that what it is? You don't like women throwing themselves at me?"

Another step. My mind is scrambled, logic long having left the party. My fingers clench and unclench.

"What on earth are you talking about, Jack?" Her chest rises and falls quickly as she backs away toward the railing. "Y-You aren't making any sense."

"Why didn't you say no? Still trying to be the nice girl?"

Another step.

Her back bumps against the rail. Her hands are plastered against the walls as she stares at my chest.

"There's nothing wrong with being nice. And I did say no. I had it handled." She fidgets, her voice barely above a whisper.

"Look at me," I growl.

She shakes her head, her hands now gripping the handrail, the knuckles white with tension.

I clasp her chin with my fingers, a frisson of electricity flowing through me at the contact. Her plump lips part in a gasp as I tilt her head up, her beautiful eyes finally meeting mine.

"You have it handled, huh? Even though he was one second away from groping you? Is it because he's rich and powerful? You need to handle him with kid gloves, protect his ego? Or is being Ms. Nice Girl more important than your own fucking safety?" My words come out on a hiss, my lips so close to hers I can feel her breath coming in quick pants.

Sarah freezes, her mouth dropping open, and I curl my lips to the side. At her silence, I take a small step back and turn off the emergency stop and the elevator whirs in motion again.

Sarah steps forward, apparently regaining her voice, and shoves my chest, but barely moves me an inch. "You asshole," she seethes.

"The claws are reserved for me only, huh?" Another inch closer.

My hands bracket her face as my nose skims hers, the contact lighting a fuse inside me. My cock stands at full attention, the heated blood not distinguishing between lust and anger. A distant alarm sounds in the deepest recesses of my brain, trying to warn me this is against all the rules, but that is quickly snuffed out by the scorching inferno between us.

I don't see or hear anything except for her. Her fluttery breaths. The fire burning hot in those golden eyes.

I want, no, *need* more.

Slowly, I flatten myself on her, every inch of her touching every inch of me. She lets out a whimper and my dick throbs in response.

"Tell me no," I rasp, my nose trailing over her cheek, relishing the soft skin, the sweet scent. Intoxicating. "Say no and I'll stop."

My mind has gone mad, or perhaps it has been slowly driven crazy by her Siren song for all these years.

Sarah's eyes flutter shut as her hands latch themselves to my back, her sharp nails digging into my muscles, and I groan.

"One last chance. Say no. Fuck. Tell me no."

She parts her lips and lets out a quaking breath before tilting her head to the side, baring the fluttering pulse in her slender neck for me.

"Fuck."

Curling one hand on the back of her head, I slam our lips together and let the madness overtake us. Our mouths war with each other in passion, our bodies carrying on the heated conversation with bites, licks, and swirls. She tilts her curvy hips toward mine. I curl a fist around her hair and tug. She gasps as I deepen the kiss, taking advantage of her parted lips to swipe my tongue inside her mouth, tasting her sweetness, her essence, sucking on her tongue as if it were my lifeline. Her tongue duels back, snaking out to lick my lip ring before her teeth clamp down and pull, the flash of pleasure mixed with pain an electrical overload of my nerves. My cock throbs in my pants, as hard as I've ever been, and we're still fully clothed.

She grapples with me, her hands clawing my back, each drag a heady burn, a pleasurable drug, and I grind myself against her, letting her feel my steel cock, threatening to break out of the confines of my pants.

"Jack," she moans, "oh shit."

I trail my lips down her neck, sucking every delectable inch of her, my tongue laving at the spot where the orange blossoms are the strongest. My teeth nip softly on her flesh and she cries in ecstasy, her body shuddering against me, as if I can make her come just like this, with all the layers between us.

"Fuck, angel. I knew it'd be like this with you." She curls one shapely leg over my hips as she chases my hardness. My dick hits the sweet spot between her thighs. I grind. She glides. Our sounds are the sweetest music. "You want to come, don't you?"

Sarah mewls in response, her other leg coming up as I place my hand on the soft flesh of her ass.

Ding.

The elevator doors open, letting in a breeze of cold air, and she freezes before pushing me away. I pant harshly as I struggle to reel in any semblance of sanity and slowly back away from her to the opposite corner, taking in her bee-stung lips, messy hair. Her eyes. Heavy-lidded. Dilated, the hazel a molten brown. She slowly raises a trembling hand to her lips as she breathes in gasps of air.

An elderly couple alight the elevator, and I nod, my lips trying to twist themselves into something resembling a smile as I grip the handrail behind me, my mind not trusting my hands to not haul her against me and finish what we started with an audience.

Soon, the elevator doors open to the fifth floor and Sarah darts out, a flash of orange and red, fleeing the scene, leaving me with a raging erection, her sweet taste on my lips.

My heart clenches. Once again left in the dust.

CHAPTER 5

Jack

"**O**kay, now that everyone has gotten to know each other better, time to take things up a notch. Gentlemen, please take off your jackets and shirts and Sarah, if at any time you feel uncomfortable, just holler. This is a safe place for everyone. Same goes for you, Drew, and Kevin. If Kevin is copping a feel at you, Drew, let me know."

The room erupts in laughter as Amelia starts the next day's shoot with her wisecracks. Drew gives Kevin a friendly shove. Kevin rolls his eyes in response. I sip the steaming-hot coffee in my paper cup as I take my position in the chair facing the settee, where the photos will take place today, my eyes glued to Sarah, who refuses to look me in the eye this morning. An ache appears in my chest and I stop myself from rubbing it. Swallowing the lump in my throat, I try not to let her demeanor affect me.

What did you expect her to do? Jump in your arms to finish what you started in the elevator?

I close my eyes and bring the cup to my lips again and inhale the rich scent of coffee, focusing on the nutty and smoky notes, letting the aroma wash over me, distracting me from the sharp slice of disappointment piercing my gut.

I exhale, my eyelids fluttering open once more and my gaze can't help but focus on the woman who is occupying most of my thoughts these days.

She looks delectable. A temptress.

Her hair is blown out, her waves curling around her tits. Her eyes are rimmed with black, her lips fire-engine red. She's wearing a strappy, silky negligee, which ends mid-thigh. Her feet are clad in these black, fuck-me heels, which make her legs look miles long. Her entire ensemble makes her look like a devil with an angel's face. And it's not only her looks that's drawing me to her, it's the perfect blend of sweet shyness and sexy confidence that's making it impossible for me to tear my eyes off her.

She's starred in my lurid dreams in the middle of the night before, but nothing compares to reality.

Absolutely nothing.

My cock throbs in response, even though I practically chafed my dick with the number of hand jobs I've given myself between last night and this morning, reliving the scorching kiss in my mind.

"These are going to be my best promo materials ever." Juliet leans against me, too close for comfort, and I shift away.

"Sure thing."

She places her hand on my arm and stares adoringly at me. "You're such a consummate professional, Jack, flying across the country for me, helping me model, and now with overseeing the set."

I fight the urge to snort, my lips curving in a half grin instead. "We at The Orchid pride ourselves on our superior customer service." I add a wink for half measure, not wanting to sound too curt.

I don't tell her I stepped in as her last-minute model because Sarah is part of the photoshoot.

I don't tell her I'm doing this to keep an eye out on my angel, because I know she's nervous and this is out of the ordinary for her.

I don't tell her I'm here because I don't trust any men around Sarah, because they always seem to want her for all the wrong reasons.

Juliet grins and backs away, as if sensing my need for distance. I release a soft exhale and fight the urge to rub the bridge of my nose. The fine line between superior customer service and curbing unwanted attention is one of the most exhausting parts of the job.

Amelia switches the music to a sultry R&B beat and dims the lights in the room for an intimate setting. My eyes are glued to Sarah as she stands in front of the sofa with Kevin behind her, one hand beneath her breasts and the other one on her hip, dragging the hem of her negligee up, revealing more of her smooth thighs.

I take a large gulp of my coffee, the black drink tasting especially bitter this morning as my shoulders tighten, and a corrosive heat burns in my chest. Drew adds his hand on her other hip as he dips his head toward her neck, his lips inches away from the spot I kissed her yesterday.

My spot. My fucking spot.

She isn't yours, Jack.

My teeth gnash against each other. My vision constricts, focusing on their hands on her. Touching what they shouldn't be touching.

Crinkle.

"Your hand is all wet! Here are some napkins for you." Juliet fawns over me as I belatedly notice the slickness of the coffee on my fingers, the burn barely registering, the paper cup crushed in my palm. She blots my hand as my attention turns back to Sarah, finding her eyes on me for the first time today. Her nose twitches, her ears red, her lips pressed in a thin line.

She's pissed. Jealous.

Somehow, the thought makes me smile for the first time on this trip. Juliet whispers something in my ear and I nod noncommittally, not caring what she just said.

The flush spreads from Sarah's ears to her face and she narrows her eyes at me before looking away.

Amelia snaps her photos, doling out directions left and right. The flashes brighten the room in bursts of light. The assistant brings out a fan and turns it on, the wind courting with Sarah's strands, making her seem every inch the angel from heaven. Kevin picks up a lock of hair and brings it to his nose for a sniff.

I crack my neck, fists throbbing with a violent impulse as I imagine what he's smelling. The sweet orange blossoms.

No one should be that close to her.

Not even you, Jack. Your street smarts can only get you so far in life. What can you offer her? A Winstead?

Swallowing the gravel in my throat, I stare at the scene before me, unable to move. Unable to breathe. Unable to do anything other than helplessly watch two men touch what's mine.

Not in your wildest dreams, Jack. She hates you. She'll never be with you.

Whatever yesterday was in the elevator, it must've been a fluke. Perhaps a figment of my imagination because the scathing looks she has been slicing me with today are as effective as any blade.

Amelia is now conferring with her lighting assistant as they look over a few shots on the camera's screen. Drew is looking in their direction with curiosity in his gaze. Suddenly, Kevin murmurs something in Sarah's ear, his lips twisting in a sick smile, and his hand drags her slip farther up her thighs, his fingers curling under the hem, groping her skin.

Sarah's eyes widen in alarm as her hand slams on top of his, attempting to stop his ascent. He shows no sign of stopping as he peels her grip off of him, and my sanity, already hanging by the thinnest thread, snaps.

Tossing the napkins to the ground, I stand, adrenaline scorching through my veins, my vision blurry and red, the need to decimate stronger than my will to live. I stride toward them, ready to kill him, to—

"I said, stop it!" Sarah's sharp voice draws everyone's attention to her. She elbows his chest, and he grunts in pain. "Don't touch me, Kevin."

I skid to a stop, the thumping pulse loud in my ears, the rage warring with a twinge of pride. *She stood up for herself.* Amelia cocks her head to the side. "What's going on?"

"Kevin is touching me inappropriately. I don't feel comfortable with this at all."

Kevin drops his hands and raises them in the air. "I didn't do shit. The bitch is making this shit up."

"Okay, that's it. You're out, Kevin. I don't care what you did or didn't do, but this," Amelia swirls her fingers in a circle at him, "is completely unacceptable. Zero tolerance."

"I'm supposed to have two more days of photoshoot time!"

"Not anymore. Pack up and leave. If you cause a scene, we'll call security." Amelia crosses her arms, her face stern. No doubt this is not the first bad actor she's encountered before.

Kevin's face turns red, his eyes flashing in anger as he grabs his clothing and stomps toward the exit. Right before he leaves the room, he turns back and bares his teeth at Sarah. "You're a cunt. Just because you have porn star tits and ass and a rich daddy, you think you're better than all of us. I was just teasing you. I heard you're trying to branch off on your own. Fucking penniless. You should be grateful I'm paying any attention to you."

"And you're a piece of shit, Kevin." Sarah's eyes flash with anger and she narrows her eyes at her tormentor. "No means no. Or is that too difficult to understand?"

Kevin growls, baring his teeth, and strides toward her, his fist rearing back.

I don't think, I don't breathe, I just react.

With two quick strides, I cover Sarah with my body, flinching when Kevin lands a solid punch on my back. The next moments blur into one as I'm filled with blinding fury, the sound of my blood roaring in my ears, my chest burning with rage. My vision is red and I only see his smug face and hear his horrible words echo inside me. My mind is held captive by scorching rage, the beast inside me wanting to destroy, to maim him.

The dipshit wanted to hurt her.

A loud growl tears out of my throat. I whirl back and slam my fist in his nose, a satisfying *smack* reverberating in the room. "You fucking asshole! What the fuck did you just say?"

Kevin howls in pain, blood seeping down his shirt from his crooked nose. "What? You want a piece of that ass too?" he wheezes, his blue eyes defiant. "My dad is a fucking senator. You think you're better than me? You think she would sleep with a junkyard dog? You're a servant, working under us for pennies."

I hurl myself at him, knocking him to the ground and land another punch to his face, relishing in the *oomph* of agony from the asswipe. "Keep your dirty hands off her." I throw another right hook, but he rolls out from under me.

Kevin clambers to a standing position, his face mottled, and he barrels into me, his head knocking the breath out of my lungs, his fists landing a few hard jabs on my ribs, but I barely notice the pain. I flip him to the ground and unleash punch after punch on him, as he does his best to block and tackle back.

"I don't give a fuck who you are," I growl. "Don't fucking touch her. No one hurts her. No. One."

He curls his lips in a fucking grin and taunts, "She'll never be with someone like you, fuckface. Pathetic trash."

Crimson mist overtakes my senses and my chest clenches. My eyes are only focusing on his unrepentant face and I didn't see him grab something with his hand until it's too late.

Whack.

A flash of pain rips through me as the bastard hits me in the forehead with something hard. A telephoto lens lays shattered on the ground. I feel a familiar warm liquid dripping into my eye.

His eyes widen and he tries to scramble away from underneath me and I curl my hand around his throat, the familiar metallic smell drifting in the air from my wound. This time, I literally see red. I clench at his windpipe and bring my other fist down.

Smack. Smack. Smack.

Faint cries of pain. Stickiness of blood running down my arms. Shrieks and screams.

I barely notice any of it as honed muscles from my days of underground boxing take my body through the motions from memory. Only one thought remains—the need to decimate, to see my enemy destroyed.

I rear back to strike again, but a pair of strong arms lock against my waist, another two sets holding on to my flailing arms. I twist my head, baring my teeth at the interlopers, finding Drew and two security guards holding me off long enough for Kevin to escape from my hold, rising unsteadily to his feet, and scamper away.

My pulse thuds loudly in my ears. My lungs heaving in laborious breaths. My mind clouded, blurry, a slave to my basest emotions.

Shaking Drew off, the bloodlust slowly ekes out of me as the thundering in my ears quiets to a beating pulse. Panting, I turn toward Sarah, finding her face ashen, her hand covering her lips, as if she's traumatized by what Kevin did. Or quite possibly, at me.

All at once, I realize what I've done, and it's like ice water pouring over my boiling rage. I never meant for her to see me like this. My angel has now seen the devil hiding beneath the suit.

My stomach twists and turns and bile threatens to make its way up my throat. I let out a shaky exhale, my hands trembling. A shameful heat rises to my face as rational thought finally enters the room.

Shit. I shouldn't have lost control.

I'm better than the delinquent getting into drunken bar fights now. I've worked so hard to shed the past, and now because of this fucking asshole I—

Sarah lets out a shaky gasp, her face still leached of color, her body swaying slightly.

Fuck. I want to chase after him and finish what I started, but the need to comfort her wins over my murderous impulse. The impulse to protect her, to draw her against me and smooth my hand on her trembling back is so strong, I bite my tongue to keep from acting on it. Swiping away the blood dripping onto my face, I step slowly toward her, my breathing ragged, the throbbing pain of my knuckles finally registering.

"You okay?" My voice comes out rough, like sandpaper. My throat is parched as my eyes roam over her face, her body, somehow afraid she's hurt.

She nods as she holds her gaze with mine, tears pooling in her gorgeous eyes. The sight of her so shaken slices me to the core, the pain much more agonizing than the flesh wounds on my knuckles. She has to be terrified...of me.

"Jack, goodness! Your forehead and hands are a mess." Juliet scrambles to my side, taking hold of my bloody fists. "I got a first-aid kit from housekeeping. Let me clean your wounds. That was so heroic. I can't believe you did that. He looked almost unrecognizable when he ran off. That Kevin is a slimeball, a villain if I've ever seen one. I may need to use him as an inspiration for my future books." Juliet takes my hand and wipes it with supplies, but I barely notice.

Sarah swallows, her eyes dropping to my hands, which Juliet is currently cleaning and dressing, and she backs away, her hand over her mouth as if in disbelief, her lips moving as if reminding herself of something.

"Let's call it a day." Amelia walks up to Sarah. "You okay, honey? Kevin is an asshole. Don't you listen to a thing he just said. Come on, let's take a walk to clear our minds." She leads Sarah out of the room, her hand squeezing Sarah's shoulder, comforting her like I wanted to.

Sarah doesn't look back at all.

. . .

Sarah

"You let me know if you want to talk more. If you decide to quit the photoshoot, I won't blame you, but I hope you don't." Amelia pats me on my arm as she walks me back to the suite after our stroll on the boardwalk where she tried to settle my nerves.

My pulse is still roaring in my ears, the sound of crashing waves in a thunderstorm, my delirious heart beating itself against my rib cage, clamoring for escape. My mind is still reeling from the events fifteen minutes ago, from how everything escalated so quickly, how Jack...

How Jack nearly beat a man to death in front of an audience because he hurt me.

How his eyes shined with concern when he checked on me afterward, even as blood was seeping through his wounds.

How his muscular body flexed with his movements, the way he shielded me from Kevin even though he didn't seem to be aware of his actions.

How my heart spasmed and clenched when I saw Juliet fussing over him, and how my impulse was to push her away and tend to him myself.

You've always hated him, Sarah. You've no right to feel this way.

My mouth runs dry and my breathing quickens again the closer we get back to the room where everything took place.

I can't think. I can't make sense of anything. All I can do is feel and there are no words adequate enough to describe the swirling storm drowning me from the inside.

"Okay? Sarah?"

Amelia's voice jolts me back to the present and I find us standing in front of the closed suite door. "I'm going downstairs to talk to Juliet and a few folks from The Orchid to explain everything. I don't want Jack to get into trouble. The door is unlocked and you can go get your things. Relax tonight, destress, and don't make any rash decisions, okay?"

I nod, my mind so muddled I can't seem to utter a single word.

Amelia squeezes my arm gently in reassurance and strides toward the elevators.

Taking in a deep breath of the faintly floral scented air of the hotel, I attempt to calm myself.

Everything will be fine. Don't let an asshole affect your self-worth. His actions speak more about him than about you.

I release a ragged exhale, my thoughts still swirling, before my mind latches on to something else, or someone else in this case.

The imposing man, someone who irks me to no end but came flying to my rescue today. Someone who didn't care about his well-being or his job when he pummeled Kevin in front of me.

Someone who used his body to shield me from what would've been a painful punch. Someone who seems to be fighting invisible demons I can finally see for the first time.

Someone who makes me feel safe.

Jack.

It's as if my mind suddenly found an antidote to the swirling madness, finally finding the reason for my rioting pulse, the thundering beats of my heart, the sickening heaviness of unease sitting on top of my chest.

Concern seems to be too small of a word to describe what I'm feeling right now. All I know is I need to find him, to see if he's okay, to ask him why he did the things he did just now.

I need to get my things.

I need to find him.

I need to see him with my own eyes.

The commands echo inside my brain, propelling me toward the door with desperation flooding in like a tidal wave.

My heart races for a different reason now, and I wrench open the doorknob.

Get my things. Find him. See him. Get my things. Find him. See—

Jack sits on the sofa, alone, his frame hunched over, his face buried in his hands.

The room is quiet except for the quiet hum of circulated air blowing out from the vents.

Wetness mists my eyes as I take note of the hastily wrapped bandages on his hands and his forehead, blood red seeping through the white. Even more painful than the physical wounds is the way he's curled over himself, as if in agonizing emotional torment, as if someone snuffed out all the stars in the nighttime sky.

Somehow, at this moment, my soul seems to connect with his—a thread of shared consciousness between us—and the visceral wave of haunted loneliness, crippling sadness threatens to unmoor me.

A burn appears behind my nose, followed by a thickening lump in my throat. My heart clenches, the searing pain piercing as I quietly close the door behind me and walk toward him.

"Jack?" My voice is a whisper, but it seems to echo in this cavernous space.

He freezes, the muscles in his arms and back taut with tension before he looks up, and what I see in his eyes devastates me to the core.

Loneliness. Heartbreak. Pain.

The emotions I felt a few seconds ago now flit by in his dark eyes, as clear as day, and as he finally registers me standing before him, he shudders, his bruised lips parting on an exhale and those beautiful eyes change before me.

The irises, dark umber, flicker to life, and the earlier flashes of desolation soften as a spark returns to his gaze.

"Sarah," he whispers, staring at me in what looks to be awe, like he can't believe I'm standing in front of him.

Unbidden, I walk over to him, drawn by his magnetized gaze, the wonder in his raspy voice. I step in between his thighs, my knees sinking into the soft carpet and my fingers reach out, trembling, to stroke his face. In a span of days, everything feels upside down and yet...everything feels just as they should be.

My vision clears as my fingers trail the sharp edges and the smooth planes of his cheeks.

He swallows, his throat rippling, and he leans into my touch.

"Why?" I breathe out, my voice thick with emotions I can't begin to understand.

He winces as my fingers trail over the bloody bandage on his forehead. I slowly unwrap the bandage, my heart seizing at the ragged gash above his eyebrow. I reach for the first-aid kid next to him and retrieve fresh bandages.

"Why, Jack?"

Jack swallows again, the sounds of his breathing heavy in the inches between us. "I can't let him hurt you." His voice is raspy. Rough. "I'd rather him hurt me a thousand times over than hurt you."

My lips quiver and my breath freezes in my throat. I blink rapidly, an unfamiliar ache spreading from the spot beneath my sternum, and I carefully affix a new bandage on his forehead before I reach for his hands.

"I-I've never been nice to you before," I whisper as I hold up one of his hands, so large and rough compared to mine, my fingers trailing over the hardened callouses used to manual labor, and I swallow once more. The ache becomes a painful throb, my swirling emotions all colorful threads intertwining, winding around my heart. It's as if my words are a bucket of water on my head, rinsing off the muck on my body, the dirt in my eyes, allowing me to really see, really feel for the first time in a long time.

How could I not see him, the real him behind the façade? The Jack sitting in front of me, surrounding me with a cloak of safety, treating me as if I'm the most precious thing he's ever beheld. The man who threw himself in front of me without a second thought. The person who is covered in scrapes and bruises, but instead of caring about himself, the first words out of his mouth were concern for me.

He reaches out and wipes the wetness on my cheek. "Don't cry for me. I can't bear to see you cry."

My lips tremble and I bite my cheek, unwrapping and rewrapping his knuckles with fresh bandages. I sniffle at the sight of the deep lacerations on the back of his hand, swollen, bruised.

Somehow, in this quiet room, the rope binding my heart has been sliced away, and now it's bruised, aching, feeling all too much and understanding far too little.

"Sarah," he rasps, his voice gentle, and I glance up, finding his eyes swirling with intensity, his lips curving into a familiar, yet unfamiliar smile. "I think these cuts add to my rugged handsomeness, don't you?"

A soft laugh escapes my lips, the heaviness on my chest lifting slightly, and I shake my head, my fingers working on redressing his other hand.

"There we go. That beautiful smile," he murmurs.

The sweetness in his voice causes a flip in my stomach and I wet my lips, my hands shaking. I fasten medical tape on his hand, the warmth of his words wrapping around me like a soft blanket on a cold winter's morning.

"Don't believe anything he just said. You're so much more than your name and your body. So much more." Jack's voice is husky, barely above a whisper, and yet his words burrow deep inside me, cutting through the carefully erected walls with the ease of a scalpel to flesh.

The beating organ in my chest pumps harder and my breathing falters. Setting his hand back on his lap, I glance up once more, ensnared by the depths of the bottomless pools of his eyes, a fire burning brightly within.

His gaze rakes over me, as if trying to ascertain if I'm all right. The teasing expression arrests on his face, his nostrils flaring slightly, and the grin slips away.

The air stirs between us. Sultry. Sweet. Spicy. Every atom of my body vibrates like a tuning fork and suddenly, I realize the precariousness of our positions; me kneeling mere inches before him, his head dipped low, his attention focused solely on me.

A small shift, a tilt of our heads, and our lips would touch.

Raw heat flashes through me, and I let out a breathy gasp. Jack's pupils widen and the tension thickens, unbearably so.

The sudden hunger in my veins shocks me and my eyes flutter shut of their own accord.

Suddenly, a chill sweeps through me when Jack draws back his heated presence. I blink, my hazy vision focusing in front of me once more, finding Jack leaned back on the sofa, his bandaged hands gripping tightly on the soft seating.

"Thank you, Sarah." His words come out clipped, the muscles in his neck taut. Jack clenches his jaw and slowly rises from his seat. His eyes are still the color of the darkest hours of the night before dawn, his irises and pupils indiscernible from each other.

I quickly stand up and move out of the way, my heart thumping a chaotic beat once more. He clenches and unclenches his hands, his feet striding toward the door like he's desperate to leave. He pauses, his hand on the doorknob, and turns around.

He flashes a quick grin, one that doesn't reach his eyes. "I'm glad you're okay, Sarah."

Jack slips out of the door, taking the tempest of swirling emotions away with him, and an unsettling silence befalls the room.

My hand flutters to the lingering ache in my chest, knowing somehow, everything has changed.

Sarah

Dabbing more concealer under my eyes, I let out a ragged sigh as I squint at my reflection in the mirror in my hotel room in Santa Monica, which I've opted to stay at instead of being scrutinized by my parents in their lifeless, palatial home. Plus, they're still giving me the cold-shoulder treatment, so no love lost there.

I realize no amount of makeup will hide the dark circles—courtesy of tossing and turning most of last night—when I was tormented with a myriad of thoughts and feelings regarding my current situation in life, my future, and mostly...

Of him.

The fury in those beautiful obsidian eyes when he charged toward Kevin yesterday.

The rage in his voice when he heard what the asshole said to me.

The way he threw himself on top of me without hesitation to take a blow clearly meant for me.

His bloodshot eyes. The vicious violence.

Unhinged. Possessive. Protective.

For me.

Perhaps I should fear the way he went from zero to one hundred in a matter of seconds, exceeding every bad boy scenario I concocted in my imagination when I was younger. Perhaps I should frown on fighting violence with more violence.

But I can't deny the flutters in my gut when I remember how his dark eyes connected with mine as Kevin dashed off—a coward through and through—how despite the blood dripping on the carpet and the swelling on his hands, those intense eyes, dark as the deepest levels of hell yet no less hot, were brimming with concern for me. As if I was the most important thing to him, the brightest spark in his universe. As if he'd rather hurt himself than see me cry.

Then there was the way he reacted when I bandaged his wounds, his impassioned words, and gentle touches. The way my body craves him and how he seems to need me in return.

Nothing makes sense.

My mind is still struggling to connect the Jack I've known in the past to the version of him I met yesterday.

He's Casanova Jack, the poorer version of my dad, breaking hearts wherever he goes, spending nights with different women, or perhaps with multiple women at a time if there is any truth regarding the rumors, never settling down. His salacious reputation precedes him. Whether it's the girls in the country club back in high school trading sordid stories of their nights of passion with him like a badge of honor, or the models he's seen photographed with over the years, even when we've lost touch. And don't even get me started on the ladies who fawn over him at The Orchid, which is impossible to ignore after our paths collided once more five years ago.

I can't reconcile the flirtatious man who winks at women of all ages, who seems to go through women like some sort of sport, who appears to live life without a care in the world, to the passionate defender of my virtue from yesterday. I can't recall a time when I saw him lose his cool. He's always unruffled, never seeming to take anything too seriously, and always in control. *Other than the time in the elevator, you idiot.*

The familiar quickening of my heart echoes in my ears as images of him flood my mind. His scorching kisses. The way he claimed me with his mouth, his tongue. The way he made me lose my mind, a slave to the pleasurable sensations he elicits inside me. My cheeks feel warm to the touch and I draw in yet another ragged breath, feeling unsettled.

The way I wanted to kiss him again yesterday.

Our kiss in the elevator... At first, I thought it was Jack the philanderer trying to prove something to me, how even I'm not immune to his charms. But after yesterday, the way he stared at me as I bandaged him, his eyes glowing with intensity, the way the air thickened between us, everything feels so damn real. Like perhaps Jack, the Casanova, is a mask he wears and there's something deeper, enticing, hidden underneath.

Nothing makes sense anymore.

Ding.

The chime of my phone interrupts my troublesome thoughts. I swipe the screen and the raucous thudding of my heart changes tune. A heaviness seeps into my chest, curling around my insides, strangling me from within.

> **Dad:** Your mom told me what you're up to. You won't be getting a cent from us if you quit the company and move to New York. I'm serious. That trust fund of yours won't see the light of day. This is your last chance to make the right choice or else you'll force my hand.

Groaning, I set down my cell phone on the desk, unsurprised by Dad's text and thinly veiled threats. Nausea roils in my stomach, my mind darting through the various situations my dad may whip up. And if the lawsuits his former employees have filed against his company are any indication, he can be quite creative and ruthless toward anyone who goes against him. A brief flash of fear makes an appearance, but I sweep it aside. Closing my eyes, I take a few deep breaths, feeling my pulse settling.

What type of thirty-year-old still lets her parents dictate her actions?

Not this one. Not anymore. I've done more than my fair share of duty toward the family. And I don't care what they throw at me. If I don't care about the money, my grit can carry me through and there's nothing much they can hold over me.

I take a sip of ice water, the chill a welcome respite to the discomfort inside me, the way your muscles hurt when you start a new exercise routine, the first time you step out in the freezing winter cold to jog around Central Park.

This is a damn good pain, Sarah. Think about the "muscles" you'll gain.

After the internal pep talk, I flip open my laptop and check my emails, seeing if any of the companies I applied to sent responses back, especially my top choice, The Gallagher Foundation, one of the world's biggest nonprofits assisting with low-income or underserved families. Giving all the players on the board an equal chance to win. Something I vehemently believe in, despite my affluent upbringing.

Inbox zero.

My chest falls at the lack of replies, the invisible rope constricting my lungs even more so than before. It's been three weeks, and while I know the job market is tough, and nonprofits especially may not have the funds to invest in open positions, so there'll be more applicants than there are openings, but I was hoping I'd at least hear from a few companies. My resume is stellar. My education is above average. This time, I used my mom's maiden name for the applications, knowing if someone interviews me as a Winstead, they may be doing it for my connections to my family. But now I wonder if that might not be the best choice.

Chugging a gulp of water, I gnash my teeth together and open the job search website to send a few more applications out. I just need one to say yes. One company to give me a chance. It's a numbers game and I'll be damn sure to come up as the winner.

• • •

"Sarah! Welcome back!" Emily shrieks and wraps me in a big hug, her signature koala hug, as our friends like to joke because of her petite stature.

"Let me in the door first, woman." I laugh as I half-carry, half-drag my firecracker of a best friend back inside her spacious two-story penthouse apartment she shares with her husband, known to the world as the reclusive billionaire Adrian Scott instead of the Adrian Callahan we knew in high school, after he changed his last name due to some elaborate revenge plot he set into motion to avenge some tragedies in his life.

Emily grins as she disentangles from me, her glossy brown hair almost whipping my face. She prances down the entryway, her steps echoing on the marble floor, a flash of bright-purple silk, the sweet scent of lilies in her wake.

"Anna is preparing dinner for us. How does filet mignon, mashed potatoes, and sauteed string beans sound? Liz is in the bathroom, but Jess can't come. Last-minute work trip up north and James is playing house dad."

The rich aroma of butter and spices wafts in the air and my mouth waters. Their housekeeper slash cook is very talented, and her meals are to die for.

I snort, having a hard time imagining the imposing, sardonic man wrangling the rowdy kids by himself. "Has he called for help yet? I'd think it'll be hard for him to hold down the fort while being his Chief Data Honcho. But darn it, I miss your sister. We keep missing each other the last few meetups." Jess's husband is a top executive at an investment capital firm, and is hopelessly, completely head over heels in love with his wife.

"He's doing all right, actually! But we're on standby in case he needs us. For all I know, he's probably pulling his hair out right now, but too stubborn to ask for help. Jess and I are actually flying out to the Big Apple next week to visit Steven. You're heading back out there for the rest of the photoshoot, right? We'll look you up then."

"Yes, the timing of the New York set works out with the move as well. By the way, thanks for helping me with the movers for the final few boxes of stuff at the apartment. And of course you better look me up! And tell your brother to stop working so much. I barely see him when I'm over there. If I'm lucky, I'll have a sighting somewhere in The Orchid."

Emily shakes her head and sighs. "You and me both. That guy is certifiable. Asking him not to work is probably the equivalent of medieval torture methods to him. No wonder he never brings any ladies home when he visits."

"Not for a lack of interest. Whenever I run into him at The Orchid, he always seems to have adoring fans fawning over him." I follow her as we head into her spacious living room, which is a statement of clean lines and tall ceilings.

She veers to the right to grab a basket full of snacks from the marble island by the kitchen as I wander over to the windows and admire the glorious views of the downtown LA skyline at night. The city is quiet as dusk settles, unlike New York, which never seems to sleep. But there's still a hum of energy in the streaks of light as the cars, as numerous as the pedestrians in the Big Apple, line up against each other in gridlock traffic, an emblem of the entertainment capital of the world.

Adrian saunters up from the hallway, every inch the handsome billionaire in the news, even if he's clad in a form-fitting T-shirt and gray sweatpants. His dark hair is casually arranged, a look that's masculine and not messy on him, his sky-blue eyes glinting with humor as he wraps me in a one-arm hug.

"Emily has been yacking my ear off, waiting for you to come visit so she could hear about your adventures in New York. I can't imagine how she'll be when it hits her you're over there for good," he murmurs, quirking his lips in a rare smile he seems to reserve for all things related to his wife.

My chest aches at the thought of being so far away from Emily, but our friendship has survived even when we were on opposite coasts for college and she visits her brother so often, I'm confident we'll still be the best of friends. We must be. A tendril of wistfulness swirls to the forefront, but I push it away.

I tilt my lips up in what I hope to be a convincing grin. "Of course she'll miss me. I'm her oldest friend. Her ride-or-die. And she owes me many drinks next time we go out since I helped with the cover shoot fiasco."

He chuckles, his deep voice warm. "Send the bill my way, but if my wife gets drunk at a bar, call me so I can pick her up. Need to keep her safe." He snakes an arm around Emily and pulls her to his side to press his lips to her hair, his normally icy demeanor melting, and he whispers, "Pixie, I'll be in the office. Let me know if you ladies need anything."

Emily blushes, her body softening against her soulmate.

I look away, not wanting to intrude in their simple yet intimate moment. My heart pinches, wishing someone would look at me like I hung the moon in the sky.

Like I'm all they need in life. Just me.

Adrian saunters away as Emily stares after his retreating form, the love practically seeping from her pores.

"Look at you, the girl who once said she'll never settle down," I tease, softly nudging her with my arm.

"Oh, shut up."

I'm so happy Emily found her happiness with Adrian. They went through years of heartache to get where they are today, and they deserve every ounce of their happily-ever-after.

Perhaps someday, it'll be my turn.

Intense eyes. Midnight hair. Charming grin. Brooding countenance.

Snippets of an infuriating man dance across my consciousness.

My brows scrunch at the direction of my thoughts.

"What's going on, Sarah? You've got this look on your face." Emily stares at me quizzically, her eyebrows quirked up. Like a shark sensing blood in the water, she narrows her eyes and peers at me as if I'm a mystery she can't wait to unravel.

"Sarah! You're here!" Pounding footsteps alert me to the presence of Liz, her scent of vanilla reaching my nose before she wraps me in a soul-crushing hug. She is Emily's and Jess's sister-in-law, and one of the most kindhearted souls I've ever met. She pulls back, her blue eyes wide as she looks me over. "Something's going on with you?"

I huff out an exhale. "I think I need a drink first." Giving her arm a soft squeeze, I walk over and plop down on the large sofa and she follows suit, pursing her lips, ready to be a listening ear.

Emily hurries back with three wineglasses, a bottle of red wine, and fills them to the brim. "There's more where this came from. Now spill."

Taking a large, fortifying sip of alcohol, I relish the full-bodied richness of wine with a hint of a chocolate aftertaste. An expensive varietal, no doubt. I set the glass down, finding the ladies staring expectantly at me, and recount the events of the last few days with them, skimming over the insanity of the kiss in the elevator and ending with the violent rage from Jack yesterday and our encounter in the room after my chat with Amelia.

"And I haven't talked to him since. He pretty much ran out of the room after I bandaged him."

Emily's lips are parted, her eyes blinking, as if stunned into silence. Liz mouths something unintelligible under her breath before taking a few more gulps of wine.

"Hold on, this is Jack you're talking about. Adrian's Jack. Jack, Jack. Big flirt, Jack. Tattoo and lip ring Jack. Jack of—" Emily recovers her voice and rambles a mile a minute, her hands gesturing as she speaks as if she's a commentator to some sporting event.

"Yes, that Jack. Jack Szeto. I only know one Jack." I slide my hands over my warm face, trying to convince myself the heat is from the alcohol and not from thinking about the infuriating, insane man.

The sexy, great kisser.

The touch-her-and-die madman.

"Stop it, Sarah," I grumble to myself, my fingers still covering my eyes. "He's a flirt, the type of man you despise. Maybe yesterday was a fluke, effects of adrenaline."

"She's talking to herself. She's losing it," Liz stage whispers as Emily snickers in the background.

"You thinking what I'm thinking, Liz?"

"Sure am, Ems. Sure am."

Clink.

I look up, finding the girls clinking their glasses together in cheers, grinning from ear-to-ear, wagging their brows at me. Looking absolutely ridiculous. Like puppies. Completely ridiculous. As if puppies can ever be ridiculous.

I'm going crazy.

I narrow my eyes at them as they take hearty sips of wine. "What are you guys cheering about? What have you figured out? Care to enlighten me? I'm so confused. This is Jack, the guy I can't stand! We've *never* gotten along, ever!"

"Uh huh." Liz lifts her brow. "If you hate him so much, why are you so worked up over him? Why did you care about him getting hurt?"

"And your panda eyes...don't think I didn't notice that half-baked makeup attempt under your eyes there. You didn't sleep last night, did you?" Emily curves her lips to the side, an impish smugness radiating from her petite frame. Her knees bounce as if she's beside herself with excitement. "You know the saying 'there's a fine line between love and hate'—"

"Ooooh, I got one too! In the regency romances I read, they always say reformed rakes make the best husbands." Liz and Emily stare at each other before dissolving into cantankerous laughter.

"Oh my gosh, look at her face!" Emily whispers, her hand swiping the corner of her eye. The damn woman is laughing so hard she's crying.

I glower mutely at them, suddenly finding myself at a loss for words.

Emily leans forward, her hands clasped over her knees, and she clears her throat. "I've talked to Jess enough to pretend to be Marybeth." Marybeth is the therapist her sister sees on the regular for her anxiety, someone who's also helped Liz's successful husband, Parker, with his grief and other issues relating to his first, and late, wife. Needless to say, Liz and the Kingsley siblings think Marybeth is some sort of genius.

Emily coughs exaggeratedly into her fist before relaxing her frame into what she probably envisions a professional therapist will look like. She lowers her voice by an octave. "So, Sarah, what feelings are going through you when you think of Jack?"

Liz cackles, her cheeks pink. She tosses her golden-brown hair over her shoulder and leans back on the sofa, her blue eyes filled with mirth. All she's missing is a bucket of popcorn.

I roll my eyes. Fine, I'll humor you. "Anger, shock...and surprise?" My brows pinch at my answer.

"So, based on what you told me, the shock must be from his beating of the asshole, which I'm not really surprised, given what he's done to your crappy exes—" Emily blathers on, completely breaking character.

Liz elbows her and Emily hiccups, her eyes as big as dinner plates, and she grabs her wineglass and takes a large sip of wine. She flushes, and my eyes narrow at her.

"*What* did he do to my exes?"

Emily shifts in her seat and laughs, her voice deceptively light. "Huh? I was saying, I'm going to call him personally and thank him, 'cuz I want to kill this Kevin person myself. Slice him in half. Ground him up and toss him to the wolves. And then—" Her tone turns vicious, her hands rubbing together, no doubt imagining all the ways she can make Kevin suffer for being a creep and sleazebag. My ride-or-die. My chest warms, my insides turning to mush.

But not enough for me to forget her slip up.

"Ems." I quirk my brow and pin her with my stare.

She grins wider. "You mean Marybeth. I'm the therapist."

"Nice try. You forget I know all of your tells and the way you're twirling that strand of hair is the look of guilt. Spill. You said Jack did something to my exes?"

Emily stares at her index finger, which is wrapped around a lock of hair, and Liz tsks beside her, shaking her head. "Just tell her the truth, Ems. It's about time."

My pulse kicks up in speed, pitter-pattering in my ears, and I just know from the deepest parts of my gut whatever Emily says next will somehow shake me. Turn my world upside down. I tap my feet in a nervous rhythm on the floor.

Emily lets out an exaggerated sigh and releases the hair she's been torturing for the last minute. "Fine. You got me. I was sworn to secrecy because Jack told Adrian and Adrian told me and Liz only knew about it because Adrian also told Parker and Parker told her, but we were all not supposed to tell you—"

"Cut to the chase, Ems."

"Jack saw Tim with an escort at The Orchid and he overheard Evan talk about all the things he'll do with the Winstead connection once he marries into your family at the gentlemen's club there. He had a *chat* with both of them, and the breakups happened soon afterward. I think he knew some secrets they'd rather not see the light of day."

"What!" I growl, a scorching burn rushing through my veins at the new sleazy revelations of my exes, who were apparently more scum of the earth than I expected. Then, my mind finally processes the rest of Emily's words involving Jack.

Jack, who secretly chased away bastards I would've dumped sooner had I known their true colors.

Jack, who somehow has been defending me behind my back and not letting me know.

Jack, who takes my barbs and half-insults without ever correcting my thoughts of him.

My breath catches mid-inhale and my heart pounds a rioting rhythm behind my rib cage. My gut swooshes and freefalls, and I grip the sofa for support. I know I probably should be angry he interfered behind my back, but somehow, after the last few days especially, instead of the boiling rage I'd expect, my mind is a riot of emotions, but a sweetness rises to the forefront, the enticing taste the beginnings of a sugar high, and my traitorous beating organ flutters harder, and I feel—

"I-I don't know what to say," I murmur, still trying to process everything. My face feels hot and I grab my wineglass and take a sip.

Emily pats my hand. "You should ask him. Talk to him. I mean, if only Adrian and I had a heart to heart sooner and revealed all of our secrets, we wouldn't have—"

Liz elbows her. "Getting off track, Ems. Or, ahem, *Marybeth*."

Emily clears her throat, and her voice flattens once again. "So, now you know about your two sleazeball exes. Ahem. Let's explore the other two emotions. Let's start with anger. Why are you angry at Jack? What has he done to you in the past?"

I squint, my lips pressing into a thin line. My thoughts trail back to the exasperating man, someone who has riled me up on every occasion I've encountered him in the past decade. "He hasn't done anything *specifically* to me, per se, but his behavior is despicable. I can't stand men like him, or better yet, what he represents."

"What behavior?"

"He flirts with anything that moves. You can't take anything he says seriously. He walks around with this 'I'm so sexy, oh look at me' swagger. He changes his women quicker than some people change clothes. He acts like his ability to dole out orgasms makes him the king. It's revolting."

Liz interjects, "Hold on a second. You're upset with him because he's a flirt and has swagger...and knows how to use his dick?" Then she raises her brow. "Aaaand you find him sexy?"

Emily nudges her hard, her lips trembling in a poor attempt to not laugh. "There can only be one Marybeth, the therapist, and that's me." Another ridiculous stage whisper and Liz makes an exaggerated show of bowing down to Emily.

"My bad, Ems. Or I mean, Marybeth, please continue."

I grab the multicolored cushion next to me and toss it at them in mock anger. The girls dodge and snicker, seemingly entertained by this entire conversation. I perch my head on one hand and narrow my eyes. *I'm not amused,* I mouth to the ladies. Emily bites her quivering bottom lip, trying her best not to break character once more.

"So, Sarah, let's dive deeper. Do you have an issue with a single man embracing his sexual self if the women he engages with are otherwise unattached?"

I scoff. "Twenty-first century, go sexuality. I have no problem with that. If you can get some, good for you." And I believe that. Sex shouldn't be something dirty or something to be ashamed of.

Ems nods and makes a show of jotting down notes on an imaginary notepad. "And if Jack hasn't done anything to you other than impress upon you his confidence and charm, do you think your anger is really toward him or someone else? Is there someone you associate his behavior with that's perhaps conflating your feelings?"

A lump forms in my throat and I stare at Em's piercing brown eyes. Shrewd. Inquisitive. As if she, too, realizes she's asking the right questions. I attempt to take a breath, but a heaviness seeps into my chest, rendering me mute. Upon my silence, she raises one elegant brow, as if to say, *got you.*

A familiar emotion crawls inside me. Slithering, slinky, sticky. Something that has been lying dormant in the darkest corners of my mind for a long time, something I've refused to acknowledge, to name, until now.

Guilt.

The same dark threads twining around my heart yesterday, only to be released by Jack's smiles.

There's really only one man whose womanizing habits has hurt me. Only one man who's really turned me off against most men in the world. Only one man I find revolting, disgusting, despicable.

My dad.

Liz sits back up, her stance excited, and she points a finger at me, the wine almost sloshing out of her glass. "That's it. Whoever you're thinking of right there. That's who you're really pissed off at. Maybe you aren't fair to Jack at all."

My mouth is dry, my throat feels like it's been stuffed with cotton balls. The weight on my chest is heavier, as if lead has lined my lungs, preventing me from drawing a full breath.

I'm afraid of what this all means.

The scorching kiss. The heated gaze. The raw magnetism unlike anything I've ever felt before. The way every nerve in my body zings whenever I'm around him. The way my heart reacted to the news of him no doubt scaring the living daylights out of Tim and Evan. I used to blame my emotions and reactions to him on hatred, on anger, on disgust.

But now...I'm afraid maybe I'm just screwed.

"So, Jack, you were telling us you're taking photos for work?" Mom inquires, her brows furrowing as she peruses the leather-bound menu of an Italian restaurant nestled inside another five-star hotel near my work. At sixty-five, she still looks young for her age, but I can't help but notice the additional streaks of white hair interlacing with the black. A harpist is playing in the corner of the dining room, her fingers flying across the strings, strumming a soft and soothing holiday melody.

"Thirty-five dollars for a spaghetti carbonara? That's highway robbery," Dad grumbles and pushes up his glasses, which are always sliding down his nose.

"It's half the price in that little restaurant next to our apartment. Why are you spending so much in this fancy place?"

"I'm doing well for myself and I want to treat you guys. It's okay, really. The chef here is amazing and they say this is the next best thing to going to Italy."

No matter how many times I tell them I want to treat them to the fine dining that was denied to us when I was younger, they'd insist I was wasting hard-earned money on frivolities. I guess you can't change the frugal mentality from first-generation immigrants.

They came to Los Angeles from Hong Kong back in the seventies and spent most of their lives toiling away at a dry-cleaning store they opened with their savings. Then, after I moved to New York for The Orchid and they could see I was settling down on the East Coast, they retired and moved to Flushing.

My parents *tsk* underneath their breath but the tilts of their lips into half smiles tell me they're secretly pleased. Like many traditional Chinese parents, they're not overtly physically affectionate, but it's these small quirks and tells that ultimately give them away. I shake my head, letting them complain about the prices, but I know they'll eat every morsel on their plates.

A waiter comes by in his sharp uniform of a black button down and gray dress pants and takes our order. My parents stuck to their favorites, the spaghetti carbonara and the spaghetti Bolognese, all the while murmuring under their breath how costly everything is.

"So, what is this photo thing you are doing? They're not demoting you, right? You're still the entertainment manager? And why are your hands all torn up again?" Mom sips a glass of water and brushes her silver-streaked hair behind her ears. Her eyes are inquisitive, her brows pinching again, seemingly worried about my job prospects, even though I've never given them any cause for concern since I started at The Orchid. And from her laser focus on my bandaged knuckles, I assume she's thinking back to the scuffles I have gotten into in the past.

A sliver of heaviness settles on my chest, and I heave out an exasperated sigh. It seems like no matter how well I do for myself, delinquent Jack still trails me like an incessant shadow. *Or maybe, you're afraid you'll slip up too.* I swallow the dark thought.

"Why are you bringing this up again? I told you before, work is great. No one is getting demoted, if anything, I may be up for a promotion soon. And yes, I'm in a photoshoot for one of our clients there who needs a last-minute model. It's part of our job description to make them happy, so I'm actually going above and beyond by helping them. This may help me move up faster. Better salary and benefits. And I've developed a good network with powerful people now. Things are going really well for me." I don't mention the photoshoot will include half-nudes and sexy poses. There are certain things they definitely don't need to know about.

I take a sip of water, noting my mom's furrowed brows, her lips still pursed in concern. "And my scraped-up knuckles were from an accident at work. Trust me, I'm not getting into trouble again."

Mom's face softens at my reassurance, and I can't say it doesn't hurt to see her still worried if I'm going down some imaginary slippery slope again.

But I can't blame her. After all, sometimes, the past colors people's perception of you, and those were mistakes I need to own up to.

Dad nods. "Good, Jack. Doing more will ensure you have a good standing with your boss. You have such a good, secure job. Make sure to try your best. These jobs don't come easily, with that pay, and you know you barely graduated college."

"Hardworking and steadfastness wins the race," Mom echoes with Dad dipping his head in agreement. "You need to be content with what you have. Don't have your head in the clouds. We're in the working class. Accept your station in life. Don't pretend you're anything you're not. Remember, you're working for the rich crowd. Doesn't make you one of them. Slow and steady, okay, Jack? We don't want you to fall back into bad habits."

The heaviness in my chest presses down like a ship dropping its anchor into the seas, and I take a deep breath, attempting to loosen up some of the pressure gathering there.

They just love and worry about you, Jack. It's what parents do. It's not their fault you were such a screw-up as a kid.

Maybe in time, they won't be so concerned.

Maybe in time, I won't feel like I'm still lacking somehow.

I force out a halfhearted smile. "I got this. Really, don't worry about me. I'm not the Jack from the old days anymore."

Mom reaches over and pats my hand, giving it a soft squeeze. Her voice softens and she says, "We know, honey. We're just looking out for you. Your dad and I have been in the real world for a lot longer than you and have seen many things. We just want you to avoid any hiccups or mistakes if you can." She smiles, and gives me another reassuring pat. Then her eyes widen and she sits up as if she remembered something important.

"By the way, how did the date go with Mrs. Lee's daughter, Stephanie? Did you like her?" Mom perks up at the mention of the blind date she arranged for me a few weeks ago. She's been giving me hints left and right about settling down and I honestly just humor her for the most part. It's better than to argue each time about how I didn't need her introductions when I can meet plenty of women on my own.

"It was fine, but we're more suited as friends," I murmur before taking a sip of my water. Actually, Stephanie was very boring and throughout the dinner, my mind kept flitting back to a certain redhead who makes my body sing whenever I interact with her, even if it's just trading insults and jokes. I can barely remember what Stephanie looks like, to be honest.

Mom deflates and sighs, her eyes raised skyward. "You never like any of them. We aren't getting any younger, Jack. It'll be nice to see you settle down and give us grandbabies."

I quirk a grin and wink. "Don't worry, I have many options. One day, I'll bring someone home. You won't have to worry about that."

Mom's lips flatten at my teasing expression. "But—"

"Hush. You can't rush these things. Let him be. He still has time," Dad murmurs to Mom and they trade a glance, an understanding seemingly passing through their eye contact, then he swivels his head toward me. "Jack, I know we worry and nag a lot, but we are happy to see you doing well." Dad punctuates the thought with a firm nod.

A gentle heat flows into my body, melting away the lingering heaviness in my chest, and I lean back as the server comes by with our entrees. I blow out a deep exhale and smile at my parents.

There are consequences with every action, and their nagging is a result of my past behavior because I didn't inspire a lot of confidence in them back then. But in time, I hope they'll finally see the man I've become, and perhaps, the old Jack Szeto will finally be ashes in the wind, figments of the past.

And the new Jack Szeto will be enough.

The rest of lunch passes by without a hitch and before long, we part ways in front of the restaurant and they're headed back to Queens to visit with friends and I'm returning to work.

Tugging the collar up of my thick coat made from the finest wool, a luxury item the nineteen-year-old me would never dream I'd one day own, I stride down 5th Avenue, the bracing winds whipping against my face, my mind mulling over my parents' concerns for me. The skies are dim and gray, a brief respite from the snowfall the last few days, and I skirt around the black sludges of ice and snow on the streets, a last-ditch attempt to keep my shoes relatively unscathed.

Don't have your head in the clouds. Accept your station in life. Don't pretend you're anything else you're not. Remember, you're working for the rich crowd. Doesn't make you one of them. Mom's words echo in my brain, as if I need a reminder. If I were in their crowds, perhaps I may have a chance with her. My heart constricts and the insidious ache of unrequited longing penetrates my insides once again. I empty my lungs, the white plumes of my breath lingering in the air as my cell phone chimes with an incoming message. Tearing off my glove with my teeth, I swipe open my phone while navigating the throngs of black-and-white blurs of fellow New Yorkers rushing around me to their next destination, all of us participants in the same rat race.

Ryland: I heard about the photoshoot problems in LA. Don't want you to worry about it. From what I gathered, it seems like we had a sexual assault on our hands and the asshole deserved what he got. Senator Townsend was pissed, but he knew if this went public, it'd look bad for him. I issued a ban on his son from any of our establishments. If you ask me later, I'll deny this convo as Fleur Entertainment doesn't condone violence. Drinks on me next time.

Smirking, I type back a response to my boss and friend, Ryland Anderson, the second-oldest sibling of the Anderson Family, who wields considerable influence in New York as they own Fleur Entertainment, the international entertainment and hospitality conglomerate, which of course includes The Orchid as part of their portfolio. I won't even ask how he heard about the photoshoot. The man has eyes and ears everywhere.

Jack: Thanks, boss. Drinks are definitely on you even before this incident since my job definitely doesn't include taking off my clothes and stepping in to model for a romance book cover. And now, I need to be in some of the more intimate shots. Flashing off my ripped physique is not what I have in mind when I get up to go to work. So, you definitely owe me one. And by the way, if you want to be off the record, you shouldn't have texted me. I will screenshot this exchange and frame it on my wall.

Ryland: As much as the douchebag brought it upon himself, you did cause the problem by punching him out, so it makes sense you need to step in and remedy the situation. Jack-of-all-trades, right? And please, I'm sure having more women drool over your body is a hardship for you. And I have resources that can make these texts disappear, jackass.

I grumble, my lips twisting up in a smirk before sliding my phone into my pocket as I weave past a small group of tourists with their phones out, no doubt taking some photos of the infamous street. But who the fuck stops in the middle of the sidewalk?

"Miss, it's really okay. I can do this myself."

"Nonsense. I'm early anyway, and you clearly need the help." The sultry, smoky voice is resounding amidst the cacophony of taxis whirring by honking horns, city sounds I've grown very familiar with in the last ten years.

Glancing up, my feet skid to a stop as I take in the scene before me, a faint feeling of déjà vu prickling my senses.

Sarah, her hair tied up in a loose bun, with wavy tendrils skimming her round cheeks, flushed from the wind chill, hoists a large cardboard box from the back of a delivery van emblazoned with the logo of a nearby restaurant to the side entrance of The Orchid reserved for smaller deliveries. This is the first time I've seen her since I escaped from the room after she attended to my wounds last week.

I was a coward, hanging by the last vestiges of control, trying to protect the remnants of my heart because if I kissed her, I knew

I'd give her the last remaining bits of my bloodied up organ and one day, when she woke up and decided she wanted to find someone better, someone more capable and suited to be her partner, those last precious pieces of me would shrivel up and I wouldn't recover.

A middle-aged woman wearing a gray puffer jacket limps after her, carrying a few more boxes in her hands. "I twisted my ankle this morning, but the restaurant is understaffed, so unfortunately, I'm still on the delivery schedule. Family to feed at home. Gotta pay the bills, you know?"

Sarah nods, her brows scrunching as if she truly feels for the woman's plight. Her eyes hold no artifice, even though I'm sure she's never worked a day of manual labor in her life. The kindhearted angel. The last twelve years have only made her more beautiful, more ethereal. My breath strains in my lungs as my fingers twitch, wanting to curl her in my arms, to protect her tenderhearted soul. Even if she can't see that about herself. Even if she thinks she's doing what anyone in her position would do.

She turns toward the van after setting the box inside the door and, as if my senses suddenly awaken, my vision sharpens, my heart sending heated blood through my veins and my feet move of their own accord, reaching them in a few strides.

"Let me do it." My voice comes out hoarse and thick as I take the new cardboard box from Sarah's hands and carry it to the side entrance, where a doorman hurries to greet me and bring the box inside. "It's cold out. Why don't you head in, Sarah?"

Sarah nods, her eyes pinned to the ground, the pink in her cheeks deepening, her eyes unwilling to meet mine in an unfamiliar display of...shyness?

"Sarah?" I frown, taking in the odd expression on her face.

Her head snaps up and her eyes sweep over me, pausing slightly at the healing wounds on my brow and hands. Her elegant brows pinch when her gaze falls to the scabs on my hands. She doles out a quivering smile. "Sure thing, Jack."

She glances at the delivery woman and calls out, "Good luck with the rest of your workday." In a whirl of orange and red, burning flames in the middle of a morning of grayscale, she disappears inside the main entrance, leaving me in a cloud of orange-blossom-scented air. And I find myself once again mesmerized as my lungs rake in the chilled air, the cold finally invading my senses, as if my body is bereft without her presence and her warmth.

"A New Yorker stopping and helping. Will wonders ever cease?" The woman pauses next to me, her hand lifting in a wave.

"She's not technically from New York, but I'm sure even if she were, she'd do the same." I smile inwardly before another doorman and I help the woman unload the rest of her boxes.

One hour later, I step into the mostly empty suite we've commandeered for the next two days to wrap up Juliet's photoshoot and park myself onto one of the stools near the open-concept kitchen. Today will be a makeup of the botched session from a week ago. My swollen and bleeding knuckles and forehead cut have since healed, the gashes scabbed over and the makeup artist applied some liquid to camouflage and to cover up the scabs on my hand.

Fucking bastard. I grit my teeth as my mind trails back to Kevin and the disgusting words he said to Sarah. The way she flinched as if he physically assaulted her. It's a good thing Ryland put him on the blacklist because I can't be responsible for my actions if I see him walking in the halls of The Orchid again.

"Jack, dear, thank you for stepping in. I'll be sure to let your boss know how you're going above and beyond to please me." Juliet's saccharine voice is especially grating today, and she leans in, the wispy frills of her couture dress, which unfortunately makes her look like a sickly ostrich with molting feathers, tickle my face. She places her manicured hand on my shoulder and squeezes.

I can't wait for this to be over. Willing myself not to recoil, I instead twist my lips into a half grin. "I caused the problem by punching out Kevin. Seems fair for me to step in. And thank you for changing your character to Asian for me."

"You were a hero that day, a complete inspiration! I also modified my manuscript to add that scene into the third act. I'm sure..."

Nodding noncommittally, I glance around the dimly lit room, noting Amelia and her new lighting assistant are setting up, clearing the living room area, and laying the plush, black blanket over the long sectional by the window, similar to the scene in LA. Snowflakes flutter outside the window amidst a sea of dreary gray, and the thick, blackout curtains are drawn halfway, the streams of cool daylight hitting the settee like a spotlight.

A small, wrapped package on the side table closest to me catches my attention. I pick it up, my brows furrowing at the inscription, "To: Jack," written in feminine script. My fingers tear at the tape on the wrapping, my mind wondering what this is and who—

The bedroom door opens with a *creak* and Sarah steps out, her hair and makeup in place, clad in the same silky negligee from a week ago. I swallow, setting the package back on the table, as I greedily rake in her appearance. The expanse of snowy, creamy skin. The dark shadow of her cleavage on display. The plump, kissable lips. The long, svelte legs I can imagine wrapping around my back as I pump into her.

The blood rushes straight to my cock at the sight of her luscious curves swaying gently with each graceful step. My mouth runs dry, my eyes feasting on the goddess in front of me while she strides up to Amelia, her hands locked behind her back, fingers twisting, as if she's unsure. Hesitant. As if she isn't aware of her effect on men.

Drew whistles next to me. I almost forgot he's here. "Damn, Kevin is an ass, but she *is* really hot."

I curl my hands into fists. "Watch it," I growl, even though I was also admiring her mere seconds ago. Because I'm a fucking hypocrite.

He raises his hands in mock surrender. "Just admiring. Looking, not touching. What's with you two, anyway? Isn't she a member here? I thought there was a no fraternization policy?"

"We're nothing. Just friends." If even that. But friends don't kiss me back the way she did in the elevator, her moans still ringing in my ears. Friends don't look at me the way she did after she bandaged my wounds the other day. Friends don't shed tears for me. My dick stiffens some more, and I shift on my stool, attempting to hide my situation down there.

Drew hums, his brows sky-high. "Nah, I don't buy that at all. And if that's what you're telling yourself, well, good luck being delusional."

Soon enough, Amelia calls us over and asks us to strip out of our shirts. Unlike Kevin the asswipe, I have tattoos snaking down my right arm. Amelia offered to have the makeup artist cover them up, but Juliet nearly shrieks in response, saying my tats are "perfect."

Sarah keeps her beautiful eyes on anything and everyone except me, no matter how hard I try to catch her attention. I want to know everything going on in that beautiful mind of hers. I want to know if the week of distance between us has brought clarity to her, or if she's scared of me after what she saw me do to Kevin last week. I want to know if she hates me even more because of my temper, my display of violence, or perhaps if she'll bestow me the tender smiles and soft touches the way she did when she cared for my wounds. I'm desperate to see what lies in those green-rimmed hazel eyes, even if it's ultimately revulsion reflecting at me.

"Okay, Sarah, you know the drill. If you feel at all uncomfortable, speak out like you did last time. We have zero tolerance for any funny business."

Sarah nods, her hands playing with the hem of her negligee as she continues to pretend I don't exist.

"Drew, step behind Sarah and cradle her waist. Dip your head down so your nose grazes her neck, like you want to smell her perfume. Jack, stand next to Sarah and tease the hem of her dress, pulling it up slightly and look into her eyes. Sarah, stare at Jack as you arch your neck to Drew. Remember, you're all lovers and you can't get enough of each other."

Drew steps into position as Sarah stands rigidly in front of him, her luscious lips parted in an "O," as if she's trying to get in quick breaths of air. I step closer, my heart threatening to break out from my rib cage, the beats of my pulse thundering in my ears. Flexing my hand, I stand in position, my body mere inches away from the one woman who's always out of reach, the angel too pure for the likes of me. I feel dirty, like by touching her I'm somehow soiling her, but I can't help myself. The smoothness of her skin and the heat from her beautiful body beckoning me like a lighthouse in the dark seas. I can almost feel her caress, even though we haven't touched yet.

Raking in a shuddering inhale, I place my left hand on her negligee, my fingers grazing her soft thigh as I bunch the silky material up. Each slide of my fingers grazes her hips and the pounding in my ears becomes a thunderous roar. My fingers tingle at the ends and I grip the hem of her dress tighter in my fist.

The scent of orange and sweetness fills my nostrils and I'm drunk from this closeness, from the soft pants of her breathing, from finally having an excuse to put my hands on her. Sarah trembles and lets out a small, almost imperceptible whimper. Heated blood rushes straight to my groin at the small sound—something I never thought I'd hear from those beautiful lips of hers. A pink flush lights up her skin, spreading from her mouthwatering cleavage to the delicate arch of her neck. Her face is still facing forward, as if she still can't bring herself to look at me. Her lips quiver and her eyes dart from side to side.

"Angel," I rasp, my right hand trembling from restraint and I reach out to touch her chin, gently tilting her face toward mine.

Her shiny pink lips part on another exhale as her large doe-like eyes finally settle on mine. Her pupils are dark and hazy as if she's trapped in the same burgeoning storm as me.

"W-What did you call me?" she breathes, her chest lifting and falling in rapid succession. Her tongue darts out to swipe her plump bottom lip.

"Baby," I murmur. My gaze snags on her lips, the sweetness I can taste almost from here, mere inches away from her, our bodies grazing in an erotic dance with a thin silky nightgown separating us.

"You dazzle me," I rasp, my heart thudding so fast I swear she could probably hear me. "You're perfect, an angel upon mankind."

She stills, her eyes widening as a flash of something registers on her face. She cocks her head to the side, her forehead crinkling, her gaze intent on mine. "*What* did you say?"

My fingers smooth out the grooves on her forehead, trailing down her face with reverence, grazing her parted lips. She swallows as the blacks of her pupils slowly overtake the greens and golds, bottomless pools. Drawn by the invisible pull between us, I lean in, wanting, no, *needing* to taste those lips once more, to see if we can create a firestorm once again.

"Perfect. This is perfect. That's a wrap!"

Sarah flinches at Amelia's voice, jerking away from me as the room slowly comes into focus, my body finally registering my surroundings. The spotlight shining on our faces. The rustling of the assistant moving equipment around the room. The slight breeze from the air blowing in from the vents.

My body stays frozen, my feet tethered to the ground as my eyes are pinned to Sarah, who's walking away from me toward the bedroom, watching what can be described as bewilderment cross her face.

A clearing of a throat draws my attention to Juliet and Amelia, who are reviewing the photos and talking in hushed whispers. Juliet stares at the camera before glancing up, a puzzled frown appearing on her face. Her shrewd eyes trail to Sarah's backside, then back at me, then narrow into thin slits.

A nagging kernel of unease plants itself inside me. I don't know what Juliet is seeing in those photos, but I need to be more careful, so the whole world doesn't learn of my obsession with the one woman I can never have.

The one woman who's too good for me.

The one woman I'll protect from afar because she deserves someone who can give her the world.

I look at Sarah again, finding her gazing at me, her eyes darting meaningfully to the half-opened package on the table before stepping into the dark room.

I grab the present, rip open the wrapping paper in urgency, and find a small note affixed on top of a silver box.

Jack,

Perhaps you're my guardian angel.

Thank you for what you did in LA.

Sarah

My hands tremble, and I carefully remove the lid of the box. A gleaming pair of silver cufflinks lay on a bed of dark-blue silk. Intricately carved angel wings, each feather tipped in rose gold, every stroke, every detail artfully crafted. A lump forms in my throat, my fingers lightly tracing the ridges and the curves of the jewelry.

She called me her guardian angel.

My heart leaps and flies against my rib cage, a heated flush spreading throughout my body as I marvel at the most thoughtful gift I've ever received.

"Friends, huh? It's like watching the goddamn *The Young and the Restless* just now." Drew snorts, clapping me on the shoulder before trudging off to retrieve his clothes from the chair.

Shit. Even Drew is catching on.

A rush of warmth cloaking my insides smothers the slither of foreboding. Carefully, I close the lid to the box, and clutch it tightly in my hand.

I barely spare him a glance, my eyes still trained on her gift, my lungs heaving in heavy breaths, and I feel my world shift on its axis.

"**G**ood night, Julia." I nod to my curly-haired assistant, who's peeking into my office at the door. She gives me a half wave and dashes off in a hurry, no doubt to pick up her kids from daycare. Closing my eyes, I rub the bridge of my nose and finish reviewing the client event requests that came through the system earlier today.

It has been a rough day onsite with two house representatives from opposing parties duking it out in the cigar club because they wanted to reserve the same ballroom for a wedding and a graduation party...for two years in the future. And it doesn't matter there are four other equally grand ballrooms to choose from. Pacifying two grown men reduced to squabbling toddlers in public while taking care of their delicate egos took most of my patience. But what's making my blood boil and the vein throb in my forehead is the email on my computer right now.

Clenching my jaw, I glare at the request from one Edmund Winstead, who's requesting half of Catania, our onsite Michelin-starred Italian restaurant to be cordoned off for a private party, for which the attendee list is sparingly short, one Sarah Winstead and one Charles Vaughn of the old money Vaughn Family with a note to decorate the place with flowers and even hiring a string quartet. The word "romance" is bolded and in all caps.

I've been working here long enough to recognize a blind date setup a mile away. Gnashing my teeth together, my fingers hover the mouse over the delete button, knowing that won't solve anything. Another request will just funnel through if I ignore this one. This is who Sarah should be with. Someone rich, handsome, and successful. CEO of Bank of Columbia. Someone who can buy her the world. Someone who can give her the lifestyle she deserves.

My chest spasms in pain, the agony far exceeding anything I've ever experienced in the past, far worse than the broken bones from fights as a kid, or the surgery I had to fix my ruptured spleen during a particularly memorable illegal boxing fight in an underground ring in college. I still won that match, though. The other guy looked worse than me.

"Fuck," I huff under my breath and rake my hand through my hair, no doubt disheveling it from its immaculate styling. Pushing out from my desk in frustration, I grab my wallet and keys.

She's not for you, Jack. She's never for you. Humans and angels don't belong together.

The thoughts litter my mind, javelins to my heart as the blood churns in my body.

I need to escape. I need to snap out of this madness. I need to accept my fucking station in life. *Be content with what I have,* as my parents said. Mr. Good Times, not Mr. Permanent. And definitely not good enough for her.

Storming toward the staff elevators, I press the button to the rooftop bar, which is usually quiet at dinnertime, as most of our patrons are frequenting our onsite restaurants or enjoying other services.

The hydraulics of the elevator are quiet, without the usual hum to dull my thoughts, and I attempt to take a few deep breaths, trying to calm the ruckus in my mind, to soothe the lingering soreness in my chest. Seconds later, the doors open, and I walk through several corridors, all part of the intricate labyrinth of staff passageways to allow us to get from one place to another efficiently, all part of the "to be seen and not heard" standards of the establishment.

Banking a right, I push open a door, revealing a winter wonderland, already adorned with the spirit of Christmas. A clear covering the staff must have set up earlier today encloses the expanse of the rooftop, with lush green shrubbery and vines decorating the quiet bar. Thousands of fairy lights are draped up high toward the clear ceiling, lighting the space in a dim, warm glow, while giving the appearance of stars suspended in midair.

Private seating is sectioned off by the towering greenery to offer privacy to its patrons. A few folks linger in the common areas, enjoying the heated lamps and the view of the New York skyline with a light dusting of snow falling all around us. A cluster of tall, faux-snow-tipped Christmas trees, already adorned with glittering ornaments and silk sashes of dark reds and golds, draw your eyesight to the center of the space. Even after all these years of working here, I can't help but marvel at the beautiful scenery before me, something I wouldn't have dreamed possible back in the day. My mind flits to the sad-looking Christmas twig in front of Grocery for Less all those years ago, when my angel first noticed me watching her.

How life has changed. And yet, some things remain the same.

The lash of unrequited longing is still as vicious as ever, the barbed ends scraping my body repeatedly, the blistering wound scabbing and reopening in a tormenting cycle I don't see myself getting out of.

Rubbing the aching spot on my chest, I stride out, determined to drown my sorrows in scotch or bourbon, when the lilting voice of Sarah interrupts my thoughts.

I've gone mad and am hallucinating. I'm now delirious from want.

I must be.

A few moments later, her voice travels across the space again.

"You guys are leeeeeaving already? It's sooooo early."

I frown, my eyes rove my surroundings, finding Sarah sitting at the bar, her normally poised figure slouched sideways. She's dressed in the same dark-green wrap dress I saw her in weeks ago, the one that brings out the reddish-gold streaks of her hair and makes her look like a lush forest nymph from fantasy realms.

She's pointing to Emily, Jess, and the back of a tall, striking man who's turning a few heads from other females around the bar. He turns—fucking Steven Kinglsey, my good friend, fellow member of The Orchid, and the youngest of the Kingsley siblings. He should've been the model in the damn photoshoot then I wouldn't be in this crazy mess. And he'd probably be better at it since he regularly graces the covers of top financial magazines and newspapers as one of the richest and most eligible bachelors in New York.

But the thought of him wrapping his arms around Sarah, his fingers grazing her smooth skin makes my fists clench and my blood boil.

I laugh mirthlessly under my breath at my ridiculousness as I stride toward them. I haven't seen the Kingsley siblings, minus Steven, for a few months, but they fly out to New York often enough for work, so it always seems like no time has passed.

"You're such a lightweight, Sarah! Come on, let me get you back to your hotel room." Emily giggles as she hops off her seat and sways unsteadily on her feet.

"Ems, you can't even stand, and you're saying *I'm* a lightweight?" Sarah lets out an unladylike snort, her luscious ass hanging precariously on her stool, before she throws her arms around a wobbly Emily standing in front of her, who is now supported by Steven.

A tingle of amusement filters through the chaos inside me. Quirking a grin, I murmur, "Drunk before seven? What's going on?"

Steven rolls his eyes as he hoists Emily up. "Hey, Jack, didn't expect to see you here at this hour."

"I do work at The Orchid. You're bound to run into me from time to time when you're a member. And I work around the clock," I respond and flash a wry smile.

Stevens looks at his sisters and Sarah. He glances heavenward and lets out an exasperated sigh. "Man, I have no fucking clue what's going on. We were supposed to meet up and then these two," he points to Ems and Sarah, who are cackling like they're at a standup comedy show, "decided to hit the bar first. Adrian is heading over in a bit to join us for dinner."

"I tried to stop them, but Sarah said she needs to drink her money's worth of alcohol from Emily because she got her into this photoshoot mess." Jess's raven hair gleams under the fairy lights, her eyes twinkling. She seems marginally sober, which makes sense, given her careful, responsible, older-sister personality. "Nice to see you again, Jack."

I tug her close for a hug and slap a hand on Steven's back in greeting. "Glad to see my favorite sibling friends again."

"I bet you say that to e-everyone." Sarah hiccups, her index finger pointing at me accusingly as her body sways toward me. "I thought your favorite sibling friends are the Andersons."

She stares at her finger like it's the most interesting thing on the planet and mumbles, "I mean, you seem awfully chummy with Ryland and Lana. And she's so *beautiful*. She's so smart. She's gorgeous. They're all gorgeous. Spectacular people. Good head on their shoulders and know how to live their lives independently. Don't have a philandering, embarrassing dad." She furrows her elegant brows, her lips twisting in a cute pout, and pitches forward on her stool. I quickly steady her, my arm curling around her slender waist.

"I got her. She lives at the Kensington next door, anyway. Why don't you guys head out?"

"You sure?" Jess steps forward, mother hen in action. She pinches her brows and narrows her gaze at me, as if trying to read my intentions.

Emily shoves Steven away and staggers to her older sister, pulling her head down, and whispers something in her ear. Then she doles out an impish grin, a devious light flickering in her eyes. I can totally see why Adrian calls her Pixie. "Jack, take care of my ride-or-die, or else! And no funny business, okay?"

Holding my hand up, I cock my brow. "Scout's honor." Even though I was the furthest thing from a boy scout when I was younger.

Steven exchanges a glance with his sisters before staring at me, his piercing eyes threatening to laser me on the spot. "You got it, Szeto?" His voice is rumbly laced with a hard edge. Despite his emotions can go fuck themselves attitude, the youngest Kingsley is a closet protector, something I'm sure even he isn't aware of.

"Yes. Go, please."

His piercing eyes narrow as he assesses me and he straightens to his full height, an inch or two taller than me. Leveling a chilling glare at me, as if to warn me, *don't mess with Sarah, dipshit,* he backs away slowly as I give him a curt nod in acknowledgement.

Jess and Steven haul a hiccupping Emily away. As I stare at their retreating figures, Emily turns around and mouths, "I'm watching you, Jack. Don't hurt her. Take care of my girl." Her eyes glitter with mischief.

I nod, amused at the current situation, until a loud, unladylike belch draws my attention to the tempting woman currently leaning against me.

"J-Jack?"

"Yes, angel?" I murmur, unable to resist leaning down and dropping a soft kiss on her golden strands, which she has braided in a half updo. Closing my eyes, I inhale her sweet scent and relish in her body heat, the earlier tension slowly dissipating. It's as if I can finally breathe deeply with her by my side.

It's as if she's the elixir to heal the aching tightness in my chest.

Perhaps humans are not supposed to be with angels, but aren't saints humans in the first place?

Like you're a saint, Jack. I bite my cheek, the sharp pain jolting me back to reality.

Sarah slides down the stool, her feet finding unsteady purchase on the floor. She's wearing the fuck-me black heels again. She grasps my jacket with one hand, her other hand making its slow and arduous journey up my chest. I can feel her teasing touch through my thin button-down gray dress shirt, my tie already loosened at the neck. Heady sensations dance across my skin, sparking the nerve endings in my body.

"Jack?" She pokes my chest.

My dick strains at her breathy whisper, the hardness making a tent in my pants. Sweat beads at the back of my neck as I dip my head down and find her staring at me, her eyes heavy-lidded, pupils blown.

"Yes, baby?"

"You're gorgeous too." She doles out a sweet smile, gazing at me as if I'm her knight in shining armor.

I swallow, suddenly at a loss for words. My heart skips and tumbles. She leans closer, her hands linking behind my neck, pulling my head down. Her sweet breath puffs against my face.

"You're more gorgeous than any of them."

"What, baby?"

"The Andersons." Her exhales now glide over my ear and my muscles freeze in tension. My sanity hangs on by the thinnest thread as I feel my head get dizzy with exhilaration and my muscles drunk with elation. Screw scotch and bourbon. This is the intoxicating hit I need to make me forget about all my worries. My hands feel clammy as I fight the intense urge to bend her over and kiss her senseless.

To tell myself and convince her to forget about the world and leap into madness with me.

She tilts her head back and looks at me, her eyes hazy but soft. With an infinitesimal smile, she trails her hand over my face, skimming my day's growth of facial hair, my cheekbones. Pleasure sparks like fireworks inside me and my eyes close as I lean into her touch. She rakes her fingers over my hair and gives it a soft tug.

Biting back a groan, my eyes flicker open once more, finding her gaze intent on me. "I've always wanted to do that, to tug on your hair and see what happens. To see if it's fake because it's too beautiful."

"And did that satisfy your curiosity?" My voice is hoarse as wetness seeps from the tip of my cock. This is the worst torture I've ever experienced.

She shakes her head, swaying slightly in my arms before murmuring, "If anything, I'm more confused. I think you're not who you pretend to be."

I curl an errant lock of hair behind her ear, watching her pale skin bloom in color. Her lips part in a soft gasp, as if she too feels this electric current between us.

Sarah's tongue swipes her lips, and a growl escapes mine as I dig my fingers into her waist, pulling her closer to me, so not a slither of air separates us.

"You're a good person, Jack. Strong. Smart. Capable. I used to think, n-no, I wanted to t-think…" She falls silent as her sweet breath lingers in the space between us and I inhale, dragging any part of her inside me, my body craving her like oxygen.

"And you were so sexy the other day." A crooked grin. Teasing. Adorable.

The pounding in my chest is so loud I can barely hear anything else.

"Really now. How so?" I'm not above fishing for compliments.

"The way you beat Kevin to a pulp. So manly."

Her hands are back on my neck now. She plays with my hair again, the soft tugs sending sharp jolts of arousal through my body. My hand trembles on her back. I want to throw her over my shoulder, haul her to an empty suite, rip off the dress, but the fuck-me heels stay on, and—

"So you're my avenger now? Protector of my virtue?" She leans in and presses her soft lips on my jaw. I feel that kiss on my cock and the loosened tie around my neck suddenly feels like a chokehold. The simmering blood in my body is laced with a drug, laced with addiction, laced with her. My skin is feverish. Sensitive. Every graze inflaming the nerves one hundred-fold.

Closing my eyes, I release a shaky exhale. "Come on, let's get you back to your hotel room. You've had too much to drink, angel." Using the last of my willpower, I guide her toward the guest elevators.

The doors slide open with a *ding* and we step in but I couldn't help but think back to the last time we were in the elevators, when she was grinding her hips on me, her fingers clawing at my back as she kisses me with fire, with fervor. The best kiss of my life. The best sexual experience of my life, and I had my fair share of sowing my oats.

"I think I'm a smart person. H-Hardworking. I have a great body...I exercise and t-take care of myself. I have a lot to offer," she mumbles into my chest, her arms wrapped around my waist. Her voice is not as slurred as before but is tinged with sadness.

Tugging her closer to me, I rub light circles on her forearms. She gasps, goosebumps pebbling on her skin, and that little sound inflames me even further. "You're perfect. Beautiful. Smart. Kind."

"Why can't they see it?"

"Who, sweetheart?" Wetness seeps through my shirt and I glance down, finding her long lashes tipped with tears. My other hand automatically reaches up to swipe the tears off her face, a scything pain slashes my insides at her tears, the anguish in her voice. "Why are you crying, baby?"

"The m-men I've dated in the past only saw me as dollar signs or a pretty girl to have sex with. Kevin, the asshole, thinks I'm a piece of ass he can just grope and get away with it. I-I know none of this is my f-fault, but it makes me so sad sometimes." The fury banked in the background leaps to the forefront once more and I want nothing more than to find each and every one of these bastards and slowly tear them apart piece by piece.

Because they hurt her, this wonderful soul in front of me.

Sarah hiccups and I rub reassuring circles on her back, wishing I could do something to ease her pain.

"You know, I-I quit my family company and am searching for a j-job using another last name but no one got back to me. Even the Gallagher Foundation. They don't respond unless I use my last name. As if all I am is just a Winstead, like plain old Sarah doesn't have anything to offer. I j-just want to make it out here by myself, because I, I..." More tears pour out of her as she gasps for breath, her face fully buried in my chest now.

"You're smart," I rasp, the lump in my throat growing. My heart aching for her, her tears shredding me from the outside.

The familiar torment of feeling not enough is not something I'd wish on anyone, least of all her.

"I'm smart," she whispers after me.

"You're kind."

"I'm k-kind." She snuggles me closer, her body plastered against mine in all the ways that matter. I close my eyes briefly, savoring her softness against mine, wishing I can convey the truthfulness in my words with my touch, that somehow, my presence soothes the bleeding wounds from her words, washing away the painful sting.

"You, Sarah Winstead, are much more than your name."

She pulls away slightly, her face tilting up to look at me. Mascara and eyeliner streak below her eyes, the tip of her nose red, her lipstick smudged around her lips. She stares at me, the golden pools blurry with tears.

She's breathtaking.

She's glorious. She's everything I want that I don't dare dream for myself.

"I'm much more than my name," she whispers as the elevators open to the first floor. She sways on her feet once more, her eyes fluttering shut as she struggles to stay awake. "Damn right...I'm awesome." She hiccups again, her lips quirking in a bittersweet smile. "I-I'm a sad drunk, Jack. That's so silly 'cause I'm awesome. Badass..."

I wet my lips, my throat parched, clogged with emotions, as I swing her up in my arms and cradle her against my chest, carrying her swiftly through the quiet lobby, dipping my head at colleagues or patrons, ignoring their whispers and pointing. I'll carry her in my arms and shoulder her burdens. I'll shield the doubts with my touch and block any strikes toward her with my body.

I'll damn well destroy anyone who dares to make her cry.

Heat rushes to my face, knowing I'd send tongues wagging as I'm straddling a thin and delicate line of fraternization with members in public. But I'll tell people I'm helping a friend and member home after she had too much to drink.

Nothing is going to happen. No lines will be crossed.

My breathing is uneven and I utter these reassurances to myself, even if the devil inside me wants to laugh at my ridiculousness. *Call it whatever you want to call it, Jack. You know you want to cross all those damn lines with her.*

I usher her through the connecting hallway between The Orchid and the Kensington Hotel, one of the hotels under Fleur Entertainment. My heart pounds in my chest at the thought of the wonderful woman quaking in my arms. I wish I could take away her doubts, her tears. Or make her see herself in my eyes.

Another bright hotel lobby. One more elevator. A dim hallway. A few closed doorways.

Swiping my hotel master key, courtesy of my position at The Orchid, I open the door to her room.

Entering the dark bedroom, I gently place her on the bed, tuck a pillow underneath her head, and take off her heels. I walk to the bathroom and scan the counter, finding some wet wipes. Plucking a few from the pouch, I stride toward my sleeping maiden, who is moaning incoherently on the bed.

Smoothing my hand over her delicate strands—the colors of my favorite season, fall—I carefully dab her face, removing the makeup from her skin, wiping away her tears. As I watch the streaks disappear under my tender touch, it's as if I could somehow remove her pain with each swipe of my hand, each caress from my fingers, until the evidence of her sadness has disappeared, but even then, the ache in my heart is still splintering, still unrelenting.

My eyes drink her in, the only woman I've admired, and perhaps even loved from afar, my gaze committing every detail to memory. The creamy skin with the specks of brown, more on her cheeks than on her nose—kisses from the angels, I'm sure—the way the color of her lips is naturally rosy. My chest feels tight, like a rope has bound my lungs in a vise, and I rake in a shuddering breath. Closing my eyes, I dip down, kissing the soft skin at her temple.

She doesn't stir. I stand back up, straighten my jacket, take one more look at my sleeping maiden, and step toward the door.

Suddenly, her hand snakes out, clasping my wrist. Her fingers trail over my cufflinks. The angel wings she gave me.

"J-Jack?"

Swallowing the lump in my throat, my hand spasming from the last vestiges of restraint, I glance down at her, finding her beautiful eyes on mine.

"You wore my present. I'm so happy." Her lips tip into a loopy grin.

"Of course, you gave it to me. They're the best cufflinks I've ever owned." I move to tuck her arm back inside the covers, but she grips me tighter, a frown marring her face once more.

"I-I heard you chased Tim and Evan away." She hiccups, her unfocused eyes staring at me.

I gently place the covers over her shoulders, making sure she's all snuggled in. "They were assholes who didn't deserve you. They wanted you for all the wrong reasons. You deserve the best," I whisper and watch her eyes misting over as her lips tremble.

She's a ball of emotions tonight, rough waves in the dark seas, and each crest calls out to me, begging me to leap into the waters and let myself drift out into the storm with her.

"I want to feel good. To feel happy tonight." Her tongue dips out and my balls tighten, my hard dick pressing against the confines of my dress pants. "Can you stay with me tonight? Just one night? That's all I need."

Images of me losing myself in her wet heat, teasing out every moan, making her cry out my name in ecstasy as she leaks her cum around my straining staff flash before my eyes. My cock aches, my balls throb. Suddenly, my lungs cease to function, and I can't breathe. I tug the tie off my neck, my hands needing to do something other than ravishing the woman before me.

"No, angel. Not like this." I lift her hand up to my lips, pressing a firm kiss, the motion earning a whimper from her.

"Why is it fine with the other women and not with me? I only want one night with you. One night with the Casanova..." Her lips wobble at the end, her eyes clouding with sadness once more. She blinks before closing her eyes again.

After a few minutes, her breathing evens out and her hand falls limp in mine.

A familiar ache forms in my chest and I release a shuddering exhale, softly placing her hand under the blankets. Leaning down, I whisper against her ear, "Because one night won't ever be enough for me. Because once I have you, I won't be able to let you go, and I can't be that selfish."

Inhaling her sweet scent, I repeat the words I wrote her all those years ago, words I memorized as soon as I put them on paper because they're so true, "The world hasn't met the real you yet and when you step into the sun, everyone will be dazzled by your sparkle, your energy, and most of all, you."

I smooth my hand over her hair, grazing the silky strands. "Now is your time to shine, angel. And I'll be on the sidelines watching you, cheering you on always."

Quietly stepping away, I take a last peek at her slumbering form before I close her door with a *click*. The aching want has slashed me open from the inside out, but every ounce of pain is worth it because every interaction with her, however small, is a treasured memory I'll lock away in my heart forever.

She asked for one night only. Not anything more. One night with Mr. Good Times, the person you fuck once and move on. The person you don't settle down with.

And as much as I want to give in, I can't.

Because I know once I do, when she inevitably walks away, it'll fucking kill me.

The sunlight streaming in from the windows rouses me from a fitful sleep. A throbbing pain pounds inside my head and I cover my eyes with my hand, wanting to drift back into sleep so I don't feel this discomfort anymore. My tongue feels thick and furry, a sour taste lingering on my tastebuds. I shift on the bed, my dress from last night sticking to my sweaty skin. Squinting, I blink my eyes as the fuzzy cobwebs slowly clear from my mind.

Laughing with Emily and Jess at the rooftop bar for a few drinks before dinner.

Steven grumbling about being the only one sober and responsible for most of the night.

Steven cutting off our drinks after the fourth...no, fifth shot of flavored vodka.

Jack...

I sit up, the ringing in my ears intensifying and I wince, my splitting headache practically cleaving me in half.

Jack telling me I'm perfect...I'm beautiful.

Him carrying me in his arms like I weighed nothing.

Me inhaling gulps of his rich cologne, a spicy blend of bergamot and leather, feeling protected in his arms.

And then I freeze. No, please tell me I didn't.

Did I seriously ask him to have sex with me? Begged him to give me one night?

My hands touch my heated face, my heart kicking up into an erratic rhythm. Groaning, I bury my face in the blankets, dreading what I'll do when I see him next...which is, inconveniently, in a few hours for the last day of our photoshoot.

The most intimate photoshoot in *lingerie.*

Kill me already.

Another thought slowly shoves its way to the surface, a nagging sensation, a phantom itch slithering into my mind.

Him gently tucking me into bed and murmuring something...

Gasping, I scramble off the bed, nearly tripping over my heels on the floor, and dash over to my purse that's sitting on the reading chair in the corner of the room. I pull out my leather wallet and carefully retrieve the laminated message I keep with me always.

My eyes skim over the message, slowing down at the passage I swear I heard Jack repeat as I was falling asleep last night:

The world hasn't met the real you yet and when you step into the sun, everyone will be dazzled by your sparkle, your energy, and most of all, you.

And he calls me angel...it can't be, can it?

All these years in the shadows, waiting, watching over me...

The thudding in my chest intensifies in response, echoing in my ears, answering the question lingering in the back of my mind for the last few weeks. A lump forms in my throat and I suddenly find myself short of breath.

Ding.

Fingers trembling, I pick up my phone and read the message on the home screen.

Jack: I asked housekeeping to drop off two ibuprofens and a bottle of water on the table in the entryway. If you need today off, I can ask Amelia and Juliet to postpone the photoshoot. Just let me know.

My nose burns as flutters gather in my stomach. My mind is replaying every interaction with him in the past, witnessing the memories change shape and flavor as my heart kicks into a desperate rhythm. Swallowing the large knot wedged in my throat, my fingers fly over the keyboard.

Sarah: No need to postpone. I'll be there. And thank you, Jack...for everything.

Hovering over the send button, I suck in a deep inhale and press send.

. . .

"Okay, we're done. You look gorgeous." Macy smiles at me in the mirror as I take in my appearance. Today is the last photoshoot for Juliet Marceau and it's the most intimate session of all, one requiring me to be in lingerie and from what Amelia described, it sounds like a classy make-out session. "Thanks for letting me work with you. Your face is a wonderful canvas." With a wink, Macy wiggles her fingers and disappears from the bedroom, leaving me with my thoughts.

I raise my hand and touch my hair, which is carefully curled into loose waves once more and set with a special mist, making my hair shimmer like the glittering stars in the Milky Way. My eye makeup is a dramatic cat eye completed with a luscious set of false lashes, and my lips are painted with a pale-pink gloss. The look, combined with the gemstone-studded black lace bra and panty set, and a matching pair of high heels, makes me appear innocent yet sexy at the same time. The type of woman to drive a man wild.

My fingers skim the delicate straps of my bra, so thin I wonder if they'll hold up my curves, but I guess that's the appeal. The lace pushes my breasts together, as if serving them up to the admirer for a taste. My nerves flutter as I guide my hand over my pale stomach to my generous hips clad in low-cut panties, the fabric cupping my ass just enough to not flash anyone, but highlights the smooth cheeks in a peek-a-boo manner.

I blow out a breath, the fluttering in my gut more pronounced, and I can't decipher if I'm nervous or excited about this photoshoot. To have Jack see me like this and to hold me against him. Somehow, in the span of a few short weeks, he has unwittingly dismantled my misgivings toward him, however unwarranted they were.

Perhaps it's because he's shown me more than his flirtatious side.

Perhaps it's because he has held himself back even when I all but offered myself to him.

Perhaps it's his whispers of angel and letting the world see me sparkle.

Or perhaps...I'm finally seeing the man behind the Casanova mask. Someone who feels deeply, is caring, capable, someone who knows my wealthy background and has never asked for more. Someone who is simply there, teasing me but never crossing the line.

Someone I've been extremely unfair to because of my hatred for my dad.

A slicing pain flashes in my gut as I remember the glimmer of hurt I've seen occasionally in his eyes in the past. I was so unfair to him, so prejudiced.

I never gave him a chance.

Swallowing, I rub my chest where the ache has gathered, wishing I could turn back time.

The *creak* and *click* of the suite door opening then closing alerts me to someone entering the premises. A few seconds later, Amelia pops her head into the bedroom. "Jack is here. We're ready for you. It's just going to be the three of us today, a small private photoshoot, and you'll do great."

A drumming beat echoes in my ears and my senses sharpen, as if I'm finally seeing the world clearly for the first time, like I've been living underwater for the last few decades.

My heart has migrated to my throat and my hands feel clammy. Staring at my reflection one last time, I breathe out a calming breath.

"I can do this," I murmur to the vixen in the mirror. Standing up tall, squaring my shoulders, I stride out of the bedroom.

I spot Jack standing next to the scene staged on top of the Persian rug on the center of the floor, with various lamps and reflector panels strategically staged around the room. Amelia opted for the living room instead of the bedroom because the larger area was easier for her to work with. The overhead lights are dimmed to a warm glow such that most of the light comes from the professional equipment pointed toward the burgundy-colored, silk-covered mattress with large pillows and a plush blanket of the same shade strewn about. The setting looks like the perfect place for a sexy romp, for lovers to lose themselves to the pleasures of each other with smooth, luxurious fabrics slipping and sliding on their skin.

Heat travels from my chest to the rest of my body, my core involuntarily clenching as my gaze moves to Jack, staring at his muscular backside, so thick, sculpted, and strong. My mouth waters as if I can smell the predator in him all the way across the room. Sultry jazz music plays from the speakers and I shake my head, trying a last-ditch effort to knock the lurid thoughts out of my head, and clear my throat, alerting Amelia and Jack to my presence.

Jack slowly turns around and freezes, his eyes flaring as they leisurely rake down my body, the muscles in his throat rippling. A hot flush sweeps through me, and I'm sure my pinkening skin is giving me away, but I force myself to stand still for his perusal. His lips part, his chest lifting and falling in rapid succession as he drags his gaze back up, settling on my eyes.

The browns of his irises are eclipsed by onyx, a mysterious black hole in space you read about, threatening to devour everything within its reach. The searing intensity of his attention feels like a caress, as if his fingers are trailing over my body, eliciting shivers in their wake.

I greedily take him in, something I didn't get a chance to do the other day in the throes of denial, as I try and fail desperately to ignore his powerful presence. My eyes drift over his sculpted figure, the dips and valleys of his muscles, which are clearly familiar with the gym, trailing to the chiseled Adonis belt, partially obscured by black boxer briefs, and if the bulge is any indication, he's packing serious heat inside his pants.

The ache between my legs is quickly turning into a throb and I feel the telltale sensations of wetness seeping into my panties. My breathing quickens and I stare at him, like I'm seeing him for the first time. It's as if this man before me is a stranger, yet someone familiar and everything feels different.

Quickly, I look away and focus on his powerful arms, the biceps contracting before relaxing. Intricate tattoos, usually hidden by his dress shirts, decorate one arm, Chinese calligraphy from appearances, only add to his mystique. His long fingers spasm before clenching into a tight fist, the enticing vein on his forearm flexing, as if he too is having a difficult time reining in the emotions, the sensations, even though we aren't touching.

I feel more turned on than I've ever been in my life, and this isn't even sex.

How am I going to survive this photoshoot?

"Thank you, Jack, for stepping in with Drew sick. But I think this may work out better," Amelia muses as she glances up from her camera. "Are you both ready?"

I nod, unable to find my voice to speak. Jack grunts in the affirmative.

"Okay, this session is just the three of us as Juliet can't come due to a conflicting appointment. We're all friends here, so again, if anyone is uncomfortable, just tell me. I'll be shooting from farther away, so you don't feel like the lens is right in your face. I want this to be natural. According to Juliet, she wants some steamy bedroom shots for her main couple, so I'll guide you both into various poses and scenarios, but it'll all be casual and open for you both to improvise so the photos and videos don't feel artificial. Jack, let's start with you on the bed and Sarah, crawl on top of him on all fours."

Jack gulps, his Adam's apple bobbing before he slowly strides to the mattress to lie down.

"Um... S-Shoes on or off?" My voice comes out as a breathy whisper, and I can hear Jack's breath hitching.

"Definitely on. Those are very sexy shoes."

My legs wobble, but I somehow make my way over to the mattress and slowly crawl up Jack's body. He lets out a hiss as my calves brush against his thick thighs. The sexy beats of the music fade into the background as every atom in my body is concentrated on the masculine specimen below me. My hair cascades over Jack's face like a curtain of fire, and for a moment, I glance down, finding his burning eyes on mine. His hungry, desperate eyes. It's as if there's only the two of us, without cameras, without Amelia's instructions. As if this is all too real.

"Brush your hair to the side so I can see your face. Jack, reach up and bury your nose in her neck. Remember, you're desperately in love with her and you finally get to have her to yourself."

A low grunt emits from his throat as he arches up from the mattress and curls one warm hand over my neck, bringing me down a few inches. He lets out a ragged, tormented exhale, as if he's hanging by a thread, and presses his soft lips on my neck, his nose digging into my tender flesh. His fingers knead my tender flesh and I can feel him trembling underneath me and reality and pretense cease to exist.

Sharp bolts of heat spread from the simple contact and my nipples bead into sharp points, no doubt poking through the thin material of the lace bra. My panties are embarrassingly wet, and it's only the first pose. I swallow a moan and my breathing falters. My fingers clench the silky sheets in a death grip.

Amelia continues to dole out instructions, but my brain can't compute, can't understand a word she's saying. I'm a slave to my body, a slave to the heated sensations spreading on my skin like wildfire. The need to touch him overpowers anything else. My head dips back, my eyes fluttering shut and my hands find purchase on his strong shoulders, my fingernails digging into his muscles, earning myself a rough hiss.

I faintly hear the shutter clicking and words of praise, but it's as if I'm swept away in a sea of pleasure, where every molecule of my body is aflame and nothing else matters except for his touch and how he makes me feel.

Cherished. Sexy. Safe. Enough.

Jack curls his hand tighter against my neck before he applies a gentle suction to a fluttering pulse point, his tongue darting out and swiping the spot quickly, as if he couldn't help himself.

I let out a whimper, my body involuntarily pressing down on his, my sex almost grazing his rippling abs. "Jack, what if she sees?"

I know I should shift away, but I can't bring myself to move. More wetness seeps between my thighs, as if the idea of an audience suddenly thrills me.

"She can't see. She's on the other side." His voice is hoarse as he guides me into another position, one where I'm sitting astride his lap while he grips my ass, and he buries his face in my cleavage. "Fuck me." A guttural groan. He sounds desperate, famished, and is slowly being driven mad by the maelstrom that is us.

Biting on my lip to prevent more errant sounds from escaping, I sink down fully onto his lap, feeling his steel-hard cock digging into my core through the thin layers of fabric between us. His breaths feel hot and wet on my breasts as he turns his head to the side, his mouth mere millimeters away from my distended tip.

I ache. My breasts feel swollen and heavy, my clit throbs, my body craving release. And somehow, the fact Amelia is watching, capturing these moments on camera, seems to inflame me even more.

His lips ghost over my neck, barely touching, and he rasps in my ear, "Baby, you're driving me crazy. I can feel how wet you are. How turned on you are." As if demonstrating his knowledge, he swivels his hips up, his cotton-covered cock grazing my clit, the lacy fabric only adding to the erotic torture. "I can smell you and I'm dying to taste you."

"Jack," I moan as he groans in response, our breaths heavy in the air.

He pulls my head down and stares intently into my eyes. Fevered, midnight pools pin me in place. I can see the reflection of myself in his pupils, a blurry image of creamy skin and fiery hair. I bite my bottom lip as I lose myself in his adoration.

"You're captivating. Ethereal. A fucking angel on earth." His voice has a tinge of gravel, and my lips part, wanting to capture his words with my mouth, to kiss his parted lips, to see if he still tastes like whiskey or bourbon, as masculine as the rest of him. To determine if my memory of our tryst in the elevator is a fluke.

My pulse rushes in my ears, deafening like the roaring waves in the middle of a storm. A cyclone. One I'm willing to drown myself in.

Amelia mentions something about taking photos under the covers and giving her a look of ecstasy, but I can barely hear her, my body thrumming for the virile man who looks like he's famished and wants to devour me whole.

Jack turns me over, so I lie supine underneath him. He tugs the soft throw over our hips as he cages me in with his arms, his bulging biceps flexing with the movement. He lays the bottom half of his body in between my parted thighs, emitting an audible breath when his cock settles perfectly on top of my clit once more.

Leaning heavily on one side, he slides his hand underneath the blanket, curling beneath my thigh as he angles himself toward what I presume is Amelia's sightline, but I don't care anymore.

I'm so hot I can combust at any moment.

My skin is on fire, my panties are ruined, and I thank God they're black, so it won't be as obvious.

"Almost finished, my beautiful angel." He trails his lips to my ears, barely touching, but I can feel each vibration of his words all the way down to the soles of my feet.

His hand under the blanket slowly moves, imperceptible to anyone observing and I suck in a breath as his fingers lightly graze my sodden panties.

"Fuck. So fucking wet," he groans, his other arm shaking. "My angel wants to feel my cock inside you, don't you?"

I moan, unable to stifle my sounds, and I gyrate my hips slightly, so his extended finger rubs against my aching clit.

"Fuck yes, you need me to take care of you, baby?" He presses harder on the swollen nub over the lace, and I bite my cheek at the sharp ecstasy spreading from the simple touch, the pressure climbing at supersonic speeds.

Turning toward him, I find him staring at me, a flush on his strong cheekbones as he takes in my movements, my expressions, as if I'm an instrument he's desperate to master.

My mouth parts as I take in quick pulls of oxygen. I want to tell him I'm so close; I want to tell him to put me out of my misery, but the pleasure has stolen my voice.

His eyes darken even more, the eyes of the devil. Even without words, he understands what I'm trying to tell him with my quickened breaths, my desperate gripping of his arms, my body rubbing against him with every movement.

Keeping his eyes on mine, Jack slides his finger deftly underneath my panties and rubs my slick clit. "Come, baby. Come for me," he commands, his deep voice barely above a whisper.

One swipe, two swipes.

And that's all it takes for me to explode underneath him, white-hot pleasure shooting through my body. He pins me down with his torso, so my shuddering doesn't show as my pussy spasms and I claw at his forearms, my fingernails digging into his flesh, my lips parted on a silent scream.

He trembles as he holds me flush to him, his steel cock digging into my belly, his harsh breaths in my ear.

"And that's a wrap. Smoldering chemistry, you guys. I feel like I need to take a shower after this shoot. Juliet will love these." Amelia's shrill voice from afar penetrates my pleasurable haze. She snorts and chuckles at herself.

The room comes into slow focus as Jack hovers above me, his chest heaving as he pants, as if he just spent the last hour fucking me into oblivion.

It sure feels like it, Sarah.

He slowly gets off me, his big cock digging into my flesh as he lifts his body. His eyes are wild. His skin flushed pink. He looks drunk...drunk on me. He caresses my heated face, his fingers skimming over my eyelids, my nose, and grazing my lips.

Jack dips his index finger into my mouth. Just the tip. The same finger that bestowed upon me the best orgasm of my life.

Unable to stop my response, I suck him in, my tongue swiping the calloused flesh, tasting myself combined with the saltiness of his skin. I give it a quick bite.

"Fuck." He slams his other hand on the mattress. "I can't be the person you need. I won't survive you." His words are deep, breathy whispers, yet carving themselves into my mind.

He swallows. His glittering eyes are pools of anguish and longing as he slowly disentangles from me. My forehead pinches at his cryptic words, clutching the blanket tighter to my chest and a hollow pain spreads from the center of my chest.

Jack rolls off the mattress and strolls to the bathroom with a desperation of someone fleeing impending doom. He doesn't look back, doesn't stop or pause along the way. My fingers grip the blanket tighter against me as my eyes are pinned to the space he was in, and I feel breathless, bereft, the sudden chill cloaking my skin, seeping into my bones.

Five minutes later, he breezes by, fully dressed in his impeccably tailored suit, nodding to Amelia as he passes, barely sparing me a glance, and promptly exits the room, the sound of the door closing reverberating in the large space.

My heart squeezes as an ache reappears in my chest and the sudden barrage of emotions hit me all at once, my mind incapable of deciphering what I'm feeling...the hurt, the pleasure, the attraction, the longing, the confusion. Anything and everything swirls in the madness inside me.

Slowly, I walk back to the bedroom, my legs feeling like jelly, a pleasurable throb between my legs with each step, reminding me what just happened definitely wasn't a figment of my imagination, wasn't a fevered dream.

My heart is pounding so hard, I'm afraid it'll give out on me. I can't make sense of the one person I've always kept at arm's length all these years, who is suddenly invading all my dreams, burying himself deep inside me. I can't understand how the intensity I used to attribute as hatred, is suddenly so intoxicating, so exhilarating, and absolutely everything I've been missing in my life before.

The chaos in my mind slowly settles, as each rioting feeling disappearing down the swirling drain, until all that remains is a cozy heat spreading from the beating organ in my chest.

Warmth floods my veins at the thought of his charming smiles, which once repulsed me.

My pulse dances at the thought of his smooth voice calling me his angel, which I once would roll my eyes at, thinking this is all part of his shameless flirtation.

It's as if I belatedly realize, perhaps I've always sensed the man behind the Casanova mask, a shield he wields to the world. Perhaps because of my past, my relationship with my dad, I've never wanted to acknowledge the beautiful and multifaceted layers of this man who has always made me feel too much of everything. Perhaps I've never truly opened my heart to let anyone in for fear of disappointment, just like how my dad was to me my entire life.

And now, the veil has been lifted, and my heart pumps with a different desire.

I want to pierce through his armor with my javelin.

I want to memorize and kiss his battle scars.

I want to surround myself with his warmth.

I want to be his angel.

Because, I have a sudden realization... Jack Szeto may be the only man who sees the true me. Who has *always* seen the true me. Who has never asked me to be anything but myself.

He may be the only person who thinks I'm enough, just as I am.

The screen of my cell phone flickers to life, and I pick it up, noticing a new email. Swiping it open, I quickly scan the contents of what looks to be an automated message, my heart fluttering when I notice the sender: The Gallagher Foundation.

> Thank you for following up on your application to The Gallagher Foundation. Our recruiters are still reviewing the applications submitted through the portal. Thank you for your patience. If we have additional questions, we will contact you.

Exhaling a ragged sigh, I can feel an added weight on my chest. I knew this process would take some time, having been on the other side of interviews when I worked in the family business. I gnaw on my lip and dip my head in a terse nod.

It doesn't matter. My persistence will pay off because I'm capable, I'm qualified, and I'm a fucking badass. Watch out, world. Sarah Winstead is coming, and it's time for me to shine.

• • •

Jack

Fuck.

What the fuck just happened?

My mind is a swirling muck of madness as I stride to the nearest stairwell, dashing toward my office like a madman. Because if I stop moving, my legs will drag me back to the suite to finish what we started on the mattress. Because I fucking lost control again and almost took her in front of an audience.

Because when Amelia asked me to pretend to be in love, she didn't know how I'm Adam and she's tempting me in the garden with the luscious apple that is Sarah.

I don't need to pretend; I can barely leash down everything I feel for her.

And just now, with Sarah only a hair's breadth away, her eyes glazed over in lust and passion, I could almost believe everything is real.

That she could be mine.

My cock is throbbing, making a damp spot on the front of my boxers, cursing me for doing the right thing, for walking away from my angel, my Siren in disguise.

Her moans. Her whimpers. The way she rubbed her body on me. The way her nipples pebbled against her bra, her tits heaving, trembling, beckoning me for a taste. The way she shuddered against me, the pretty flush lighting up her neck and face as she threw her head back, her eyes glazed in the throes of orgasm. It's a sight that'll forever be burned in my mind, more beautiful than anything I've ever seen in my entire life.

A sobering thought makes its way to the forefront, the chill seeping into my bones, rioting against the inferno inside.

I took advantage of the situation.

It was supposed to be a photoshoot. Something professional. Instead, I turned it into something sordid. I seduced her, touched her in an arrangement where she's vulnerable.

I'm a fucking asshole.

The burn of self-hatred rushes through me, my conscience stepping in last minute, stopping me from doing something irrevocable.

And it's the last strand of integrity which has me barreling out of the room, not even able to look at her, to see if disgust or hatred shines from her eyes once the lust cooled down.

My heart pounds loudly in my chest, my shoes thumping against each metal step of the stairwell, and sweat gathers on my forehead as I fly down the stairs.

I see coworkers waving, calling my name, but it's as if I'm trapped in the prison of my mind, and I can't respond to them as I turn a corner, and another.

Minutes later, with my hands quivering, I unlock my office door and step inside. The lust is still hot in my veins, the images of Sarah lying in my arms playing in my mind like a never-ending erotic slideshow.

I pull out a bottle of whiskey from my shelf and pour myself a glass, downing the alcohol in a few large gulps, my throat barely registering the burn. Staggering to my desk, I collapse into my leather chair and bury my face in my hands. I'm standing at a crossroad where every direction feels incorrect even though the compass in my heart is pointing due north. But what if the path will lead us to destruction?

Now that I've had a taste of her and know how she melts in my arms when she comes, how will I ever be able to resist her?

I adjust the satin mask on my face and smooth my hand over the V-wire, notched neckline of my dark-red velvet gown while I wait behind a few couples in line to enter the towering, intricately carved double doors ahead of me. Even though I grew up in this world, where price tags are inconsequential, penthouse-living and wearing couture from Parisian fashion houses are commonplace, my mouth drops open the moment I take in the transformation of the magnificent ballroom.

The large space has been transformed into old-world glamor and I feel as if I stepped through a time machine and landed in Regency or Victorian England. The usual modern light fixtures have been removed and, in their place are elaborate crystal chandeliers completed with ornate, gold furnishings, and candelabras with real candles. The walls are covered with fabrics of dark, shimmering gold, and the ceilings have been painted with Renaissance-style art, no doubt for authenticity. The Orchid doesn't do anything by half measures. And I suppose when money isn't an issue, a transformation such as this shouldn't be surprising.

The Christmas ball at The Orchid, which is usually held on Christmas Day, is the pinnacle event of the season where the elite from around the country, and in many cases, from around the world, try to secure an entry to the coveted affair. This year's theme is the midnight masquerade. Like many things with The Orchid, money can't buy invitations to the ball, and the months leading up to the event always have the rich and famous on their toes, wondering if their tickets are in the mail or if they'll be snubbed. But unlike the usual rules of the establishment, this is the one and only instance allowing for press photographers. Of course, none of the usual paparazzi antics are allowed—the strict "be seen and not heard" rules apply to them or they risk removal from the premises and being blacklisted for the future.

Needless to say, the exclusivity of the event in a mysterious, nearly impenetrable establishment is the place to see and be seen. My parents still aren't talking to me other than a few terse text messages and Dad instituting a "deadline" of the end of the year for me to return home with my tail between my legs before he enacts his "mysterious" threats against me. In a rare occurrence, they couldn't make it to the ball this time around, and Dad demanded my presence here to represent the family. I could say no to him, but I figured I'm already ruffling enough feathers with them, one less point of contention the better. Plus, enjoying a wonderful night in luxury plus being able to network with some of the most powerful members in society seems like a win-win to me.

"Beautiful event, right?" a familiar, sardonic drawl comments from behind me as I stand by the side, marveling at the dazzling atmosphere, the patrons all decked out in beautiful gowns or sharp tuxedos, donning masks as expected of a masquerade.

"Steven. If you didn't open your mouth, I wouldn't have recognized you." I sneak a glance at the tall man who's made his way next to me. The tuxedo fits his body to perfection and his angular and handsome face is mostly covered by a silk black mask.

"Who can recognize anyone with their faces half-covered? I feel like a raccoon crossed with a penguin in this getup."

I grin. "I think the masks make it more fun, don't you? We can gawk at others to our heart's content."

He grunts, shifting beside me, impatience rolling off his frame in waves. "I'm going to stay here for an hour or two and attempt to locate a few folks, if that's even possible, then I'm heading out."

"No Kingsley family gathering this year?"

"Jess and James took my parents on a vacation to Europe with the kids. Emily and Adrian are in the Maldives, doing God knows what for his birthday. Just poor old me alone this year." He taps his foot on the floor. "But I have a work event tomorrow anyway, so I probably wouldn't have been able to go anywhere."

"There are so many things wrong with that statement. First, there's nothing poor or old about you. And the 'alone' thing is by your own doing. You can easily find a girl or someone to spend the holidays with. And second, you really have to stop working so hard. You'll keel over from a heart attack before you reach forty."

A waiter clad in a simple tuxedo sweeps by with a tray of champagne and Steven hands me a flute before responding, "I have no use for girlfriends or relationships, and I already have two older sisters, don't need another one, Sarah."

"Can't help it. I watched you grow up and still remember you as the awkward, pesky little brother with more legs than torso who pulled pranks on us."

He lets out a rare grin, transforming his usually serious face—or in this case, half a face, since the rest is covered by the mask. "The good days. You girls were so easily riled up."

"The time you snuck a frog onto Ems's bed is a classic."

"It was originally supposed to be a snake, but I thought Ems would kill me."

"She definitely would." I laugh, still remembering Emily's high-pitched screeches when Kermit was leaping all over the place. It took an hour to catch him. Then Emily tearfully asked me to take care of the frog for her, since her overbearing mother would never let him stay in the house, and that's how I ended up with my first pet at fifteen.

The orchestra strikes up a new melody and more couples gather on the dance floor for the next set. Steven grabs my glass and sets it on the nearest table.

Extending his white-glove-clad hand, he murmurs, "A dance, Sarah?"

"My pleasure. Let's see if you have two left feet."

He leads me into the fray, and swings me into proper position, whirling with the other couples.

"Merry Christmas, Sarah. I didn't ask last time at the rooftop bar because I didn't want to be presumptuous and others were there, but I still want to offer, nonetheless. Do you need help...with the job search or your parents?"

My chest warms and I stare at the normally cold and stoic man in front of me, his hazel eyes softening with concern. "Thank you, Steven. I want to make it on my own this time...I think I need to prove that to myself."

He keeps his eyes on me for a beat and nods. He dips me for a quick second, the movement smooth and confident, before pulling me back up. "I can understand that. If you ever need help, you only need to ask."

"Thank you. And I'm surprised you haven't stepped on my feet at all so far."

He chuckles, shaking his head and opens his mouth to reply, but his frame freezes suddenly, his eyes pinned on something behind me. His mouth curves into a sly smile and he relinquishes my hand, dips into a bow, and backs away just as another man stands before me.

Obsidian, searing eyes, thick locks of black hair, full lips tilted in a familiar half grin, but this time, there's a thread of uncertainty in the smile and banked tension in his gaze. He swallows, the muscles in his neck rippling, before letting out a ragged exhale, like he's grappling with something inside him. We stare at each other on the dance floor, the moment somehow seeming suspended in time, and he slowly straightens up and squares his shoulders, as if he's reached some conclusion in a puzzle he's solving in his mind.

The scents of bergamot and leather waft to my nose and I inhale sharply. The tuxedo drapes over his muscular body like a second skin and while he hasn't said a word, his frame is vibrating with intensity, with coiled power. He takes my hand, the gentle touch at odds with the current of electricity zinging through my veins. He guides me into a waltz, his arm curling around the bare back of my velvet dress, the fingers on his other hand intertwining with mine, the slow and sensual slide of his fingers sending frissons of awareness through me. Goosebumps prickle on my bare arms and my pulse ratches up in speed.

Even though he doesn't have his lip ring in tonight, and he's as indistinguishable as the other gentlemen here, I'd recognize him anywhere.

"Jack," I breathe out as he twirls me around the dance floor, his steps sure and flawless.

"Siren. My beautiful angel in red." The deep voice. The sexy rasp.

I swallow as a sultry heat spreads through my body, awakening every inch of my skin. It's as if I'm a flower blooming under his presence. "How did you recognize me? I'm not the only strawberry blonde in a mask here."

"You're the only one that matters," he murmurs, "and I'd recognize you anywhere." Pulling me closer, his mouth dips down, his breath grazing my ear. My nerves spark alive, and a bolt of pleasure gathers in my core. He presses a gentle kiss on the outer shell, the simple touch ratcheting up my breath, before whispering, "I don't think there'd be a world where I wouldn't recognize you."

His words echo in my ear. They sound like a promise. A vow. One I want to bind myself to and be swept away by the tsunami of my emotions. The butterflies in my gut take flight, and I close my eyes, losing myself in the warmth of his embrace, the whiskey-smooth tenor of his voice, the feeling of safety and being treasured.

For the first time in my life, I feel like I'm at the right place at the right time, with the right person.

I feel whole.

Laying my head on his chest, I listen to his thundering heartbeats, bask in his loving embrace, and he clasps me tighter in his arms. It's as if I'm a flower, struggling under endless days of dreariness and rain, only to finally see the first rays of sunlight break through the clouds, marking a brand new beginning.

"I want you to know that you, Sarah Winstead, are dazzling, even without your family's wealth, without your looks, without your name." He pulls me closer and tips my head up, ensnaring me with his passionate gaze. "Because it's your soul that's beautiful, and no one can ever take that away from you. You've shown time and time again how you help those in need, how loyal you are to your friends, and what a good heart you have."

He lets out a shuddering exhale, as if somehow those words were buried deep inside him for years and are finally expelled from his lungs. His words are a balm to my ragged soul, an acknowledgement I never realized I desperately needed to hear. His words cloak my heart in warmth, filling every crevice with light. And somehow, knowing this is how he sees me for all these years, how he's been silently standing by waiting for me to truly see him has my heart twisting in pain. My vision blurs, wetness welling in my eyes, and I marvel at the beautiful man before me, wondering how I could've been so wrong and so blind in the past.

Jack slides his thumb on my cheek, wiping away the small bit of moisture. His lips curve into a smile, a genuine smile, nothing like the ones he doles out in his Casanova façade. His eyes glint behind his mask, a sheen gathering in the midnight seas.

The flutters in my gut are now a swarm, my heart galloping in my chest as time slows and ceases to matter. The world is a blur of sparkling color and glittering lights, but I don't notice anything other than the man before me, someone who has lurked in the shadows all along, but really shines the brightest of them all.

Jack slowly lets go of me, bringing my hand up for a searing kiss as the last chords of the music fade into silence.

"Merry Christmas, Sarah."

Dipping into a curt bow, he backs away, keeping his eyes on mine until a few people call to his attention. A fluttering pulse beats loudly in my ears, my mind pushing me to follow him, to shorten our distance once more but I stop as an unmistakable silhouette of Juliet Marceau sidles up to him, her glove-clad hand slides on his chest as she leans in to whisper something in his ear. He smiles politely and murmurs something back before stepping away, his eyes finding mine once again. One split second of searing heat from the obsidian gaze and I stand there, transfixed, watching him as he turns away, servers and attendants trailing after him. He disappears behind a hidden door earmarked for the staff.

Juliet whips her head toward me and takes off her gold mask, her eyes narrowing before widening. I quickly turn away, disappearing back into the crowd, knowing it was probably too late and she must've recognized me and seen us dancing together. I just hope this won't cause Jack any trouble.

I let out the breath I was holding and recounted the last few magical moments. The way he spun me in his arms, his gaze solely focused on me, as if I'm the most important thing in his life.

He looks at me like I hung the moon in the skies.

He looks at me as if I'm the only thing he needs in his life.

My heart thuds a resounding rhythm in my chest.

It can't be, can it?

· · ·

The evening passes by in a blur of conversations, laughter, and merriment, but I can't seem to focus on anything other than this innate pulling inside me, this desire for me to find him. It's as if my soul has finally awakened, recognizing the call of its other half.

Ridiculous, Sarah. This has to be just infatuation. Or is it?

I bite my cheek and exit the ballroom, stepping away from the crowds, eager to find a spot where I can hear myself think. My feet traipse through the quiet halls and corridors in the labyrinth. The pounding of my heart hasn't subsided in the last few hours. I find myself searching for him time and time again in the sea of tuxedos and black masks, hoping I can spot the familiar set of penetrating eyes and feel his heated gaze on my skin. I crave the way my skin sparks and tingles whenever he touches me, the way the warmth spreads throughout my body whenever I'm in his presence, something that has been happening all these years, but I've just been reluctant to recognize it.

And I realize, my body has been giving me signals the past twelve years, my subconscious waving flags in the form of the thrill I feel when sparring with him, the blistering intensity of my emotions whenever we interact, but I've chosen to interpret these signs differently, sweeping them away as if they are nothing of importance.

The way he tugged at his lips the first day I saw him at the grocery store like he was perhaps nervous on top of flirtatious, followed by a flash of crestfallen disappointment when I didn't respond.

The way his eyes would light up whenever he called me Siren.

The way he picked the seat next to mine at Carnegie Hall during Adrian's surprise proposal to Emily and kept me company when there were so many other open seats available.

The way he gently teased me but never crossed the line, respectfully backing away when I rebuffed him in the past.

All fragments I missed or distorted in my colored lens of prejudice—automatically writing him off as someone like my dad when he's anything but like him.

A sharp slice of regret pierces my chest and a wave of belated agony floods my heart. How he must have felt all these years. How lonely he must have been to have others only see him for who he is on the surface, never bother to look behind the mask.

How he must've wished someone could see the real him, the soulful man behind the charm.

My throat constricts, robbing me of breath, and I wrench open the glass doors to an outdoor terrace, overlooking one of the quiet courtyards hidden in The Orchid. A burst of frigid air cloaks my skin and the loud city sounds remind me I'm in the heart of Manhattan.

I reach out to turn on the heat lamp, the orange embers providing a soft glow in the darkness. Staring up at the nighttime skies, the stars hiding behind a layer of smog and clouds, my eyes close and I breathe, my mind filling with memories of him over these years. Every look, every smirk, every teasing grin. I grip the handrail for support.

The air shifts, and the doors open behind me before shutting in a soft *click.*

It's him.

It's like he knows I'm searching for him.

"What are you doing out here by yourself?" Jack's voice is gentle and I can feel his heated presence. My eyes are still closed, but I can imagine the crinkle of his brows and his eyes darkening with worry. Moments later, I smell another whiff of his heady scent and a jacket is draped over my shoulders. My eyes flutter open and I clutch the fabric tighter against me, surrounding me with his warmth.

"Thinking. Wondering how I have been so blind all these years."

He leans his arms on the railing, and I keep my focus on the water fountain in the gardens. I can feel his gaze skimming over my face, something I used to think was flirting but now recognize is concern.

"Do you know what you want in life, Jack?"

He lets out a gruff chuckle, the raspiness renewing the shivers inside me. "For the longest time, I just wanted to matter. My parents were busy with their business, barely had any time for me. My friends were all moving on in life, going to good colleges, lining up internships, checking all the boxes while I lagged behind, blending into the background. I think that's why I got into so much trouble before. The tattoos, my lip ring, the drunken brawls, the illegal boxing …everything that got me attention, even if sometimes it wasn't the right kind of attention."

He releases an exhale, the white plume of smoke flittering away into the night. "My parents were so disappointed with me, and they tried everything to put me on the 'right path,' but I didn't have the grades, hated studying, and just didn't see the point of trying only to fail. But at least, it's attention. And then I realized the ladies liked the way I looked…again, more attention. And you…you hated me, but then, that was also…"

"Attention," I whisper, finishing for him. The ache between my rib cage worsens and my eyes burn, thinking about how I missed all these calls for help.

"But Adrian, my man, saved me, pulled me out of the muck. Got me a job here even though I didn't have any qualifications, and gave me a purpose, an identity other than a delinquent so close to being on the wrong side of the law. Gradually, I realized I'll be fine, even if I don't have all the zeroes in my bank account, a powerful job title, but I'll survive in this world. Even if I'm still known as Mr. Good Times, a Casanova. That this'll be enough. More than I ever thought I deserved."

Jack falls silent, as if willing me to look at him. With my heart in my throat, I turn, finding his smoldering gaze on me.

"And for a long time, I thought that'd be sufficient. But then...I realize, there's a hole inside me I never filled, and I still want to matter...to this one person who probably will never feel the same way about me, because I'll never be able to be who she needs—"

"Shhh." I press my finger on his lips, stopping him from denigrating himself even further. "Jack, you *matter*." My hand drifts to his chest, on the spot above his beating organ. "You matter so much, you wonderful man. If anyone can't see that, then they don't deserve you."

He intakes a sharp breath, his chest lifting and falling heavily, his eyes darkening, a swirling pool of turmoil.

"S-Sarah," he chokes out, his frame vibrating with tension. "I...I—"

A burning need scorches through me and I reach up, gripping his hair to bring him closer, and I do the one thing I've wanted to do ever since the madness in the elevator.

I seal my lips to his and kiss him.

CHAPTER 11

Jack

She kisses me.

Of her own accord. Without cameras, without taunts and challenges.

Her soft lips on mine are the focal point of every nerve ending in my body. I forget how to breathe, how to think, how to move. I'm not sure if I'm dreaming, if I'm dead and already in heaven, if any of this is real or a figment of my tormented imagination. I freeze, my mind warring with my heart, warning me how this may change everything. How I'm breaking the cardinal rule of The Orchid. How I may lose *everything* I've worked so hard to achieve. How I may lose the job which pulled me out of the gutter.

Sarah applies gentle suction before her teeth make an appearance, nibbling on my bottom lip. A bolt of lust shoots straight to my cock, which hardens within a millisecond, and the rest of my body finally catches up, and suddenly, it's as if everything else doesn't matter except her. Because she's worth it. Because everything else fades in importance, mere grayscale to her brilliant hues.

Letting out a guttural groan, I take over, my mind blanking, my heart and my body in sync, doing what I've always wanted to do with her, ever since I saw her all those years ago at Grocery for

Less. I wrap my arms around her and pull her flush against me, one hand dragging up her back to clasp her nape, curling my fingers in her thick, glorious hair, and I bend her over the railing, my lips chasing hers, my tongue teasing the seam, invading, licking, tasting her sweetness. She moans as she melts against me, her body pliant against mine while she clutches my back, her nails digging, scratching, as if trying to meld herself with me.

"Yes, baby, you fucking drive me crazy." My lips trail kisses down the sensitive column of her throat before my tongue travels back up, licking, laving at each pulse point, her loud mewls turning me wild.

My teeth find her collarbone, nipping at the sensitive divot, earning me a shuddering gasp before a lusty moan when I soothe the pain with a gentle suction, my tongue licking away the bite marks. I lean back, watching her fair skin turning red, and my inner caveman roars with approval, wanting to mark all over her silky skin so the world will know she's mine.

But she isn't.

This is one night only, Jack. A Christmas present to yourself. Then you need to let her go, so she can find someone who can give her the world, someone with the proper background and education. Someone in her station. Someone who is worthy of her.

My mind, the villain in my story, tries to warn me, to wave the red flags and catch my attention. But I'm in too deep, too far gone.

I need her with a desperation of a starving man, finally finding a feast before him. I need her as much as my lungs need that next breath of air.

Sarah pulls on my shirt, her fingers fumbling with the buttons and the shrill sound of a loud horn in the distance jolts me back to the present. Barely. I haul her back up, my eyes greedily raking over her flushed face, messy hair, swollen lips, and dazed eyes.

Taking her hand in mine, I drag her back inside and find the nearest guest elevator. As the doors open, I usher her in before letting go of her, my hazy mind still aware of the security cameras recording in the steel cage. I lucked out last time when the camera was temporarily out of order for maintenance, but I don't count on it happening again. Swiping my badge to press a button, we stand in silence, watching the lights flicker, indicating the passage of the levels.

Sarah shifts closer, her hand moving to grab mine.

"The cameras." My voice is hoarse. Rusty. Uttering the two words I'm only capable of at the moment. I fight my body to keep from hauling her back against me, from feeling her curves and drawing out her sighs.

She exhales, her hands twisting in front of her, and we wait in strained silence, the tension in the air so thick I can smell it. Taste it.

Our breaths are loud in the small space and the seconds feel like minutes. Finally, in what feels like forever, the doors open to our floor. I step out, stalking toward one of the empty suites, and she wordlessly follows suit. Reaching the door in question, I swipe my master key and step inside, waiting for her to enter the dark room before closing the door.

At the soft *click*, I turn around and face her, finding her backing away slowly, her body a dark silhouette against the moonlight streaming in from the windows in the living room. My dick is a steel rod in my pants, my hands clenched into tight fists and I wait to see what she'll do. Upon reaching the living room, she slowly reaches behind her and the erotic sound of the zipper echoes in the quiet room.

I let out a shuddering breath as the gown pools at her feet. She turns sideways, the moonlight bathing her skin, highlighting every delectable curve. My feet slowly move toward her as the strapless bra joins the gown on the floor, followed by a tiny black thong.

"Jack," she whispers, her smoky voice tinged with arousal. She slides her hands slowly up her body and my body is heated, on fire.

I need to touch her, to taste her, to be inside her.

I prowl toward her, my eyes glued to her soft body, watching the swaying of her perfect teardrop tits with every breath she takes.

The dim light is just enough to illuminate her actions as she pinches her distended nipples, the room far too dark for me to tell what color they are. A dusky rose? A soft brown?

She moans, her fingers pulling at the hard buds. My cock throbs and my balls ache. I approach her, my hands shedding my clothing at the speed of light, until I'm as naked as she is, standing mere inches from her heaving body.

My restraint is hanging by the thinnest thread, the last remnants of logic beckoning me to ask, "You sure?"

I would die if she says no.

"Fuck me, Jack."

Growling, dark urges obliterate my senses, taking over, I grab her hips, plastering her against me. I hiss at the contact, the way her soft flesh feels against my hardness. I slam my lips to hers, sucking, drinking her essence, and my tongue invades her mouth, swiping, obliterating, conquering. My hands grip her fleshy ass, the perfect, silky globes, and I lift her up, her legs hooking around my back. Grunting, I rub my cock against her wet heat, sliding between her slippery sex and white-hot bliss sizzles my skin.

"Fuck. You're so wet, sweetheart. You're so primed for me."

She emits a long mewl as my dick glides against her clit, her body shuddering against me, her fingernails digging into my shoulder blades, and I hiss from the pleasure-pain.

"Right there, oh my God, right there," she whimpers and I hit that spot again. And again, my hands clutching her thighs, grinding her body against me.

My nerves are raw, my mind drowning in a sea of madness as we grapple with each other, trying to find a soft surface in the dark. There's no way we'd make it to the bedroom. My lips suck a trail down her neck, my teeth scoring the skin, and she thrashes against me.

"Yes, baby, rub yourself on my dick. But don't come. I want to feel your pussy strangling my cock when I make you scream."

Sarah moans in response, and we fumble around the room, finally finding a sofa. Laying her down, I hold her legs wide, poising my rock-hard shaft at her entrance. Pulling back, I watch her face in the darkness. Wide eyes, parted lips, blown pupils. She bites down and shudders as I insert the head.

"You like it, huh? You like it when I talk dirty to you," I murmur against her lips.

She grows impossibly wetter as she clutches me tighter against her. "Yes, oh my God, yes." My dick hardens even more and I growl under my breath.

"Fuck me, your cunt is swallowing me like a good slut," I rasp and she whimpers, arching her back while my dick slides in a few more inches, her tight, wet heat driving me wild with pleasure.

"Y-You're so big," she moans, "it'll never fit, oh fuck."

"Halfway there, baby." I grit my teeth and push in, her pussy gripping my shaft in a perfect vise, my eyes already seeing stars.

My hand snakes down between us, finding her swollen clit, and she lets out a keening moan, the sweet sound hardening my cock even more. I groan as I feel more slickness from her tight channel, easing the way as I slide the rest of my dick in until I'm balls deep.

She feels so good. So wet. So hot. This is what heaven feels like. If I die right now, my life would be complete.

I gnash my teeth together when I realize why everything feels extra sensitive, extra intense.

"Shit. Condom."

I don't want to take the time to go to the bedroom and find one in the nightstand.

Sarah trembles, her pussy clenching my cock as if it needs me as much as I need her. "I'm clean."

"I'm tested. Me too."

She looks like a goddess in the dark. A true Siren. She brings my hands to her heavy tits. My hands curl automatically around the heavy globes and squeeze. "Fuck me, Jack. Make me come with your big, hard cock."

Just like that, I snap.

My hips pull back and surge forward, ramming inside her as she clings to me for dear life, her hands grabbing my forearms.

I pinch her nipples and she shrieks.

I slap her heavy tits, watching the way they jiggle as my cock pistons inside her, the pleasure building at the base of my spine, my vision blurring at the edges. I watch my thick shaft sliding into her wet heat, glistening with her wetness. This is heaven and hell mixed in a blazing inferno of torture and rapture.

This is filthy. This is bliss. This is my personal cocktail of madness.

It has never been this good, this perfect, before.

Her tight channel clenches me in a death grip, her back arches. Her eyes flutter closed and I can feel her walls spasm. I know she's close.

"Angel, look at me. I want to see those beautiful eyes as I make you come."

Sarah's eyes flutter open as she stares at me, her mouth parted, an erotic vision permanently imprinted on my brain.

Smack. Smack. Smack.

The sounds of skin slapping against skin joins with her keening wails and my grunts. Her heavy tits sway with each thrust and I lift her hips, slamming into her harder and faster.

"Yes! Yes, oh my God, I'm so wet." Her voice is pure sex. She bites on her bottom lip to leash down her cries.

I rut into her, angling my dick deeper, swiveling it until I feel a fleshy part inside her and she lets out a long scream, her legs shuddering.

"Fuck yes, scream for me. I want to hear every sound as I fuck you so hard you see stars," I roar, sweat dripping down my forehead and I pummel inside her, the smacking of our bodies loud and lurid.

"Oh my God... Jack, what are you doing to me?" Her mouth drops open, her body arching up, and her entire frame convulses.

"Take it, my beautiful, dirty angel. Take my cock like a good girl."

With that, I pinch her clit and she comes on a wail, her juices gushing out in a torrent where we're joined, her pussy clenching, the walls throbbing.

My balls contract as fire shoots through my cock, and I let out a deep growl, my legs spasming. "Fuuuuuuck." I fall into oblivion with her, each strong pulse unloading spurts of cum inside her.

Her skin is slick with sweat, her body trembling, and I slow my thrusts, riding out the last waves of orgasm before collapsing on her, our breathing harsh.

I've never come so hard in my life.

I lift my head up, my hands cradling her face, and I stare into her eyes, my heart still racing, my mind still not computing. I want to tell her I love her. I want to ask her to stay with me, to love me back. I want to say fuck it to being merely content with life or staying in my "station."

Words are trapped in my throat, and I tell her everything the only way I can, by sealing my lips with hers again, our tongues tangling, tasting, our bodies still sliding against each other as my dick is semi-hard inside her.

I was right. How could I stop after one time with her?

I lie beneath him, my body half off the sofa, my legs still trembling in aftershocks of the most intense orgasm of my life.

My heart is aflame, my skin hot to the touch. We may be shrouded in the dark, but the spark spreads through me, every atom in my body awake and vibrating, calling to the man on top of me. Slowly, he disentangles from me, his large cock slipping out and my body suddenly feels bereft, even as I feel his cum leaking down my thighs.

He kisses me once more, seemingly rendered speechless like me, before he picks me up as if I weigh nothing and carries me to the bedroom. He lays me on the bed, my burning skin appreciating the coolness of the silk, and he strides away to turn on one lamp.

A soft glow, not too bright, but enough for me to see my surroundings, lights up the room. His footfalls are heavy as he walks back to me. My heart stutters and restarts when I take in his naked frame in the dim light.

His eyes are pitch black. Unhinged. Fevered. Possessive. His thick hair messy. His chest has faint red scratches on it, as if I clawed him too hard just now. My eyes trail down every sculpted muscle, to the dusting of dark hair leading to his thick, long cock, which is hard once more and curled against his flat stomach. The tip is dark red, a drop of white gathering on top, no doubt the cum from just moments ago, and a vein is pulsing on the underside.

Jack hauls me against the edge of the bed and spreads my legs before kneeling down on the carpet, all the while keeping his gaze on mine.

His tongue swipes out and licks his lips, like he's still famished for me.

"J-Jack? Again?"

Groaning, he parts my folds. "So pink, beautiful. And my cum dripping out, shit." He grunts as his hand reaches down out of my line of sight and his arm moves up and down, like he is stroking himself. He lets out a shuddering exhale, before murmuring, his voice a deep gravel, "You think once will be enough for me, angel? I've dreamed of this for years with you. And now, I'm here to collect."

Before I can respond, he dives in, feasting on my slit from the puckered back hole to my clit in one long swipe of his tongue. A moan is wrenched from my throat. My pussy throbs, still sensitive from the rough sex just now, and I fist the blankets, my body inching away, trying to escape from the sensitive and pleasurable torment.

He holds me down harder on the bed. "You're going to come two more times. Once on my mouth so I can taste your cream and once again on my cock, and you're going to love every minute of it."

My head shakes of its own accord and I whimper, "I'm t-too sensitive, Jack, oh my God." He doubles down, his tongue dipping into my wet pussy, slurping as if I'm everything he needs.

"Fucking delicious. Sweet, like the rest of you. I can taste myself on you." His tongue fucks me, and he uses one finger, rubbing circles on my sensitive clit as sparks gather at my core, spreading like wildfire. Then suddenly, a long finger drags the leaking wetness into my back hole, his finger breaching the tight ring of muscles.

A flood of ecstasy follows the pinch, and I clench against his moving fingers.

"I-I'm going to come," I wail, the deep burn overflowing and I detonate, my body convulsing from the combined stimulation of his fingers twisting my clit and fingering my ass and his tongue ramming into my pussy.

"Yes, angel. Give me your cum. You're leaking all over the place, shit." He laps at me and I fall back into a shuddering heap on the bed.

Then, as I'm coming down from the high, he flips me, tugs my ass high in the air before he climbs behind me and thrusts his hard cock to the hilt, meeting no resistance this time.

"I-I can't. Oh God," I moan incoherently, my ass arching back at him as if my body has a separate mind of its own.

"Oh yes you can, and you will," he growls, his voice rough and gritty. He laces his fingers with mine, our hands digging into the bedspread and he pounds relentlessly inside me. Dominating. Wild. Animals rutting in heat. Yet somehow, we're connected, body and soul.

My mind blanks, my vision darkening at the corners, and I let myself go, absorbing every thrust he's giving me, letting him fuck me into oblivion.

In a few short moments, my core vibrates once more, and I can feel another orgasm around the corner—a first for me as I'm usually a one-and-done type of girl—and I arch my ass higher in the air, my hard nipples dragging on the bed, the friction adding to the high.

"Yes, baby. Take it. Your pussy is clenching me like a good girl, like you want another load from me. That's it, you're almost there...milk the cum from my balls. Take my cum." With a loud, rusty groan, his cock thickens impossibly more, and he comes inside me, the hot seed flooding my wet channel and I cry out, bursting into a million pieces.

My mind is in a pleasurable haze, my entire body sensitive. I feel like I had some sort of out-of-body experience, and I can feel wetness dripping out of me. Our breathing slows and my ability to think, to do anything other than to feel, slowly reengages.

Jack tilts my chin to the side and snags my mouth with his in a soulful kiss. "I...I..." he begins, his voice thick, and he swallows audibly. "I..."

He struggles to complete his sentence, his eyes glittering with untold feelings. I arch higher and kiss him again, my emotions overflowing me, rendering me mute.

Our fingers slide against each other, our bodies communicating in silence. Slowly, he intertwines our digits together, the movement feeling significant and monumental.

After a few moments of soft kisses, he slowly slides out of me. His lips part on an exhale. "Seeing you spread like this, my cum dripping from you...I'll never forget this sight."

My core clenches at his words, my clit pulsing. He disappears into the bathroom and returns with a warm towel, gently wiping me down. I hiss when he swipes the cloth against my sensitive clit.

"Sore, baby? Did I make this beautiful pussy come too hard?"

Shit. It makes perfect sense why women throw themselves at him.

But he's so much more than his moves in bed.

So much more.

Jack climbs onto the bed and gathers me against him, wrapping me in his embrace. His fingers massage my scalp and stroke my hair. My mind is still fuzzy, and a heaviness weighs on my eyes. My heart pounds in a steady beat and for the first time in my life...

I feel content. I feel enough.

With the thought in my mind, darkness takes over, coaxing me into a deep sleep.

• • •

Calloused fingers skim over my hips, drawing a soft whimper from me. Morning light seeps through my eyelids. My legs move on the silk sheets, relishing the pleasurable fissures the motion creates, punctuated by a soreness between my thighs. Slowly, my eyes flutter open, my skin heating as memories of the most sexual night of my life barges into my consciousness.

"Good morning, my beautiful girl." Jack kisses my shoulder while he drags one hand up my stomach to curl around my breast. He squeezes, his finger flicking the nipple and I whimper, an insatiable need slicing inside me despite the soreness in my core. Chuckling, he lets go and murmurs, "How are you feeling this morning?"

His words appear casual, but I sense an undercurrent of concern in the nonchalance, as if he's afraid of my response.

I turn over and face him, my fingers brushing his raven hair, caressing his strong nose and sharp jaw, those full, delicious lips that gave me so much pleasure last night. Smiling, I lean closer and press my lips to his, before whispering, "Good morning, Jack. I feel...wonderful."

And it's true. Everything feels so natural between us, like this is what we should've been doing all along.

He breaks into a wide smile, his dimple showing. His eyes flash with relief and he lets out a sigh.

"I finally know why the girls are gaga over you," I tease, my lips quirking into a grin.

Jack freezes, a darkness clouding his eyes before disappearing.

Shit, stupid thing to say, Sarah. Now he probably thinks you're like the rest of the girls he sleeps with, after him because of his bed skills.

He lets out a pained chuckle and I shush him.

"I know what you're thinking and it's all wrong, Jack. You matter to me. Even without the sex. Because you're you, someone with integrity, despite what you may think, someone who makes me feel safe, and makes me feel enough. I should have known for all these years, but somehow I was blind, but now, I see *you* so very clearly in front of me, and you see me as me. And I feel so very happy with you."

His eyes turn darker, and he swallows, his corded throat rippling. "Sarah, you're so enough. What did I ever do to deserve this?" His voice is thick, clogged with emotions as a wet sheen gathers in his gaze.

"I feel the same way," I whisper back as I stroke his face and he leans into my touch. "And the great sex doesn't hurt..."

Jack barks out a loud laugh, which I can feel from his chest. "Yes, the sex is definitely a plus." He trails his fingers to my breast again and pinches the tip. "And this body drives me insane."

My fingers graze to the characters inked on his arm, the writing winding around an intricate vine which starts on his biceps and ends before the wrist. "What do they mean?"

"They're all different sayings I believe in or reminders for myself. This one, in particular," he points to eight characters buried amongst the foliage on the vines, "roughly translates to 'starlight shines far.' It's an old proverb that has been reused by many individuals in history. It means a single spark of fire can turn into a blaze and light up everything else. It's a reminder that everything we do can have pervasive consequences, and we should be mindful of our actions."

He traces the characters, stroke by stroke. "I got it one time after a bar fight when I was drunk. I didn't even remember what it was about, to be honest. I was lucky I didn't get thrown in jail. The next day, Adrian called me and told me about an opportunity here, and I knew it was a sign for me to change, to stop wallowing in self-pity and complacency, and try to make something of myself. I didn't look back."

I kiss the beautiful sentiment, wanting to learn everything about him, all the tidbits I've missed when my mind was shrouded with prejudice. Regret pangs inside me. All the time wasted. "Wow, all this from eight characters, huh?"

He laughs. "That's the beauty of the language. Very concise and efficient."

"Someday, I want to learn."

"And I'll teach you whenever you're ready." Jack smiles warmly at me.

I giggle, watching his face light up, finally not hiding behind his masks. "So, another random question I have to know the answer to... How did you learn to waltz so well?"

"Perks of working here. They make us take lessons as part of our training. Jack-of-all-trades, you know."

His words niggle at me.

"What?" He frowns.

"You work here, Jack! Isn't there a no fraternization policy between employees and members?"

His brows soften as he cups my cheeks. "Yes, and if I get caught, I'll be fired. But..." He swallows again. "Y-You're worth it. You're my spark. My choice. Consequences be damned."

My lips tremble, and tears cloud my vision once more. I couldn't care less if everyone finds out I'm with him. I'm my own woman now and he's the man I want to be with. But I know the stakes are much higher for him. I've seen how much pride he takes in doing his job well, how his colleagues seem to respect him from what I could observe in the halls of The Orchid. No one has ever treated me as if I'm the most important thing in his life, like I'm someone worth upending everything for. Upon seeing my response, he leans in and kisses my forehead.

"You're worth everything, Sarah," he whispers.

My eyes tear up and I bite my bottom lip and nod before I reach up and press a gentle kiss on his mouth, conveying everything I couldn't say in words.

"Come, let's get out of here before we truly get caught." He glances at the clock on the nightstand. "Housekeeping should make their rounds on this floor in an hour or so. Shit. I also have brunch with my parents. But I'll come find you afterward. You'll be at the Kensington, right?"

Nodding, I roll out of bed, wincing as I hobble over to the bedroom, a pleasurable ache reminding me of all the sex we had last night. I hear a deep chuckle behind me and glance back, finding the bastard smirking at me.

Two can play this game. I lick my lips slowly, my tongue caressing my bottom lip before flicking up to the top lip, watching the smile slip off his face, his eyes intense. Turning around, I slowly sway the rest of the way to the bathroom, making sure my ass jiggles with each step.

"Fuuuck. What monster did I create?" he groans and I close the door behind me, my heart skipping a beat.

Fifteen minutes later—it would've been ten minutes if Jack hadn't barged in and spent five minutes making out with me yet leaving me high and dry—we stagger out of the room separately, my soul feeling light even though I'm striding toward the elevators in the ultimate walk of shame.

He grins when I approach him in the elevator bay. His hair is still disheveled, his white shirt unbuttoned at the top, his tuxedo jacket draped over his arm. But his rugged looks only add to his handsomeness. The *ding* of the elevators sound before the doors glide open.

Jack and I look away from each other and find a startled Steven standing inside, his perceptive gaze darting between us. He looks worse for wear, sporting some suspicious scratches and welts on his neck as well, and his hair is flopping over his forehead in a rare departure from his usual controlled, pristine self.

We stand there momentarily gawking at each other before Steven speaks, his deep voice sardonic, "Coming in, you guys?"

Jack clears his throat and nods, stepping inside as I hurry in after him, pressing my lips together. The door closes and the chiming resumes as we descend toward the first floor.

"Do I even want to know what's going on with you two?"

"Nothing is going on," I mutter, not wanting to get Jack in trouble.

Jack sneaks a glance at me, an odd expression arresting on his face.

"I thought you were heading out early?" I change the subject back to Steven before he prods further.

"Something came up. I had to make adjustments." Steven quirks a brow, his dark eyes clearly calling bullshit on my answer.

Silence befalls us and I never thought I'd wish The Orchid had annoying elevator music.

"Want to give me that Rose card sticking out from your pocket and I'll take care of checking out for you?" Jack quips from the back.

My eyes widen when I see Steven let out a sigh, then slap a pink room key in the shape of a rose onto Jack's outstretched hand. Steven's lips tilt into a half smile when he finds me staring at him.

Though not a secret, Rose keys allow members to reach the few floors where adult entertainment reigns supreme—sex clubs, strip clubs, kink clubs, and special suites where members can reserve for pleasurable pursuits with their partners or hired companions. I just never knew anyone in my circle who frequented those floors. I've been curious but haven't had the opportunity to explore and didn't feel like going by myself.

I guess Steven isn't a monk after all.

The elevator doors open to the lobby and a small crowd of partygoers are gathered on the floor, everyone looking haggard or hungover after no doubt a long night of partying. The lobby sparkles as rays of light stream in from the stained-glass windows, bouncing off the Christmas tree and ornaments placed throughout the space. Staff carrying trays of coffee and snacks quietly circle the space, ensuring all patrons have their preferred form of morning-after cure.

"Have a good day, Jack and Sarah. And...what happens in the elevator stays in the elevator." Steven laughs softly, shaking his head as he strides toward the entryway to the neighboring Kensington Hotel.

I sneak a glance at Jack, suddenly feeling shy, and find him staring back at me as we join the crowd. He walks next to me, our hands not touching, but I can almost feel his caress, the way his callouses scrape against my skin. He keeps his eyes on my face, as if memorizing my features. His lips twitch, the beginnings of a smile. My heart flutters and I open my mouth to ask him when we'll meet up after his brunch.

"Sarah Winstead, lady in red, gorgeous as always." A gravelly voice interrupts my train of thought. Jack's eyes flash to my side and his face darkens.

Turning toward the voice, I break into a big smile when I see the familiar, striking blond man my friends and I jokingly say resembles a stock photo for Scandinavian royalty. "Charles Vaughn! I didn't see you at the ball last night."

He laughs and pulls me into a hug. "I wasn't there. My parents made an appearance."

"Lucky you. I had to represent."

He crosses his arms as he looks me over, his pale eyes surveying me, but not in a leering manner. It's as if he's trying to figure something out.

I pat my hair, hoping I don't look as freshly fucked as I feel. "W-What are you looking at?"

Charles cocks his brow. "Something seems different about you."

Heat crawls up my chest. "What are you talking about?" I wet my lips, my fingers twisting. "Jack, do you know Charles?" My head swivels toward where Jack was standing mere moments ago, finding the space empty.

"Jack Szeto? I've talked to him once or twice but don't know him personally. He walked away a minute ago."

My heart hiccups as slithering unease snakes inside me, winding around my lungs. "O-Oh. Never mind, then."

"So, are you ready for our 'date' next week?"

My brows are still scrunched up as I gaze toward where Jack was before he vanished, questions littering my mind about his abrupt departure. Then Charles's words sink in.

My head whips to the blond Adonis before me. "What?"

He furrows his brow. "Shit. You didn't know. They blindsided you."

"What date, Charles?"

"Our parentals decided to make it their business to set us up, and they rented half of Catania next week for a romantic evening."

"What!" My response echoes in the large space, drawing a few curious glances our way.

Charles whistles, his brows high on his forehead. "Damn, what's with the ladies not wanting to go out with me? First with Jess before she got together with James, then Liz wanting Parker, and now with you. I swear I'm considered a good catch. One of the most eligible bachelors in the city, heck, probably in the Eastern seaboard."

"Charles, I didn't know about—"

He holds his hands up, placating me. "Didn't know about the date. Yes, I already gathered that, and calm yourself. You and I are friends, and I don't hold any romantic feelings toward you, but supposedly, this request originated from my grandmother and my parents were excited about the prospect, so I thought I'd entertain them and have a wonderful dinner catching up with you while I'm at it."

The pulse races in my ears while relief floods my veins at not needing to hurt Charles's feelings by turning him down. But the respite is short-lived as an acidic burn surges inside me. "Dad's still trying to use me to further his ambitions by binding me to you. So that at least, if I stray from the family business, I'm connected to your family. A Vaughn and Winstead happy union."

Charles places a hand on my shoulder. "They can't force you to do anything you don't want to do, Sarah. I have your back."

I'm fuming at Dad's machinations behind my back after I explicitly told him I want to live my own life and be my own person. Glancing at my friend, I nod. "Thanks, Charles. It goes to say it's not you. I'm just sick and tired of this BS from my parents."

Charles leans back and murmurs, "The ugly side of old money. You have nothing to worry about from me or my family." He then straightens and throws out a teasing grin. "And I fully intend to be with someone who's head over heels in love with me."

I chuckle, the knot in my chest loosening slightly. "As you should be."

"See you around, Sarah. I'll cancel the over-the-top Catania reservation but let me know if you want to grab drinks...as friends, of course."

I nod and he walks away after bestowing me a wink.

I release a deep breath, resolve thickening inside me. Standing up tall, I stride toward the Kensington Hotel. If my parents think I'm going to back down so easily, they have another thing coming.

"**Y**ou haven't touched your food, Jack. Did they work you too hard last night?"

I stare at my barely touched smoked salmon benedict before glancing up, finding Mom's concerned gaze on me, her brows crinkling.

Forcing out a smile, I cut a piece of the benedict and place it in my mouth, doing the required chewing before swallowing, barely tasting anything on my tongue. We're sitting in Montclair's, a restaurant well known for their lavish brunches and top-of-the-line buffets. The space is well lit with large windows, letting in natural light, and a handful of small booths that are usually packed to the brim with repeat customers. But I barely notice my surroundings. My mind has been preoccupied ever since I left Sarah in the lobby with Charles Vaughn, the successful financier her family wants her to be with.

They looked so good together.

My chest aches and my stomach riots against the food.

Adrian and Emily had similar issues, I remind myself, since Adrian and I both had very humble beginnings, whereas Emily came from the wealthy Kingsley family.

Except Adrian is now a billionaire, Jack. What are you? A mere employee, clocking in and clocking out of work like a worker bee.

The elation from my time with Sarah slowly fades away. They're fevered dreams from a lovesick mind.

You matter, Jack. You matter so much, you wonderful man.

Her words echo in my mind. And she believes them. I can hear it in her voice, see it on her face. But is that enough?

"Jack? Is something going on?" Mom's brows crinkle further. Leave it to a parent to know their child's tells all too well.

Swallowing another bite, I keep my lips tilted in a grin. "No, I'm doing fine. A little tired from work. Last night was one of the biggest events of the season and we spent weeks preparing for it."

I raise my glass to the air. "Mom and Dad, merry belated Christmas. Sorry, as usual, for not being able to spend it with you. How was your day?"

We clink our glasses as Mom launches into a recap of her day spent karaoke-ing with her friends at their house in Flushing. Dad laughs at Mom's opinions about everyone's singing abilities, or lack thereof.

My heart lightens and I smile and chime in as appropriate. It appears they had a good time, and that eases my guilt for never being able to spend the day with them since I always have to be on-site for The Orchid ball.

My parents have worked hard all their lives and I've always added to their worries. For a long time, aside from disappointment with me, they were concerned I'd end up in a ditch somewhere. And now with me more or less on my feet and them getting older, it's time to be a responsible son and, at a minimum, not have my aging parents lose sleep at night over me anymore.

"Mrs. Wang told me her daughter just moved back and is staying in Brooklyn like you. She's single and is an accountant." Mom's eyes glitter at the prospect of introducing me to someone who'll hopefully make me settle down.

Except there's no one I want except for her. My angel. It has always been that way.

"I told your mom not to give you too much pressure, but we want to give you options. You're thirty-three now, not getting any younger. We'd love to be young enough to enjoy our grandchildren." Dad pushes his wire-rimmed glasses higher on his nose and sips from his cup of tea.

I finish the rest of my meal even as my stomach protests, so I don't end up with wasted food, which will earn me another lecture from them. As much as there may be generational and cultural differences between my parents and me, they've supported me the best way they can, and I do believe they try to understand me.

So, I want to be honest with them.

Taking a deep breath, I clasp my hands in front of me. "Mom, Dad, there is someone in my life right now. It's early and I'm not sure if things will work out, but...I'm serious about her."

My parents glance at each other and Mom breaks into a big smile. I'm sure she's envisioning wedding bells in her head. "Who is this girl? Is she your colleague at work? What's her background? Can she speak Chinese? How old—"

Dad pats her on the arm and shushes her. "Let your son speak."

"I'm just too excited. He's never mentioned anyone serious before."

They both stare at me expectantly.

I chug down a few gulps of ice water, my mind twisted in a convoluted mess. My love for Sarah, my longing for her, the elation from last night and this morning, the splash of reality when I saw her with Charles, the sinking doubt, all are strings tangled up in a knot I can't untie.

"She's a member there. Her family is wealthy, but she's looking to branch away from the family business. Sarah is someone I've known for a long time, ever since high school. She's best friends with Adrian's wife. And she doesn't speak Chinese, but she's interested in the culture."

Mom's mouth drops open, and I can see her trying to process everything.

"She's rich? And you're sure this is serious for her? We're not wealthy by any means. What does her family think? Isn't Adrian's wife from old-school money?"

More questions, some of which I don't have the answer to.

I give a hesitant nod. "I believe it's serious for her, but her family doesn't know. It's very new. I-I'd like to see where this goes."

"Won't you lose your job, son? I thought there were rules in your fancy club." Dad purses his lips, as if deep in thought.

"You can't lose your job, Jack! It's a once-in-a-lifetime opportunity and pays well with benefits!" Mom screeches, clearly worried about my prospects and probably tabulating one hundred and one reasons why me dating Sarah is a nonstarter.

I heave out a sigh. "Like I said, it's very new, so we haven't talked things out, but Mom, Dad," I look into their worried eyes, "I l-love her. I think I've always loved her. I can't walk away without trying. It'd be my biggest regret."

Mom's eyes soften, after all, she and Dad fell in love unlike her parents, who had an arranged marriage, so she understands the sentiment.

She reaches out and pats my hand. "We will never stop worrying about you as your parents. Once you have children, you'll know where we're coming from. You are the most important person to us. Your happiness matters, *you* matter. We just don't want to see you hurt. That's why we've asked you to find a good girl in your station and be content. And it seems like she has your heart. And she wants to learn Chinese; that's a good sign she's respectful."

"And if you're sure about her...we won't stand in your way. Regrets are a horrible thing in life, son. But we trust you. If you think she's worth it, then trust your judgment." Dad smooths his hand down his button-down shirt and smiles at me. "For a long time, we were worried about you. You lost your way, and we didn't know how to reach you. But now, you have your life together and we're very proud of the person you've become. If she's smart, she'll see that as well, and if not, it's her loss."

My parents glance at each other again, silently communicating, before they nod and proceed eating and drinking as if this rare display of sentimentality didn't occur. I bite my cheek and swallow as a tidal wave of warmth sweeps inside me, almost robbing me of breath. The nineteen-year-old me would've never thought I'd be sitting here, at a high-end restaurant, treating my parents to a Christmas brunch, and hearing how proud they are of me.

Moisture gathers in my eyes and I blink rapidly, my hand gripping the cup tightly as I take another large sip of water. I set the glass down, watching the condensation drip onto my fingers.

Buzz.

My phone vibrates in my pocket, alerting me to a text.

Adrian: Merry Christmas from the Maldives. Another year older. Where the fuck did the time go?

A photo appears a second later. It's of him and me on our break in front of Grocery for Less. The asshole is scowling at me for sprinkling ash from my cigarette onto his open textbook. I smirk at the picture. Some things have changed and yet, some have remained the same.

Jack: Didn't peg you for keeping this sentimental shit.

Adrian: Emily was going through my old photos the other day and squealed when she saw this one.

Jack: And after all these years, you finally got your girl, and now probably slumming it in some fancy ass penthouse in the middle of the ocean, bastard. But all jokes aside, happy for you, man.

He rose from the ashes and climbed to the top of the world. Something I knew he would do, but it's still amazing to be on the journey with him.

Adrian: You can have your girl too. Don't give me your usual bullshit. I know you have been stuck on Sarah forever. Go after her. What's stopping you?

I reread his text as my parents chat amongst themselves, the clinking of silverware and the background music from the speakers barely registering.

Adrian: Whatever's holding you back, know the true enemy is only yourself. You told me that before and I'm saying it back to you. I've met many people over the years, but not many have stood by me like you have, especially when I was dirt-ass poor. That tells me something about you as a person and definitely defines your character as a man. So, throw out whatever bullshit you're telling yourself and don't let what-ifs become regrets.

His words vibrate inside me, igniting a fire from the base of my spine, the warmth spreading upward. Sarah's words, my parents' encouragement, how perfectly right it felt to wake up next to her this morning, how my heart finally felt complete...all adding to the resolve building inside me.

I grew up with nothing and slowly built something for myself.

Anything I lose, I can regain with my own hands.

I am worthy. I matter. While I may not be a billionaire like Adrian, or old money like the clientele at The Orchid, I can offer her myself, my all-consuming love.

We can figure the rest out together.

My mind flits back to her drunken words to me the night I carried her back to the hotel room from the rooftop bar. Her despondence at the challenges she was facing with her job search, and suddenly a rush of resolve jolts my insides, a shot of adrenaline to my system.

There is something else I can also do for her.

I release the stale breath from the deepest corners of my lungs, my fingers twitching, my body itching to move, to get out of here, to make a call, and to find her.

Chuckling softly at myself, I draw the attention of my parents once again.

"Son? Everything okay?" Dad scrutinizes me as he slides his glasses, which have slipped to the tip of his nose again. I make a reminder to buy a better pair for him.

"I'm good. More than good. Mom, Dad, I wish I could stay longer for brunch, but I need to head out and do something important. I've already given my card to the waiter when I came in, so stay, enjoy desserts and a coffee or two."

I get up and walk over to my normally physically unaffectionate parents and wrap them both in a hug. Their frames stiffen against me as Dad awkwardly pats me on my arm.

"You're messing my hair," Mom complains, but can't hide the blush on her face.

Love comes in many shapes and forms, and this is their love for me.

"See you both next time."

I don my winter coat and grab my phone to type a reply to Adrian, then stride toward the exit.

Jack: Thanks. When you come back from vacation, I hope to have some good news for you.

Pushing open the double doors of the restaurant, I breathe in the cold, winter air, letting it settle into my lungs. My eyes close as I enjoy the refreshing chill seeping inside my body, which feels crisp instead of frigid today. The familiar sounds of cars honking and cab drivers cursing wrap around me like a warm blanket in a snowstorm.

I take out my phone and place a call, my voice raspy when a lady on the other line picks up. Clearing my throat, I ask, "This is Jack Szeto from The Orchid. May I speak with Ms. Gallagher?"

A minute later, the smooth voice of Bianca Gallagher, president of the Gallagher Foundation, carries through the line. "Jack? So nice to hear from you. To what do I owe the pleasure?"

Smiling, I reply, "Bianca, I'm hoping I can help you out. I heard you were looking for a Marketing Director and I have just the candidate..."

One simple phone call. Another gift from me to Sarah. Something only I can offer her. Something other than myself and my love.

Perhaps life is all about perspectives. The difference between hopefulness and hopelessness is nothing but a line in the sand, waiting for you to swipe away.

Iron resolve replaces the remnants of insecurity when I wrap up the quick call, and my legs break off into a run toward the Kensington Hotel, hurtling past the hordes of gray puffer jackets and black winter coats, my body weaving against the crowds, going against the grain.

I'm going to talk to her and ask her to be mine, not just for one night, but for all the nights in the future.

Because one night is never enough.

Because I, Jack Szeto, matter, just as she does, and no one will treat her better than me. Screw fancy last names and billion-dollar bank accounts. The angel I know has never cared about that shit. And if she says yes, which I desperately hope she will, we can tackle whatever comes our way.

Together.

CHAPTER 14

Sarah

"I know this is unorthodox, but thank you for meeting me here this morning on such short notice, after Christmas, no less. If I didn't have to fly out today and be gone for a month and a half, I definitely would've suggested meeting after the holidays." Bianca Gallagher sits across the table at the coffee shop around the corner of the hotel, looking every inch the pristine, powerhouse girl boss in her sleek, tan pantsuit.

"No worries, thank you for squeezing me in before your trip. I'm glad I happen to be in the area today." I smooth my clammy hands on my black sheath dress underneath the table. A last-minute interview after the night I just had…with Jack. It's disorienting, to say the least, but thankfully, I've studied everything I could get my hands on about the foundation and am as prepared as I can be, given the circumstances. At least I got time to throw on some makeup and pull my hair back into a presentable bun.

"So, I've reviewed your resume, but I always like to meet the candidates in person at least once. Promising candidates, that is." She smiles, her green eyes warm, nary a thread of haughtiness I usually see in the old-money crowds, which are definitely points in her favor, especially since she doesn't know my true last name.

"Understandable. The role will be pivotal to the image and public outreach for the foundation."

"Exactly."

She proceeds to ask me routine questions you'd expect at interviews—what-if situations, probing inquiries on parts of my resume, my thoughts on work-life balance. The conversation flows easily—she's someone I can see myself being friends with, someone who wants to do more for the community and for herself outside of her family name.

A sharply dressed waiter comes by and refills our water, stepping away with a spring in his step. The Christmas spirit is still in the air.

"Tell me, if you were the marketing director now, what are some problems you see with the foundation and how might you want to remedy them?"

I smile inwardly. This is something I've thought of, heck, dreamed of, when I was applying for jobs. Something I didn't ever get a chance to do when I was working with my family. Leaning forward, I clasp my hands together.

"I don't need to tell you how important the foundation is for families in need...everything in its mission statement. But I do sense a disconnect in the targeting of the current marketing campaigns."

Bianca tips her head to the side, her eyes sharp. "How so?"

"Currently, the campaigns are what you'd expect a nonprofit foundation to have—beautiful photos of families reunited, a touching tale or two of unfortunate situations, and an anecdote of how the foundation has helped in these situations. They are well-made campaigns and definitely tie back to your mission statement, but I think we'd be remiss if we didn't take into consideration the expectations of your target audience."

I take a sip of my latte and let her mull over my words.

"You think our marketing is mis-targeting?"

"Yes and no. I think you have a one-size-fits-all using a model I've seen many nonprofits use, so you definitely won't be rocking any boats. Nor will you be standing out either, and as a donor, there are thousands of charities and foundations to choose from, so why would they want to give their money to you and not the other options? This is where the targeting comes into play."

"To stand out from the rest."

"Exactly. So, think about your financial statements and your donor categories. My guess is, most of your donations or endowments come from high-net-worth individuals and then a smaller portion, but still significant, comes from individual donors—the everyday Joe. These are two distinct audiences, with two different expectations. The current campaign you have, unfortunately, will appeal more to your everyday Joe, not as much the high-net-worth individuals."

"Interesting. And why do you think that's the case?" Bianca leans forward too, her body posture telling me she's vested in my response, which is a good sign.

"Because folks with money, the amount that'll allow for them to grant you the large endowments, are much too far removed from the plight of the families your foundation serve. I'm not saying they're cold-blooded and unfeeling..."

She smirks. "I guess that depends who we're talking about. There are definitely some folks in mind I'd use those adjectives for."

I chuckle, completely agreeing with her statement. These folks include my parents, for starters. "Your marketing for these populations should target the interests of these individuals, which often include public image, competition with the Joneses, increasing net worth, etcetera. Now, that type of campaign should be rolled out in areas where these targets will see them, like financial or business news stations, exclusive clubs like The Orchid, etcetera."

Bianca nods, a small smile appearing on her lips. "And what type of campaigns do you have in mind for our high-net-worth individuals?"

"Well, I can't give out all my strategies for free. Why don't I tell you in detail...when you hire me?"

She throws her head back and laughs, not seeming to care if anyone stares at her. Definitely unlike most of the societal princesses I grew up with. Her emerald eyes glint with mirth. "Touché.

I like you, Sarah Merced. I like you a lot. I guess I owe Jack a drink later."

My chest spasms, the shock rolling through me like a sudden strike of lightning in the otherwise clear skies. "E-Excuse me? Jack?"

"Yes, Jack Szeto. He mentioned he knew a qualified candidate for my position and told me to dig out your resume. Turns out my recruiter had already received hundreds of cover letters and resumes and was working on them in the order they were received and since the position has been opened for the better part of the year, your application was toward the bottom. If Jack didn't tell me about you, I wouldn't have known to ask my recruiter to find your name in the huge stack."

I bite my cheek, and a burn appears behind my eyes. My heart drums a steady beat, pumping the warmth to my extremities. Jack, my silent knight in shining armor, my defender from the shadows. Someone who thinks his acts of kindness are nothing out of the ordinary, things anyone in his position would do. Someone who gave me the one thing I really wanted for myself. A new job away from my family, a new beginning, a new vehicle to freedom.

While there's a nagging pinch deep inside me, and I wish I could've gotten the interview by myself, to truly do this on my own, my heart is flooded with an overwhelming warmth and appreciation for the man who's been silently looking out for me, while asking for nothing in return. The last few weeks have been an awakening, and I wonder how I could've been so terribly obtuse and miss the beautiful, complex, intricate layers of this man, who still doesn't think he's enough.

But he's definitely enough. More than enough.

The world could use more Jacks.

I can't imagine my life without him.

Bianca glances at the delicate watch on her wrist and stands up. I follow suit, my mind still reeling from the revelation, but a sense of calmness slowly infiltrates. For the first time in weeks, I'm no longer worried about my job prospects. If this interview is any indication, I know what I'm doing and I'm very capable. Fate will take care of the rest.

"You know, I want to get your thoughts on one other thing and I'd be remiss if I didn't ask about it." Bianca leans back and cocks her head to the side, staring at me with an inscrutable expression.

My forehead crinkles and I lean forward on the table. What could she possibly be worried about?

"Not many people know this, but there's a few of us at the foundation who are heavy romance readers. And imagine my surprise when several folks emailed me a teaser clip of an upcoming book from Juliet Marceau and the short features you, Jack, and two other models."

The earlier calmness is eroded by a churning in my gut. I saw the beautiful and sexy photos in my email the other day and didn't think much about them, but of course others may have questions if they come across them, especially prospective employers worried about the image of their companies or foundations. Shit. How could I have not predicted this?

Forcing myself to relax my muscles, I lean back, hoping to convey nothing is out of the ordinary. Quirking one brow, I murmur, "Ah yes, the photo and video shoot Jack and I did as a favor to her. Is there a problem?" Ice slithers inside and I twist my lips into a smile.

Bianca stares at me for a few quiet seconds before responding, "Do you think the photos will affect the foundation's image given the racy nature of them?"

I cross my legs, my hands clenching into fists below the table. "I'm just a model in a professional photoshoot. There's nothing unbecoming about it. If anything, I think it creates interest in the foundation and how we're letting women drive their own careers, whether it be modeling or helping in important causes such as yours. My resume speaks for itself and my reputation is unimpeachable. I definitely don't believe the modeling job for an esteemed author I took will have any impact on my role at the foundation and as a professional, modern woman. I hope you'd agree."

My voice is light, but I keep my eyes on hers, emoting the confidence I feel regarding this matter. If her response is unsatisfactory, I'll reconsider my interest in the foundation.

Bianca laughs and nods. "That's what I was hoping you'd say. I had to ask because the clips have circulated, so there'll no doubt be questions floating about later, so I wanted to see how you'd handle them. I'm a modern woman and I can recognize one in you as well. Those are beautiful photos and videos, by the way. I'm sure Juliet is pleased with the results." She stands, indicating the interview is at an end. The swirling inside my gut settles and I smooth my hand on my dress before following suit.

"It was such a pleasure chatting with you, Bianca. Thank you for your time." I extend my hand toward her. "And I hope you have a pleasant trip."

She smiles, her eyes crinkling at the corners, and shakes my hand. "Likewise, Sarah. And I look forward to learning more of these ideas of yours."

I arch my brow at her response and hold my breath—is she saying what I think she's saying? Does this mean—

"Unofficially, welcome to the Gallagher Foundation, and let's talk when I get back. I think we need new blood. People with fresh ideas." With a wink and a wave, she drops a few bills on the table and glides out the door and into a dark sedan parked by the curb.

I plop back down on my chair, Bianca's words echoing in my mind.

I did it. They hired me for me and not for my last name. This is my era. My era to shine.

With trembling hands, I retrieve my cell phone and open the latest text from my dad. I type in my reply.

Sarah: Dad, my decision has been made. I don't care what you want to do with my trust fund or whatever your threats are. I got a job with the Gallagher Foundation and will stay behind in New York. I also found out about the date you set up for me and I canceled that as well. I hope you respect my decisions.

I hold my breath and hit send, watching the message go through, and exhale forcefully. The small motion seems significant somehow. My phone buzzes. An incoming text from my dad. I guess he finally sees the finality in my decision from my text.

Dad: How dare you take what we give you and throw it back in our faces. Don't make me come over there and drag you back myself. You're pathetic and—

I avert my eyes, forcing myself to stop the poisonous words from seeping into my heart, and with a deft swipe of my fingers, I delete the message from my phone. A familiar burn scalds my chest, but I now recognize how it reflects more on my parents than on me.

And I have a choice on what I want to do for myself in the future and who I associate with. Closing my eyes, I take a deep inhale, holding my breath for a few seconds before letting go of the air, the pain of the past, and everything tethering me behind.

The binds around my chest splice open. My stomach swoops and falls, a giddiness floating inside my body like bubbles in champagne. Suddenly, everything in front of me seems brighter, more colorful. The path forward is evident and my steps are sure. I bite back a squeal when all I want to do is screech and scream with joy. Clenching my fists, I strut out of the quiet café into the chaos of the city, and finally, unable to control myself, I let out a cry of victory and pump my hands into the air.

New Yorkers in their heavy coats trudge around me, not sparing a glance. A delivery man speeds by on his motorcycle, the wheels dragging up a muck of sopping gray sludge from the icy roads, the wet plop landing on the hem of my dress, but I couldn't care less, the elation filling every atom of my body as I stride back to The Orchid, needing to talk to him, to see him, to tell him the good news.

I imagine his sly grin, the tip of his tongue swirling around his lip ring, his devious winks, the warm, soul-healing embrace, the cloak of bergamot and leather wrapping me in a cocoon of love and safety.

I want to ask him to be by my side as I navigate the uncharted waters. I won't have the support or backing of my family and with that, all the privilege and luxuries I've grown up with, and I'm sure there'll be some adjustments and challenges along the way, but I know he won't mind.

My breathing comes out in pants by the time I see The Orchid in the distance. My mind is preoccupied with everything I'm going to say to him. I'm dizzy with excitement, eager to begin this new chapter in my life when suddenly I look up and spot the familiar tuft of dark hair, penetrating eyes now wild with something I can't identify, a man who cuts an impressive figure in a black coat and dress pants, his presence calling to me like a homing beacon.

His chest lifts and falls in rapid succession, as if he too ran back from God knows where and we stare at each other, silent messages passing between our eyes. Pedestrians move past us in a blur, the city fully awake and in business, the weather still gray and dreary, but my vision is in technicolor and focused solely on the man before me, the man I like desperately and someday, perhaps soon, could even possibly love.

Jack's eyes soften, and he chuckles under his breath. He looks down, his head shaking as if he's laughing at a joke only he can understand. I stand frozen mere feet away from him, waiting for a signal, something from him, my heart pounding as I watch his transformation before my eyes.

His gruff chuckles become laughter, the rich sound traveling to my ears, fanning the flames inside me further, and he finally glances up, his teeth snagging on his bottom lip. He opens his arm wide and my heart hiccups and freefalls.

Forget someday or possibly...I think love could be very much around the corner if the swarm of beating wings and clusters of shooting stars bursting in my chest are any sign. I let out a squeak and fly toward him, my arms outstretched.

Jack's smile widens, the expression blinding, forever burned into my memory, and I leap into his arms, curling my hands around his neck, burying my nose in his shoulder. He hoists me up and spins me around, his warm laugh reverberating in my ear.

My soul soars and everything feels right with the world.

"What's going on, angel?"

"You called Bianca Gallagher, didn't you?"

He pulls back and slowly releases me, his eyes scanning my face as if checking to see my reaction—to see if I'm okay. Slowly, he nods, the muscles rippling in his neck as he swallows.

"H-How did you know I applied there?"

Jack's eyes soften. "You told me the night at the rooftop bar." His hand gently cradles my face, his thumb circling my cheek in tenderness. "I don't have much, but this I can give you. An introduction, a recommendation."

"How do you always know exactly what I need?" My heart flutters and leaps as I lean into his touch. My chest aches at yet another reminder of the goodness that is Jack Szeto, wondering how I missed it all these years.

"If someone loves you, they'd pay attention to you, and they'd see you. Just like I see you." His voice is hoarse, his nostrils flaring. His beautiful, dark eyes captivating.

I grab his face with my hands, sealing my lips with his, needing to connect with him physically, to let him know how much I appreciate him for what he did, how much I like him for being who he is. I just need to have his lips on mine.

I need him, Jack, the bane of my existence before, but now the spark in my life, someone I know who'd light himself on fire if it means it'll keep me warm.

Jack groans, his mouth sucking, seeking, his tongue swiping my lips. Shards of pleasure spread inside me, gathering at my core, and I moan. He angles my chin and deepens the kiss, his lip ring gently rubbing against my sensitive flesh while his tongue sweeps inside, invading, obliterating, conquering my senses. My fingers dig into the corded muscles of his neck, feeling him flex in response, and he presses his body firmly against mine, his unmistakable hardness digging into my stomach.

"Oh shit," I gasp. We break for air, the white plumes of our breaths floating between us. I just kissed him in broad daylight in front of the most exclusive establishment in Manhattan, and people probably saw us, and the word will probably make its way back to my family. But I don't care about that. I curse myself for being so careless...for him.

"Yes, baby?" He stares at my lips, his eyes ravenous, his pupils blown.

"I'm totally going to get you fired. I should've waited until we were somewhere more private."

"I don't give a shit, Sarah." Jack leans down again and captures my bottom lip with his teeth, the sharp pleasure shooting directly to my clit, and I clench my legs together, feeling my panties get embarrassingly wet. I cling to him and he devours my lips as if they are a delicacy he can't get enough of.

"No, we're in the middle of 5th Avenue. We need to talk, to strategize. And I have so much to tell you." I push him away, thanking God for the last threads of logic my mind is holding on to.

"Fuck, you look so serious. It turns me on," he growls as he leans in again.

I laugh, a heat creeping up my face, and pull back. "Everything turns you on."

"Everything when it comes to you. I wonder how I survived these past thirty-odd years." He finally steps away, the dark chocolate brown of his eyes slowly making an appearance. He links his fingers with mine, his roughness feeling exactly right against my softness.

He lifts our interlinked hands up and brings them to his lips, pressing a featherlight kiss to the back of my hand and the beating organ in my rib cage trembles and kicks into high gear.

"I have something to tell you too." His voice is vibrating with tension, and he swallows audibly. I nod, clutching his hand tighter, and wordlessly follow him when he leads me back to the Kensington Hotel, ignoring the pointed stares of familiar faces along the way.

Blowing out a deep exhale, I roll out my tense shoulders and hang a "do not disturb" sign on the doorknob before shutting the door to Sarah's suite. I turn around, my fists clenching as I gather my courage to tell her how I feel about everything, words I've held inside me for so long.

I'm going to ask her to be mine. Not for one night. Not as a fling. Not as something casual. But for real. A relationship to end all other relationships because that's how serious it is for me.

I hope she believes me. Because, despite my spotty romantic past, my reputation as the king of one-night stands, everything in my past is history, a placeholder, a routine I mindlessly followed as I went through the motions of life. But with her, someone I haven't dared hope or dreamed would return my feelings, it's as if an insatiable hunger has sparked inside me ever since the photoshoot, a monster clawing its way out, threatening to devour everything in its path, I'm famished for her, the feelings she evokes inside me, the—

My breath is suspended in my lungs when I look up and see her standing in the elegant living room of her suite, her silhouette backlit by the cold winter light filtering through the gauzy curtains.

Déjà vu. An echo of last night. A seductress in moonlight, an angel in the daylight. An antique lamp on a delicate, gold-embellished corner table is turned on, swathing the room in much-needed warm light.

A few wispy strands of the silky amber tresses, shimmering between golds and reds, have fallen from her bun and frame her face. Her hazel eyes glow as she stares at me. She looks like a fallen angel, traipsing across the earth, leaving shimmers in her wake. Even after all these years, the sight of her still brings me to my knees.

Slowly, I prowl toward her, enjoying the way her breath quickens, a pink flush blooming across her chest and up her neck, as if my presence affects her as much as hers does me. I slide my rough hands on her face, gently caressing her icy skin to chase away the chill from the outside.

She blinks and her lips slowly break into a smile, the invisible rays of sunlight beaming straight into my heart, banishing any traces of doubt or fear in my mind.

"Sarah," I rasp, my other hand sliding to her waist, curling her against me.

"Jack."

"I know this perhaps may seem too fast for you, or perhaps you're wondering if it's serious for me given my past, and I understand only time will show you the truth."

"The truth?" She bites her lips like she's holding her breath. A pulse flutters in her neck and I want to kiss it, lick it, suck on it.

"The truth is, I'm desperately, madly in love with you. I have been for a very, very long time. Perhaps that may be hard to believe, but I always thought you were too good for me. Your heart is too pure. You're the Winstead princess—your life and everything you're used to differ completely from mine. I don't have riches, I don't have a fancy last name. Heck, I barely graduated from community college."

My pulse rumbles heavily in my ears as the words I've bottled inside me spill from my lips. "We don't make sense on paper. Your parents will hate me. I don't need to guess—I just know. I won't be able to take you to exotic locations in a private jet or have a personal chef cooking for us at home. But what I have is my heart and my soul, which only call out to you, only beat for you. I thought one night would've been enough. That it would be a Christmas present for myself, a precious memory for me to treasure always."

Sarah's eyes are coated in a wet sheen, the tip of her nose turning red. I take her hands in mine, needing to touch her, to reassure her, to reassure me. "But I realize how ridiculous that was. How one night with you will never be enough because I want all of your nights. And I know we may have hurdles to cross, challenges to face, but somehow, I know everything is surmountable if you're by my side. I know I can't give you much, and perhaps I don't deserve you, but I'll do my damnedest to make you the happiest person alive. I'm constantly dazzled by your sparkle, your energy, and, most of all, you. You are perfect in my eyes. You're an angel among mankind. I want to give you my all, Sarah. Will you be with me? Despite everything?"

Her hands tremble and she reaches into her purse and pulls out a familiar scrap of paper, lovingly cared for, from its pristine condition. It's the Christmas message I sent her all those years ago. The lump in my throat grows and I swallow, to no avail.

She kept it with her all these years too.

"You sent me this message twelve years ago, didn't you? It was you, right?" Her voice wavers while she stares at me steadfastly with bright eyes.

Swiping my tongue out, I wet my parched lips, suddenly finding myself unable to speak. I nod, watching her eyes widen, her lips parting as something like awe transforms her face from uncertainty to one of pure elation.

"You saw me, the real me, all those years ago." She hiccups and sniffles, clutching the laminated message tightly in her fist, her chest lifts and falls rapidly as her searing gaze pins me to the spot. "It was you all along. Always you."

I let out a shaky smile and take out my wallet, retrieving the worn scrap of paper I stole from the Christmas twig, the message from her. Clearing my throat, I show her the message, watching her eyes widen in surprise and wonder. "I stole it from the tree after you left it there. A little piece of you I could keep with me always." My voice is rough and I watch her beautiful eyes dart from the writing to my face, her lips trembling. "I'd like to think you meant this message for me. I'd read it time and time again when I felt like shit about myself, hoping one day I could be worthy of your sentiments."

She lets out a small whimper as an errant tear streaks down her face. My heart lurches, a cut opening, wondering if I've made her sad. Brushing my thumb over her tears, I murmur, "Don't cry, baby. I didn't mean to make you cry, I—"

"Y-You're worthy, Jack." She cradles my face in her hand, and I lean into her touch, breathing in her sweet orange blossom scent. My eyes burn and I exhale, trying to hold my composure as bottled-up emotions all suddenly coming to light. "I see you. You're enough. Much more than enough. The world needs you and I..." She swallows, her voice thick, her eyes red. "I need you too, Jack."

"Sweetheart, I don't deserve—"

"Shhhhhh." She swallows and rolls her lip inward as if overcome with emotions. "I don't care about the material things, and I think you know that. Because if those are important, I would've never been so set on breaking out on my own away from my family. It is I who doesn't deserve you, Jack. I'm the one who was horrible to you for so long, the one who was so blind with prejudice."

Her voice is urgent, her fingers clutching mine tighter, like she's scared I'll pull away. "Truthfully, I don't think I've ever really hated you. The only man I really despise is my dad because of his womanizing ways, making me a ridicule in front of everyone. And with you being so good with the ladies, it was easy to say I disliked you too. But that was never really true. I think I couldn't handle my emotions around you. You make me feel so much, too much. It's not just the anger, it's also the intensity, the way my body vibrates whenever I'm around you, the way a natural high courses through me when we trade insults. And now...I understand, my body always knew who you were... It just took a while for my mind to catch up."

She doles out a watery smile and my heart flips and turns,

the weight in my chest slowly lifting, melting away with her words. "You've always seen me. The true me without the fancy clothes and last name. You've never treated me like a piece of meat, a girl with curves and connections. You've believed in me, defended me, stood by me. You make me laugh, you make me angry, you make me swoon, you make me feel *everything*. How could I ever ask for more, Jack, when I have *everything* I need with you? Jack, I like you, so, so much, and I want to be yours—"

I smash my lips with hers, swallowing the rest of her answer, the monster inside me awakening, hungry, needing to burrow inside her this very second. Her words echo in my ears, heating the blood in my veins, spreading the addiction to every cell of my body. My tongue teases the seam of her soft lips and she whimpers, letting me in. Grabbing her round ass, I hoist her up and back her toward the windows a few feet away. I slam her to the cool glass as I devour her lips, my hands dragging the hem of her dress up to her waist and clasp her long legs behind me.

My cock is hard as steel, pre-cum already leaking from the tip and I grind against her, rubbing my clothing clad hardness against her panties. She moans, her teeth snagging at my lip ring and she sucks the delicate area into her mouth, her tongue swirling, sending sharp frissons of lust straight to my balls.

Her hand snakes down between us and works to take my cock out, the sounds of the belt buckle and zipper reaching my ears. Fevered desperation floods through me. My fingers grapple behind her, unzipping her dress, and tearing the top down so it gathers around her waist. She fumbles with my underwear before grabbing my cock, giving the long shaft a hard squeeze.

"Shiiit," I groan and thrust against her. "You like my cock, angel?"

She moans as my mouth trails down her neck, nipping along the way before I bury my face between her swollen tits, her pink nipples as hard as eraser buds on the tip of pencils.

"Your fucking nipples." I suck one in and Sarah shivers against me, her hand clenching harder on my dick and I want to burst, want to flood her with my white-hot cum.

"Sexy, fucking nipples. Do you like it when I do this?" I rasp before taking the other in my mouth, my teeth clamping hard on the distended tip. She emits a lusty cry, her hands reaching behind my back and clawing my shirt. "Yeah, baby, you like this, don't you?"

"Oh God, yes, Jack, more." She thrusts her tits at me and presses my head against her chest. My teeth bare down again, giving her another pinch and she shudders—my angel likes pain with her pleasure.

"Fuck, I need you naked, now," I grunt, sliding her down so her feet touch the floor. We make quick work of our remaining clothes, the cool daylight illuminating every part of her I didn't get to see in the dark, from the freckles decorating her right breast to the way her pussy has an enticing landing strip of auburn hair.

Sarah drops to her knees, her eyes wide, her irises nearly swallowed by her pupils, and she grips my cock, giving it a hard swipe, before she slides the tip between her lips, her tongue lapping and swirling around it like it's the best thing she's ever tasted.

"Yes, baby, take that fucking cock inside your mouth like a good girl, an angel with a devil's body." I knot her hair in my hands, pushing her face toward the base of my cock as she takes more and more of me inside her, every inch an exquisite torture, the ecstasy practically blinding me.

She looks at me, her eyes watery as my tip hits the resistance of her throat. She looks so fucking sexy with her plump lips wrapped around my big cock, her heavy tits swaying as she struggles to swallow me whole. The sight alone could make me come.

"You okay, baby?" I grunt, willing myself not to impale her to the hilt.

Sarah nods, her eyes watering, and I can feel her throat muscles relaxing as she attempts to deep throat me.

"Fuuuuck, Sarah. Shit." I heave out a few breaths, my legs turning numb from the excruciating bliss, every atom of my body focusing on her tight, wet mouth around my cock. She continues to swallow, and I can feel my balls tightening, wanting to release my load into her.

"Yes, baby, oh fuck, you give such good head. Relax your throat...yes, I'm almost there." She takes the last few inches like a champ, tears streaming down her face, and she bobs up and down, gagging, slurping, her hands fondling my balls.

The burn builds rapidly, heating my blood to a boil, incinerating my nerves. My balls throb and contract, the pressure rising in my shaft and every muscle in my groin spasms, the telltale signs of my impending orgasm. I wrench her off me, my cock releasing from her mouth in a loud pop.

"I'm going to come inside you and fill you up with my cum, angel. And the world is going to see it." Dragging her pliant body up my body, I turn her around and face her toward the windows, pushing forward until her hands and tits are flat against the glass. I kick her feet apart and arch her ass up, giving the round globes a few loud slaps.

"Fuck me, Jack," Sarah mewls, her lithe body quaking in front of me, her hands rubbing the windows, leaving her palm print as evidence of our tryst. Her heavy tits hang down, jiggling as she gyrates her fuckable ass, now pink from my ministrations.

"Baby, I can see your pretty little pussy. So wet, dripping for me." Another slap. Another keening moan when I rub away the sting.

"Ready, baby, want to show the world you're mine?" I grunt, teasing the tip of my steel shaft on her plump, pink lips below.

She arches back, offering herself to me, her glazed eyes reflecting from the windows.

I thrust in to the hilt and a lustful moan wrenches from her throat, her hands pawing the glass, trying to find purchase when I hammer inside her, all logic and sanity having left the room, leaving me with only my primal instincts and my need to conquer, to decimate, to fuck her into blinding bliss.

"More, harder. Harder, Jack!" Sarah gasps in between thrusts, her luscious frame shuddering, every inch of her skin pinkened.

The sound of skin smacking against skin is erotic and resounding. I slowly pin her against the window and I fuck her at a different angle, getting in deeper, hitting a spot which makes her cry out, throwing her head against my shoulder.

"Look at me, baby, let me see those beautiful eyes while I'm buried so deep inside you."

Her eyes flutter open, and I plow into her relentlessly from below. Her pupils are blown, her eyes unfocused, her lips parted. Incoherent sounds emit from her mouth with each smack of my hips against her ass. She looks drunk with carnal bliss.

"God, you're so beautiful, Sarah. So perfect. So mine." I kiss her soft lips, slowing down my thrusts, staving off my impending orgasm, wanting to draw this moment out, to wring out every ounce of pleasure between us. My hand slowly trails between her legs, finding her slick nub. I rub tight circles around her clit, and she thrashes against me.

"I-I need to c-come. Please make me c-come," Sarah begs, and I hasten my movements, pistoning inside her again. Deep, hard thrusts, my balls slapping against her pussy as our bodies collide, pushing us closer and closer to the edge.

Sweat drips off my brows as I watch her reflection in the window, her heavy tits slapping against the cool surface in tandem to my cock driving deep inside her.

Her legs convulse and she clutches my forearms in a tight grip, her fingernails digging into my flesh and the pain only adds to the insanity and my hips move harder, faster, jackhammering inside her until the world falls away and nothing else matters other than bringing her to the heavens.

"I think they can see you," I rasp in her ear, "see your luscious tits smacking against the windows, watching your beautiful face in the throes of orgasm, your body taking my big cock like my good girl."

Sarah lets out a loud scream and I feel liquid gush out of her, her legs giving out and I pin her with my body weight so she doesn't slide down to the floor. Her pussy throbs against my dick in the peak of her orgasm and my rhythm turns erratic, the pressure releasing from my balls, up my shaft, and implodes in a burst of incinerating heat.

"Mine. Mine. Mine." I follow her into the heavens, a low roar tearing from my lips and heavy spurts of cum shoot inside her, each pulse sending me into a tailspin while she trembles and moans in my arms.

Our heavy pants fill the air as we slowly come down from our high. The room smells of sweat and sex. The window is fogged up in certain spots with our palm prints smudged against the glass.

"Fuck me, Sarah. You've made me the happiest man on earth." I press a kiss to her hair and she giggles. My angel fucking *giggles* after the most intense sex of my life. My lips quirk to the side. "What's so funny, angel?"

"I didn't know it could be like this. I'm never like this with anyone else. I'm so damn lucky. If I post this on my smutty readers' group on social media, they'd be so jealous." She flushes and burrows her body against mine. She giggles some more. "I'm God's favorite."

"I don't care whose favorite you are, you're definitely my favorite," I murmur against her ear. "And just so you know, it's never like this with anyone else for me, either. It's only like this with you."

Sarah melts and releases a sigh of contentment. Then she stiffens. "Do you think they really can see us through these windows?"

I throw my head back in laughter. "Now you're worried? You were so turned on moments ago...a closet exhibitionist, aren't you? And no, the glass is reflective on the outside. There's no way on earth I'm letting anyone see what's mine." With that, I give her nipple a pinch, earning myself a squeak.

Swooping down, I lift her legs and carry her toward the bathroom. Her enchanting eyes are now the most stunning gold and green.

"Your job, Jack?" Sarah furrows her brows.

I press a kiss to her forehead, wanting to dissolve those lines of worry. "I'll handle it. I'm meeting Ryland in a few hours to tell him. We're not a secret and I'm going to do the right thing. Worse comes to worst, you and I may lose our access to The Orchid, but I don't need luxury when I have you. I've climbed up from the gutter to get to where I am today. I can do it again somewhere else. All I need is you by my side."

A wet sheen glazes her eyes, and she nods in agreement. She caresses my cheek with her hand.

"Thank you, Jack, for everything. And regarding the Gallagher Foundation..."

I pause my steps at the door of the enormous bathroom and smile. "It really was nothing. I knew they had a lot of applicants and knew they would miss out if they didn't review your resume. Everything is on you. I only reminded them. It's your abilities that'll convince them to hire you."

She grins, her face turning impish. "I got it."

I slide her back to the floor and cradle her face. "What?"

"I interviewed with Bianca this morning. It was extremely last minute, but she wanted to squeeze me in before she left for an extended trip. She gave me the unofficial word on the spot. And she didn't know I'm a Winstead."

Letting out a whoop, I spin her around, reveling in the sound of her laughter, watching her amber tresses flutter in the air like the dream I've always had...except this time, it's real.

Jack

Adjusting my tie, I stride down the quiet halls of the third floor of The Orchid, dipping my head at patrons passing by as my heart beats a mile a minute.

She said yes. Sarah wants to be with me.

My heart jumps in elation and free falls, tumbling toward something resembling nirvana, a high so thrilling I never imagined it could happen to me.

My feet quicken as I weave around staff members walking briskly to be on the beck and call of the rich and powerful.

A treacherous worry pierces my joy—an inevitable one. What will become of my employment at The Orchid, the place where I transformed from the delinquent into something more, the place where I truly gained self-confidence in something outside of my ability to charm women or my looks. A striking wistfulness wraps its vines around my lungs, restricting my airflow and I pause as the full reality of the situation crashes upon me like a freight train.

In the next hour, I'll most likely walk out of here without a job, having given everything up for her. I've plowed through the golden rule at The Orchid, a zero-tolerance policy. No one in the history of the establishment has escaped unscathed. I may be blacklisted from the industry from now on. To say I'm not concerned would be a blatant lie.

Tiny beads of sweat break across my forehead and I lean against the wall, trying to catch my breath. A sudden irrational fear shakes me, a voice nagging me in the dark corners of my mind, reminding me I'm someone with subpar academic credentials, someone who had a spotty past. The murky thoughts are something I've managed to brush aside until now, when they've forced themselves to the forefront, moments before a conversation which will change my life.

There'll no doubt be other problems to contend with, such as how our relationship will affect her membership at The Orchid, and how her family will react once they find out. I'm sure they'll be furious.

When you're used to swimming in disappointment, the riptide of hopefulness and hopelessness is disorienting, and my mind wants to clamp on to the doubts, as if they're lifeboats. But today, the lifeboats can go hang themselves, because I'm diving headfirst into the waters, knowing I'm forsaking the safety behind me and swimming toward an oasis, choosing to believe something better is waiting for me on the horizon.

Heaving out a deep breath, I will my pulse to calm.

I know I can climb out of this and make something of myself again. I've done it once before and with her by my side, I can do this again.

For her.

Because I'll finally get to be with the one woman who's always been out of reach.

Because she finally sees me for who I am and believes in me.

Because she's the angel to the devil inside me, my other half.

She's worth it.

Determination pierces through me, slicing through the remaining vines wrapped around my lungs, and I resume my walk down the hall, eager to get the conversation over with.

A few moments later, I stand in front of the thick mahogany doors at the end of the walkway, the gentlemen's club, where Ryland is meeting me. Of all the Anderson brothers, and there's four of them, and their youngest sister, Lana, I'm closest to Ryland. Perhaps it's because his surly personality reminds me of Adrian. But he's kind deep inside. You just need to dig through all the layers of grump to get to it.

Pushing open the doors, I take a fortifying breath and stride past the long, expansive antique bar top made of the darkest woods, shined to perfection, my eyes connecting with the bartender wiping down a few glasses. He gives me a curt nod and I return the greeting.

I scan the spacious room, searching for my boss and friend. The club is decorated in dark grays and mahogany. The walls are adorned with masculine shaker paneling, the classic lattice pattern elevated with raised circular and pyramid inserts, under lights casting a glow toward the tall ceilings, which contain matching lattice-work painted in burnt gold and deep navy. Supposedly, it was modeled after the gentlemen's clubs of the aristocracy from historical England but elevated with modern amenities. In normal situations, I'd look to see if anything appears out of place or order, an occupational hazard, but what makes me very adept at my job. But today, I can barely bring myself to care, my attention a homing beacon wanting to find the man and get the conversation over with.

Brushing past the umber-colored tufted leather sofas spaced throughout the room, some of which are occupied by men absorbed in their conversations, tumblers in their hands or on the black-marble tables in front of them, I head toward the back to the private rooms, skipping past the ones with open doors. I slow down my pace as my eyes rove over the hand-printed placards, which identify the occupants of the rooms, stopping until I reach the beveled glass doors of the room noted "Anderson."

I blow out a deep exhale and bring up my hand for a furtive knock. My lungs are lined with lead, the sudden heaviness rendering it difficult to breathe. Whatever happens, I have no regrets. Even if this means I'll walk out of this room unemployed, I'll still be the happiest man alive.

"Come in," Ryland's deep voice commands from within.

Pushing open the door, I step into the elegant private room. Floor-to-ceiling bookshelves are lit up by a Tiffany floor lamp and a large window with thick velvet curtains tied to the sides. Shards of rainbow cascade to the brocade wallpaper through the antique stained glass of the classic light fixture. Ryland and one of his younger brothers, Rex, are sitting on the sofa, along with Steven Kingsley. All three men are dressed in three-piece suits, clearly discussing business matters moments before I walked in. Rex and Steven stand as I approach them.

"Jack, I hear you've requested an audience with my brother, His Royal Highness." Rex smirks and runs his fingers through his dark-brown hair.

Ryland rolls his eyes at his brother's teasing quip. Ryland and his older brother, both brooders of the family, are nicknamed royalty by the rest of the siblings. Sometimes, it'd be "Your Royal Highness," other times, it'd be "Your Majesty." From what I heard, the siblings used to bicker over these nicknames, but now it appears Ryland has accepted his fate. Of the four brothers, Rex appears to be the most casual of them all, the one who doesn't walk around as if he's carrying the weight of the world on his shoulders, the one who seems to lighten the atmosphere of any room he occupies.

"Just something I need to run by him." I keep my eyes on Ryland, finding his aristocratic face serious, giving nothing away. It's what makes the bastard so good at poker.

"Can't tell me? That *does* sound serious."

I arch my brow. "Telling you anything will mean the rest of your family will know about it in a matter of minutes."

Rex narrows his eyes, and I bite back a grin. He mutters, "I like to make sure everyone is informed. You guys will cry if I don't send you all the information you're desperate to know, but won't ask."

Steven clears his throat and turns to the brothers. "Thanks for the drinks. I'll be in touch with more data on the investments. Rex, any plans for the rest of the day?"

Rex unleashes a shit-eating grin. "What do you have in mind, Kingsley? Are we on the prowl?"

"Let's leave these two to their 'conversation,' and we can figure out our vice for the evening." Steven ushers Rex to the door before pausing and turning back to me. His eyes scan my face, and I fight to maintain a placid expression. He furrows his brows, as if he came to some sort of understanding. "Good luck and tell Sarah I said hi."

I swallow and dip my head in acknowledgement. Taking in the perceptive glint in his eyes, I find his lips tipping into a small smile. Somehow, the bastard knows what I'm here to discuss with Ryland. I guess what they say is true; you don't have a meteoric rise to the top in Wall Street unless you're a predator with the keenest instincts. At my expression, he huffs out a deep chuckle before leaving the private room with Rex in tow.

"So, love looks good on you," Ryland comments, crossing one long leg over the other. His angular face still looks serious, if not for the twinkle of mirth in his eyes.

"Thanks." I take a seat across from him. "How did you know?"

"Very little goes on in these halls without my knowledge. One must keep their eyes and ears open when swimming in shark-infested waters."

I heave out a sigh and sink into the comfortable leather sofa. "I wanted to tell you in person."

"And I appreciate that."

"I know I've broken the non-fraternization rule, and I fully expect to hand in my resignation by the end of the day. I wouldn't have done it for anyone else other than Sarah."

He leans forward, a shadow passing over his gray eyes, his shoulders suddenly tense. A flash. A wisp. A muscle tics in his jaw. "And you think it's worth it? Giving up your job for her?"

"Definitely." No hesitation, something I would do over and over again. "If you meet the right woman, that's something you'll give up the world for."

"The right woman," he murmurs like he's talking to himself, his eyes taking on a faraway glint.

His gaze sharpens again, and he stares at me for a few beats, his brows pinching, before nodding. "The rules are there for a reason, and I can't let this go for anyone. But I like you, Jack. You're great at your job and also a good friend. And I respect you. It takes guts to be forthcoming about this, knowing the potential consequences."

Ryland takes a sip of the amber liquid in his tumbler. He stares at the alcohol sloshing in the glass, his voice taking on a quiet nonchalance. "How about I propose an alternative? You stay on, but we terminate the membership for Ms. Winstead? Few know about your new relationship with her, and while I don't want to break the rules, I'm willing to bend them for you."

My pulse kicks up, my chest lightening as I contemplate his words. To continue working here with the people I respect while being with Sarah sounds too good to be true. But I'd need to talk to her about it. It's only fair. "I'd be interested, but let me discuss this with her."

"Sounds good. You're part of management, so, I'd like to remind you, you have an allotted number of days to bring a partner or a spouse to enjoy our amenities, in case you forgot." His lips curve into a smile, softening his demeanor.

"I know you've always loved me, Ryland." I chuckle, my heart slowing to a steady rhythm. He's providing a way for me to be employed and for Sarah to come back every so often. The sneaky bastard.

"Don't let that get in your head, dipshit." He grins, leaning back in his seat, and arches his brow.

• • •

I pace back and forth in the lobby of the first floor of The Orchid, my high heels clacking against the marble in a staccato rhythm.

Much like the pounding of my heart.

A tingling heat spreads inside my body, the warmth infusing me with happiness at the thought of Jack, the infuriating man who has conquered my heart with his teasing grins and sexy drawls, but most importantly, with the depths of his soul. I want to spend the days peeling back the layers, learning all there is to know about Jack Szeto.

It has been a little over a week since we've made things official, and when Jack told me the choice his boss gave him, I laughed out loud. I remember the relief flooding my veins, calming my rioting pulse. There wasn't any hesitation, any question on what needed to be done. Jack will stay in his employment, something I know he truly enjoys, and I will visit him every so often under these management guest days.

I've moved out of the Kensington—I'd rather do that on my own terms than be kicked out once my family cuts off all my funds in my accounts—and am staying temporarily with Jack in his small, but cozy apartment in Brooklyn. I intend to find my own place and relish my newfound independence. But maybe someday, we'll move in together...for good.

The back of my neck tingles with the heat of someone's attention, and I smile. Sure enough, once I turn around, I find Jack striding toward me, clad in yet another navy suit, which seems to mold over his tall, muscular body like a second skin, his passionate eyes filled with love. His lips curve into a smile, his tongue dipping out to swirl around his lip ring.

My face heats, and I smother a laugh. I still remember how I used to hate this flirtatious behavior from him in the past, but now, seeing him walking toward me, eyes pinned on me like I'm a delicacy he wants to devour, his actions make my heart race and my panties wet. I let out a deep breath at the direction of my thoughts.

"The staff meeting took longer than expected. Sorry to keep you waiting. Not what I had in mind for your first guest day." He links his fingers with mine and brings my hand up for a kiss.

My heart hiccups and free falls, and I giggle.

"What's so funny, angel?"

"I was so dumb." My giggles become snorts, and my eyes mist over. "So dumb."

He cocks his brows, his lips twitching. "I'm not following, and I don't think it's wise for me to agree with that statement."

"You! With your hand-kissing thing. I've seen you do this sporadically over the years. You're a closeted gentleman all along."

He growls, bringing his lips to the outer edge of my ear, and rasps, "A gentleman on the streets and a freak in the sheets."

My empty core clenches, the familiar ache centering on my clit when my mind drifts to the way he has been "freaky" to me every night for the past few days. Against the wall. On the terrace at night. On the floor. On top of the counter. His inner beast was fully unleashed.

"Horny, aren't you?" His nose grazes my neck and I almost moan out loud from the way the simple touch lights up all the nerve endings in my body.

I clutch his lapels. "Maybe we should get a suite here or try the Rose floors for our guest day?"

Jack pulls back, his eyes the color of midnight, and his nostrils flare. His gaze is trained on my mouth as his talented tongue darts out and wets his bottom lip. His voice is rough when he whispers, "You're an angel in disguise, you—"

"Sarah Elizabeth Winstead! You ungrateful, worthless daughter!"

We freeze at the scathing remarks from my dad, who is strutting toward us, his thin face red with fury. I can feel the heat crawl from my neck to the rest of me, my breathing quickening. Beads of sweat gather on my forehead. I knew this would happen at some point. I've thwarted everything he has planned for me so far. I just never expected him to do this so publicly, in full view of his peers. But I guess a man with no shame who'd parade his mistresses around in public thinks little of his self-image. He narrows his eyes and points at us, his lips curling into the snarl of a rabid beast. Jack straightens up and steps in front of me, as if to protect me from someone who can probably destroy his career with a few well-placed phone calls.

My warrior and defender.

"Mr. Winstead, this is a public space," Jack calmly responds, but I can hear the undercurrent of anger in his voice.

Dad ignores him as he continues to charge toward me, his eyes scanning me from top to bottom in disdain. "How dare you turn down the date with the Vaughns! We've raised you. You lacked nothing! And now you leave the company, moving across the country. You have a responsibility to the family. At the very least, you can find yourself a respectable suitor worthy of the Winstead name, and instead, you," he points his finger toward Jack, venom in his voice, his spit sputtering from his mouth, "you choose this *nobody*. The help! A runt! And I had to find out because of a photo of the two of you kissing in broad daylight on *The Gossip Times*! And now, because you're a public disgrace, I had to fly across the country to talk some sense into you. You're worthless. A disappointment. You're *nothing* without us. You—"

"Dad. Stop it, you're embarrassing yourself! And that's rich, coming from you, who has thousands of photos floating out there with your mistresses." My eyes dart around the room, and as expected, silence has befallen the lobby as an audience waits with apparent bated breath, as if we're actors in a riveting play.

I rub my thumb over Jack's hand, feeling his barely leashed fury in his death grip. I take a deep breath, attempting to tamp down the anger long enough so I can tell him how I truly feel. For good. "I'm sorry I've disappointed you. I know you didn't get the answer you wanted in your end-of-the-year deadline."

Feeling Jack's gentle squeeze on my hand, I swallow and continue, "Actually, I take that back. I'm *not* sorry at all. I'm my own person and this is my life. I appreciate the privileges you and Mom gave me, which I know have made my life easier. But I need to live my life on my own terms and be with someone I love, not because of his last name or the number of commas in his bank account. This is something I'm unwilling to, and will never, compromise on."

Jack flinches at my mention of the word, "love," his hand shaking in mine, and I realize it's true, I do love him, and perhaps these feelings have been growing since we first met twelve years ago, starting with the intense dislike, blossoming into something headier, something flammable I couldn't name until everything came to a head the last few weeks.

I curl my arm around his, feeling his muscles slowly relaxing, and we stand united as one team before my dad, whose mottled face and furious snarl tell me he's working himself up for something terrible because he can't fathom a world where people don't bend to his will.

"You're cut out from your trust fund and all ties to our family, you ungrateful, pathetic bitch! You're coming with me," he roars. His hand grips mine so tightly, I'm sure it'll leave a bruise later.

Crying out in pain, I try to tug my hand free without success.

A growl tears out of Jack's lips and within a split second, my hand is freed, and I see Jack twisting Dad's hand at an odd angle. Dad lets out a howl of agony. "How dare you!"

"You can talk shit about me. I couldn't care less. But one more word about your daughter, the best woman I've ever met, or if you even think about touching a hair on her head, I can't promise you I won't break every fucking bone in your body. Don't. Test. Me," Jack growls, his words echoing in the quiet space. He towers over my dad, his teeth bared, his eyes wild. Unhinged. He bends Dad's arm farther and Dad lets out another pathetic cry of pain. A vein pulses in Jack's forehead and he tightens his grip before throwing Dad's hand back toward him.

"I'll sue you for assault. I'll sue this establishment," Dad rages, his bony frame vibrating, finally appearing to notice the number of eyes staring at us and the muted whispers echoing in the space.

Pounding footsteps alert us to the arrival of the security personnel. Armed guards flank Dad, gripping his arms.

"Please escort Mr. Winstead off of the premises," a clipped voice instructs behind us. A tall man strolls up, stopping next to Jack. Rex Anderson, someone I recognize in passing, glowers at Dad, his eyes flashing in anger. "Fleur Entertainment and The Orchid have a zero-tolerance policy for assault toward our staff and members. Please consider your membership hereby revoked."

The security drags my screeching dad out the doors. Rex turns to us, his grave face softening before his lips curl into a grin. "Things are never boring around here, huh? God, I love my life." With a wink, he strolls around the room, murmuring to astonished members as hordes of staff carrying trays of drinks and hors d'oeuvres seemingly appear out of nowhere, offering refreshments to patrons to soothe their rattled nerves.

A familiar brunette emerges from the fray and I fight the impulse to groan. Juliet Marceau struts over as she eyes the two of us. Jack clutches my hand tightly in his.

No hiding. No pretending.

Juliet arches her brow at the possessive gesture and quirks her lips to the side. "So, I guess the fraternization rules don't apply when it comes to her? I thought there was something between the two of you...an author's sixth sense."

"Sarah is no longer a member here, and it has always been her for me," Jack murmurs, his voice hoarse. "Thank you for understanding, Juliet."

Juliet swallows and blinks her eyes. She stares at the man next to me and lets out a wistful sigh. "Of all people, I should know you can't stop true love." She nods and murmurs, "Best wishes to the two of you and I'll see you around, Jack." Whirling around, she heads toward the elevators, leaving the two of us standing there, wondering what just transpired.

Quiet chatter and soft music fill the room once more and everyone appears to move on with their day. I turn to Jack, finding his impassioned gaze on mine. He lifts our interlinked hands to his lips and whispers, "You love me? That's what you told your dad just now." His voice is thick, seemingly filled with awe and disbelief.

I wet my lips, the thumping of my heart resounding, no doubt matching its other half in his chest. "Yes. Yes, I do, Jack." I let out a halfhearted chuckle, the binds around my chest loosening. "Guess what? I'm penniless now, and my last name is completely worthless."

"I don't care." His response is ardent. Urgent. "All I need is you, Sarah. Only you. I love you so, so much."

My lips wobble, my eyes tearing up, and I rise to my tiptoes, pressing a soft kiss on his mouth—after all, we're in public. His arm curls reflexively around my waist, and I whisper in his ear, "And I love you, you insane, infuriating man."

Jack grips me tighter, and he bestows me with the most brilliant of smiles. Fireworks burst in technicolor inside me, the exhilaration so sudden, I almost forget to breathe.

We stare at each other, mere inches of distance between us, and my life feels complete. I may be poor in the bank account but am rich in all the ways that matter.

Grinning, I murmur against his ear, "I guess...I still have my rocking, curvy body left..."

Jack laughs, the rough sound echoing in the space, once again drawing a few eyeballs our way. He rasps, "Fuck me. Your mouth. I think we should utilize one of the Rose floor suites today and I'll show you the thousand and one reasons I love you, Sarah Winstead."

A sharp heat shoots straight to my clit, a breath catching in my throat, and he leads me toward the elevators. He turns to me and gives me a wink and I bite back a smile, the fuzzy, comforting warmth in my chest spreading to every atom of my body.

For the first time in my life, I'm finally free.

"**W**here are you taking me, angel?" I grin, my eyes squeezed shut, my hand holding tightly on to Sarah's while she leads me down a few corridors in The Orchid and some...stairs?

I swear, the woman now knows more about this place than I do. Ever since she has been freed from the shackles of her family, Sarah is thriving. Her work at The Gallagher Foundation is going well, and she has formed a friendship with her boss, Bianca. She appears to be fulfilled, her eyes sparkling in a way I've never seen before. She's also doing things the Winstead princess wouldn't do in the past—hanging out with the staff in the employees' quarters here, making legions of friends naturally, exploring every nook and cranny of the labyrinth, including the Rose floors.

My cock hardens at the memory of experiencing a voyeurism kink room with her last month, watching the flush bloom on her face when she watched a couple going at it in a glass enclosure.

Then there was the time when we went on our first vacation together, a road trip to Yellowstone National Park, where we lost our wallets, our car broke down, and had to hustle our way out of the debacle by selling tires for an auto repair shop. It's a long story.

Fuck. This woman.

Just when I think I may have figured her out, she still manages to surprise me at every corner.

"Almost there, don't open your eyes!"

Biting back another smile, my hand reaches down and gives her tempting ass a squeeze, earning me a squeal.

"Ugh. At this rate, we'll never get there." I can imagine the cute little pout on her face.

"Fine, fine, fine. I'll behave for now. Lead the way."

A few more quick turns later, I hear the familiar squeak of the metal bar of our stairwell or emergency doors being pushed open. Then I'm hit with a warm, balmy breeze, the scents of wildflowers and mint swirling in the air. The sounds of the city are muted, as if we're far away from the main streets, and not mere feet away from one of the busiest neighborhoods in New York City. A few birds sing their spring songs, their melodies crisp, and the sound of leaves rustle in the air.

"Ta da!"

I take that as my cue to open my eyes, finding us standing in a small courtyard surrounded by towering hedges with dark-green foliage interlaced with long vines of bright magenta flowers.

"What is this place? And how do I not know about it?" Not that I'm surprised since The Orchid is rumored to have secret passageways and hidden rooms and gardens.

"I found it last time when I went exploring while you were working. Apparently, some employees and patrons also know about this courtyard. I've seen a few familiar faces here every so often. It's peaceful, isn't it?" Sarah beams at me, her wavy hair glowing amber in the waning afternoon sun, and my heart clenches.

Suddenly, I'm transported to that day when I stared at her from afar at Grocery for Less, when she noticed me for the first time. She's still as breathtaking—no, even more breathtaking—than the sweet girl of eighteen.

Even after a few months together, when every day has been bliss for me, even on the days when we'd be at each other's throats, my heart is a bass drum, beating in loud, reverberating *thumps* whenever I'm in her presence. I lace my fingers with hers, gently circling the soft flesh before bringing it up to my lips for a tender kiss. Sarah blushes prettily, her thick lashes fluttering slightly at the gesture, something I found she really loves.

"I love you so much, Sarah," I murmur against her hand, watching her brilliant hazel eyes flare at my words.

"Jack…" she whispers, her tongue darting out to wet her lips. My eyes snare at the movement and I wrap my other arm around her waist, drawing her closer, and lean down. I must have a taste of those sweet, red lips, and—

"You know you guys have an audience, right?" My head snaps up, the low, sarcastic voice laced with mirth from my right drawing my attention away from my love.

Steven Kingsley, in his perfectionist glory, nary a hair out of place, smirks at us. He unbuttons his dark-gray suit jacket and crosses his legs in his chair. Sitting at the long table with him are his siblings and their spouses. He arches a brow as if to say, *how the fuck did you miss us sitting here?*

My eyes rove over the rest of the folks, finding identical shit-eating grins on their faces. Emily, her dark hair piled high on her head, is biting her bottom lip as she bounces in her seat in apparent glee. Adrian has his arm around the back of her chair, his fingers tracing lazy circles on her shoulder. Jess smiles warmly—the eldest Kingsley always a picture of poise and grace—and her husband, James, someone who's known to worship the ground his wife walks on, tilts his lips in a half grin.

Two servers, dressed in the crisp, blue uniforms of Kobayashi, our onsite award-winning Japanese restaurant, carry trays and trays of an assortment of food, ranging from sashimi, hand and sushi rolls, chirashi bowls, the fish I know will melt in my mouth since the catch is fresh and purported to be flown in from the Tsukiji Market in Tokyo every morning. Platters of food decorate the table, an array of bright colors of pinks, oranges, and whites of the thinly sliced fish to the pops of green of cucumber, avocado, and side salads in sesame dressing.

"What's this?" I ask Sarah. She grins and leads me to the two empty chairs at the table.

"A surprise celebration for your promotion. I know you didn't want to make a big fuss about it, but you deserve celebrating, Jack. Everyone, except Steven here, flew in yesterday. James and Jess even left the kiddos at home with her parents to come visit."

I blink, a familiar prickle gathering behind my eyes. My throat feels dry, and I suddenly find myself at a loss for words.

Steven gets up and smacks a hand on my shoulder in a bro hug and the rest of the group follows suit, loud cheers of felicitations erupting around the table.

"Director of Special Events at The Orchid," Steven comments, his hand giving me another heavy slap across my back. "Moving up in the world, my man." His piercing eyes twinkle. "Proud of you."

"All thanks to Adrian for giving me the opportunity in the first place. And..." My voice is hoarse and I clear my throat, eager to dispel the sudden thickness gathering in my chest. "Thank you all for coming all the way over here."

The group waves me away, as if saying, *of course, what on earth are you talking about?*

"It's all you. I only provided an introduction. Even though I wonder what they saw in you, jackass," Adrian mutters under his breath, every inch the cold billionaire he's known to be in the press. Only I can tell he's joking by the slight quirk of his mouth.

"Dipshit." *Thank you, my best friend.*

"Don't fuck up." *I'm proud of you.*

Emily rolls her eyes at our exchange and shoves her husband gently in the arm. "You men will never grow up, will you?"

"Nope," Jess and Sarah quip in response.

"Hey, don't throw me in the fray. I'm a very well-adjusted, successful man, and the luckiest man on earth to be by your side," James murmurs to a blushing Jess, whose fair skin glows pink.

"You guys are all pussy-whipped," Steven comments next to me, seeming unimpressed.

"One day, it'll happen to you, Steven. Just you wait, and I'll be here to gloat." Emily narrows her eyes at her brother. "Don't come whining to me about your love troubles."

"Never." Steven arches a brow, engaging in a staring contest with Emily. From what I heard, these two have bickered since they were young, and it appears age and wealth did not change this one bit.

"You can't work all the time, Steven. Don't you want to settle down at some point?" Jess interjects, her forehead pinching, concern bleeding through her voice.

"Work is my mistress. I'm not interested in relationships. Seeing the crap you all went through only further confirms my choice." Steven's voice is flat, as if nothing will ever change his mind. He takes a sip of the green tea in his cup, his face seemingly unruffled.

Sarah and I exchange a glance before we shake our heads in amusement. We'll be here with the popcorn to watch the fall of Rome.

"You two are so adorable with your secret looks and everything. You know, I always thought you guys would get together eventually, even back in the day," Emily remarks. She picks up a few pieces of yellowtail sashimi with her chopsticks and places them on her plate.

"It would've been helpful if you convinced this woman earlier, Emily. I wouldn't have had to suffer for over twelve years."

"Love will happen when it's the right time. I couldn't force it. Sarah was too stubborn to see it." She wags her brows.

"Hey! In my defense, for someone who claims to know women well, Jack went about it all wrong with me. If he'd shown his true colors back then," Sarah glances at me, her hand over my heart, "I'd have fallen years ago."

Chuckling, I lean down and kiss her nose. "You're always right and I'm always wrong."

My statement is met with a chorus of loud groans by the men around the table. "Don't do this, Jack. You're setting a terrible example for the rest of us." I think that was James complaining.

"Completely pussy-whipped. *None* of this looks appealing." That's Steven.

"What do you think about what Jack said, Adrian?" Emily bats her lashes at Adrian, who's staring at her with the same love-sick puppy look in his eyes he had in Grocery for Less twelve years ago.

His eyes soften. He curls a lock of hair which has fallen out of place behind Emily's ears with a tenderness only reserved for his wife. "You're always right."

Steven tosses his napkin on the table in mock horror and rolls his eyes.

We laugh at his expression, my heart filled to the brim with happiness and contentment, something I'd never thought was possible for me, and yet, in a stroke of luck, here I am, sitting at a table with my friends, who've taken time out of their busy days to celebrate me, my angel leaning her head on my shoulder.

Squeaaaak.

The door behind us slams open, the sound abrupt. Jarring.

My head whips toward the intrusion, finding a curvy brunette, scantily clad in a minidress—if you can even call it that—made of strings of pearls, hooked together with some thin chains, all her important parts covered by revealing underwear, stepping out into the courtyard, tears streaming down her face. I glance at Sarah and the others at the table, finding equal expressions of bewilderment.

Standing, I ask, "Excuse me, miss. Are you okay? Do you need help?"

The girl gasps and looks up, her eyes widening as if she's surprised to find us out here.

Out of the corner of my eye, I see Steven slowly rise from his seat, a strange tension-threaded calmness emanating from his towering presence. "Grace?" He takes a few steps forward, his head cocked to the side. "Is that you?" Shock and uncertainty lace his voice.

The brunette's gaze snaps to Steven, her eyes widening for a split second before the expression is wiped from her face. She takes a deep breath and wipes her tears with the back of her arm. Her face is now placid, and if I hadn't seen her earlier outburst with my own eyes, I wouldn't have thought she was crying mere moments ago.

"Y-You're mistaken, sir." She stares at Steven like he's a stranger. She turns back to me and murmurs, "I'm fine. Just some bad news at home. Sorry for the interruption. Please enjoy your day."

As abruptly as she appears, she whirls around and darts back inside, her long, wavy hair flying behind her.

The door closes behind her with a resounding *bang*.

The courtyard is silent other than the distant honking of car horns. Even the birdsongs have taken a hiatus.

Heaving out a deep breath, I glance at a seemingly shell-shocked Steven. His forehead is creased, and he stares at the closed door. "Do you know her, Steven? From her outfit, I think she's one of the girls working on the Rose floors."

He shakes his head, murmuring something under his breath, before sitting back down. I follow suit and scan the table, finding everyone else looking as equally confused as I am.

"I must be mistaken. Sorry about that." Steven chuckles, the laugh sounding forced to anyone who knows him. "Yes, I must be wrong." He lets out a deep exhale as the tension slowly releases from his shoulders.

He reaches for his cup and lifts it into the air. Steven smirks—the perfect, untouchable Kingsley back in full force—and announces, "Cheers to you, Jack, for your well-deserved promotion. I can't wait to see what's next in store for you and to have you be at my beck and call when I visit."

I snort and the others laugh, the strange interruption apparently forgotten. We clink our glasses together. "Thank you to all of you." My voice is unwavering and I make eye contact with everyone at the table, attempting to convey the depths of my gratitude and my love for them. Turning to Sarah, I tug her to my side, feeling her melt against me. "I'm the luckiest man on earth to have all of you here."

And I realize something I should've known all along.

I've always mattered, but more importantly...

I'm loved.

$$\bullet \; \bullet \; \bullet$$

Thank you for reading THE BRIGHTEST SPARK. Hope you've enjoyed Jack and Sarah's story as much as I did writing it.

Please Review: Please consider leaving a review on the retailer website and Goodreads (https://www.goodreads.com/book/show/197397419-the-brightest-spark). Your reviews will really help this author out and will allow for more readers to find this book.

Bonus Chapters: Want to tag along with Jack and Sarah on their road trip where their car broke down along the way and they had to sell car tires and hustle? It's spicy and hilarious. Sign up for my newsletter to get THREE EXTRA BONUS CHAPTERS, new release alerts, exclusive bonus material, and more. Just click on the "The Brightest Spark Bonus Chapters" on the website: (https://www.victorialum.com/bonus)

Read Steven's Story Next: Do you know Steven and mystery girl's story will be the first book of my new series (The Orchid) based in New York City? Don't miss their story, WHEN HEARTS IGNITE. Their story is filled with angst, steam, all types of swoon, and features a broken man who doesn't believe in emotions and love and the woman who topples his walls. Don't miss it. Read it here: (https://geni.us/whenheartsignite)

Keep in Touch: Join my Facebook group, Victoria Lum's Luminaries (https://www.facebook.com/groups/576423100572205) for sneak peaks, exclusive giveaways, and to chat about all things book-related! You can also find me on Tiktok @victorialumwriter (https://www.tiktok.com/@victorialumwriter), Instagram @authorvictorialum (https://www.instagram.com/authorvictorialum/), and other sites at this link (https://linktr.ee/authorvictorialum).

ACKNOWLEDGMENTS

I can't believe in the span of one year, I've written and published four books! Thank you for joining me on the journey. This marks the end of the *LA Hearts* series, which will forever have a special place in my heart as these characters are the ones who gave me the last push to pursue my dream of becoming a romance author!

As an indie author, I had to spend hours searching on stock image websites to find the right cover models for my books and trust me, after the first hour of six-pack abs and not the right face, things would get old pretty quickly. During this time, I'd come across spicy photos of couples in various amorous positions and an idea sparked in my mind—what happens at these photoshoots? Can things get spicier than intended?

So, when Jack showed up in *The Harshest Hope* with his lip ring and swagger and the sparks flew off the pages between him and Sarah, I knew I had to give them a story, and thus, *The Brightest Spark* was born. Jack and Sarah's story was originally supposed to be a fun little holiday novella. I also quickly learned that I couldn't write short stories, because I liked to delve into a character's backstory, their emotions, and of course layer in some of the angst you and I both love. So, this little novella became the book you finished reading today!

Of course, it'll be remiss of me not to say the explicit elements in this story are completely fictional and dramatized. Professional photographers will never allow funny business to occur under their watchful eyes!

The ending of a series is always bittersweet but what makes me happy is the beginning of another one! My stories are all in the same universe, so a farewell is never a goodbye, so look out for those cameos!

As you can probably tell, the next set of stories will move to NYC and will begin with a familiar character, our darling Steven Kingsley, who we literally watched grow up in the span of these four novels. He's broody, he's broken, and I totally enjoy writing how he falls to his literal knees over a woman.

The NYC series is titled *The Orchid*, because this exclusive establishment will be a central hang out spot for our hot couples, and let me tell you, spiciness and angst are in the near horizon! Hope to see you there!

As always, thank you to everyone who has supported me, in no particular order:

My family: To my husband and my children, who always see me working around the clock, thank you for putting up with me.

Regina Wamba: Thank you for letting me bug you on the phone to get some high-level details about your day as a cover photographer and giving me some inside information. Your photos are gorgeous and utterly breathtaking. Every time I see your work come across my feed, I tell myself...someday I'll graduate from stock photography!

My editors: Theresa Leigh, Grace Bradley, and Amy Briggs, thank you as always for your edits and feedback. My stories would not be what they are without your help.

Proofreader and Formatter: Thank you to Virginia Tesi Carey and Elaine York of Allusion Publishing for polishing these babies and making them shine.

My PA: Thank you to Nikki Johnson for keeping up with my madness and keeping me on track!

Cover designer: To the awesome LK Farlow of Y'All That Graphic, thank you always being so flexible and so kind! I love the covers you've created!

Beta readers: Malia, Jenn, Jess, Fiona, and Isha, I love you girls. Thank you for being honest with your feedback and letting me bounce off blurbs and taglines with you. I'd be lost without you all!

My ilLUMinati girls: you know who you are! Thank you for being my biggest cheerleaders!

Fellow authors: So many authors have helped me on this journey—it is impossible to name everyone, but I appreciate each and every one of you.

PR Firms: Thank you to Greys Promo and Literally Yours PR for your promotional efforts and helping me get the word out especially since I scheduled this with you last minute!

My Fellow Readers: Thank you for reading my stories. I love chatting with you on Instagram or Tiktok DMs, Facebook comments or messages. Thank you for reading my stories! I hope you'll stick along for the journey! I love you all!

With love,
Victoria

ALSO BY VICTORIA LUM

Catch up on Victoria's backlist! Don't miss these swoony, romantic stories with all the sizzling spice and angst. All stories are stand-alones and can be read out of order.

LA Hearts:
The Sweetest Agony (https://geni.us/thesweetestagony)
(James and Jess)
The Coldest Passion (https://geni.us/thecoldestpassion)
(Parker and Liz)
The Harshest Hope (https://geni.us/theharshesthope)
(Adrian and Emily)
The Brightest Spark (https://geni.us/thebrightestspark)
(Jack and Sarah)

The Orchid:
When Hearts Ignite (https://geni.us/whenheartsignite)
(Steven and Grace)

ABOUT THE AUTHOR

Victoria is a lover of all things romance, including movies, books, and television shows. A hopeless romantic since childhood, she is always dreaming up stories and happily ever afters. Caramel lattes are her fuel in the morning and she can usually be found reading anything she can get her hands on. She lives with her family and a beautiful Siberian husky in sunny California.

Keep in touch!
Sign up for her newsletter below:
Newsletter
https://dashboard.mailerlite.com/
forms/289149/81041142820374109/share

Follow Victoria on social media:
Tiktok
@victorialumauthor
Instagram
www.instagram.com/authorvictorialum
Facebook Group
www.facebook.com/groups/576423100572205